Accolades for
Wandlore

"Alferian Gwydion MacLir has succeeded in writing one of those rare books that, as soon as you open its pages, you realize you have been looking for all your life. We shall be recommending it to all our druid students."—*Philip Carr-Gomm, Chief of the Order of Bards, Ovates, and Druids*

"An extensively detailed and informed history of wands including references derived from many diverse cultures and beliefs to give a well-rounded backdrop to their construction and use. I also like that the book is practical, with instructions on how to manufacture wands and examples of ritual consecrations. I truly believe that you will be happily rewarded for the time spent on this very informative text."—*Roger Williamson, founder of Magus Books & Herbs in Minneapolis*

"A born storyteller and teacher, Alferian's words weave a poetic spell that we can follow, entranced, through the forests of the world. *Wandlore* gave me a profound appreciation of the 'life' within these treasured tools of magick, as well as a deeper respect for the art of wandmaking from the finding of the wand through all the processes involved in turning it into a magical tool. It has enhanced my magical practices, enabling me to connect more deeply with the spirit realm."—*Susa Morgan Black, Druid in the Order of Bards, Ovates, and Druids and co-founder of Doire Bhrighid 817 (a Druid seed grove dedicated to Brighid)*

"Far more than just a resource on making wands, this volume deals with the elemental and magickal correlations and connections behind the intent that a wand is used to project. This must surely become a definitive work on this subject, bringing a modern perspective to an ancient device."—*DruidicDawn.org*

The person having fully comprehended
the mystery of the magic wand in its
magnitude will never do his operations of
ritual magic without this implement.

~ Franz Bardon

About the Author

ALFERIAN GWYDION MACLIR is a Druid Companion of the Order of Bards, Ovates, and Druids, a traditional British druid order. He is a 32nd degree Freemason and has served as a Grove Chief Druid and as a Professor of Wizardry at the Grey School of Wizardry. In 2001, he created Bardwood Wandry, which has rapidly become one of the leading shops for handmade wands. Visit MacLir online at www.bardwood.com.

Wandlore

The Art of Crafting the Ultimate Magical Tool

Alferian Gwydion MacLir

Llewellyn Publications
WOODBURY, MINNESOTA

Second Printing, 2012
FIRST EDITION

Book design by Rebecca Zins
Color pages designed by Lisa Novak; photographs by James Maertens, Esq.
Cover design by Lisa Novak
Cover photo by Andrea Smith-Luedke
Interior illustrations by Mickie Mueller except for Rocky Mountain maple leaf illustration
from *Trees & Leaves CD-ROM & Book* ©2004 Dover Publications, Inc.;
part five's photographs by Linnea Maertens

Llewellyn is a registered trademark of Llewellyn Worldwide Ltd.

Library of Congress Cataloging-in-Publication Data

MacLir, Alferian Gwydion, 1960–
  Wandlore: the art of crafting the ultimate magical tool / Alferian Gwydion MacLir.—1st ed.
    p. cm.
  Includes bibliographical references and index.
  ISBN 978-0-7387-2002-9
  1. Magic wands. I. Title.
  BF1623.W36M33 2011
  133.4′3—dc22
                                                                                2011011841

Llewellyn Publications
A Division of Llewellyn Worldwide Ltd.
2143 Wooddale Drive
Woodbury, MN 55125-2989
www.llewellyn.com

Printed in the United States of America

*This book is dedicated to my friend and
fellow druid Chalcedoni Piastra Scott,
whose encouragement and persistent poking
were instrumental in bringing this project
to the page. I dedicate it also to my wife,
Sarah, and my daughter, Linnea, whose
love and support are so important to me.*

Acknowledgments

I must acknowledge my many druid friends and colleagues without whose teaching, interest, and support this book could not have come to fruition: Philip Carr-Gomm, Nigel and Caryl Dailey, Donata Ahern, Vivyan Minouge, Leslie Gentilin, Kernos, Oakwyse, and Loosh, all of OBOD. Thanks also to the editorial team at Llewellyn Publications, especially to Elysia Gallo for her incisive criticism of the early manuscript and its many tangents.

Thanks also to my irksome colleague-companions of the Imaginary Royal College of Enchanters, whose quibbling about the nature of dryads over many samovars of tea helped to refine my own theories. And thanks to my brother Masons of Lake Harriet Lodge, who kept me grounded in the world of matter and inspired my soul with the square of virtue. Further thanks to all the wand clients I have had the pleasure to serve over the past nine years.

Special thanks to my guides and confidants from the otherworlds, Princess Rantir D'Ascoyne and Dr. Endymion Westmartin of the University of Mara Sylvia's Department of English, both of whom provided me with answers when I needed them regarding the magical properties of trees and those knotty bits of magical theory. And finally, last and first, my humble respect and gratitude to my sensei, Aarondel the White.

Contents

....

PART THREE
Wind

....

PART FOUR
Stone

....

PART FIVE
Water

Introduction

WELCOME TO THE world of *Wandlore*. The making of magic wands is an ancient art and one central to the practice of wizardry, yet it has not been presented fully in any book ... until now.

This book weaves together the physical and spiritual dimensions of the craft of the wand-maker—or, at any rate, my experience in this craft. I have made nearly two hundred wands for clients around the world, each handmade and unique. Back at the turn of the century, I was working on my formal studies with the Order of Bards, Ovates, and Druids, the largest international order of druids today. Among my studies was working with trees and their energies, or spirits. I found myself picking up fallen branches wherever I went to talk with trees, and I was directed by my spirit guides to take up the making of wands.

When the Harry Potter books started to come out, Mr. Ollivander and his shop captured my imagination, and I remember how eager I was to see how the director of the first film depicted that scene where Harry chooses his wand—or, rather, it chooses him. I realized then that wandmaking was one of the most important of the arts of the enchanter, and it was a particular specialty among wizards. When I was in college, my magical studies led me to attend college for a year in England—in the city of York, the crossroads of Anglo-Saxon, Roman, Celtic, and Norse cultures. There, in 1984, I turned my energies decisively to the history and craft of wizardry.

Something that happened in that year came back to my memory when I began to ponder wands in the context of druidry years later. I had found a catalog through some metaphysical shop, a catalog of a British wandmaker. I do not recall his name, only that his wands were advertised as containing the living dryad spirit of the tree. I ordered one but it never arrived before I had to leave the country. That incident strikes me now as a curious turn of fate. I was not ready for a wand, and it would not be for many more years that I would finally make my own wand of linden wood and conjure its dryad myself. But the life of a wizard is full of curious happenings like that.

It must be said that *Wandlore* covers a lot of ground. There are many wandmakers, and each has his or her own style. Some wands are made of metal and stone or even resin, but the traditional and ancient method of wandmaking was working with wood. It is believed that the druids of old used branches of trees to convey their magic. Working with wood in a physical sense forms part of the craft of wandmaking. Working with wood in a spiritual sense is also part of *Wandlore*. The contents of this book are organized around the five elements of the craft, which are related to the five alchemical elements. These are the metaphysical elements through which wizards, druids, and witches contemplate the world. Usually in the West, we refer to the four elements (air, fire, water, earth) and the fifth, aether, as an element that is of another order, which is that invisible essence from which the other four manifest their forms. I will refer to the four elements throughout this book, and when I refer to *five* elements, you will know I mean the four plus one that is the great mystery of all magic.

The first part of the book is some general history and theory of wandlore. Knowing the background of what you are doing is always the best first step in any adventure. The rest of the book takes each part of the wandmaking process in turn. You will begin with selecting the type of wood to be used and learning the powers of the trees. That is the stuff of elemental fire—the spirit and will in the tree and its dryad spirit.

Next comes the consideration of design—the stuff of elemental air and intellect. If the wand design includes stones or crystals, then the next part of the book, regarding the magical properties of minerals, is important. It is no surprise that this part is given to elemental earth.

Part five explains the art and craft of wand carving, setting stones, finishing, and all the practicalities that bring together the flow of your creative imagination and the flow of the wood itself. In my experience of ten years as a wandmaker, this is a matter for elemental water. Feelings, visions, and intuition are of this element and are just as necessary to the wandmaker as a sharp cutting tool.

Lastly, we will study the element of quintessence—the summation of all elements, also known as spirit, or aether—that invisible, intangible essence from which the other four elements emerge into the material world. This is the element of enchantment itself, and under its aegis I will reveal the secrets of enchanting a wand core of unicorn hair or phoenix feather. You will also learn the way to use enchantment to bring together the parts of a wand into a single, coherent being. This part also features how to dedicate a wand and how to use it for magic.

The text of *Wandlore* is not intended merely as a "how to make a wand" book. It is an "everything you ever wanted to know about wands" book. It has been three years in the writing, accompanied by my practice and teaching. Bardwood Wandry is a shop for wands, a place where magic wands are crafted, and a place for wands to find their wizard. Through my practice and my website (www.bardwood.com), I have had the pleasure of meeting numerous clients and many more magical people who feel the same call to wandmaking that I felt years ago.

This spiritual calling is a phenomenon of more than just personal significance. It is as if the denizens of the higher realms are causing the rebirth of a craft into a level it has probably never had before. If there were professional wandmakers in premodern times, I have never heard of it. The making of wands was a matter for the wizard, witch, or druid personally; they made their own. But I suspect that some of the more skilled and wise mages passed on their knowledge of working with the trees and their wood. Today, there are so many magical practitioners (because there are so many more people on the planet) that professional wandmakers are desired. Both the furniture of our lodges and the implements of our work may now be bought from those with the special skills to make them. Specialization in the wizard's world shows that it has grown large enough to join the other professions. Physicians do not make their own medical devices; auto mechanics do not make their own tools. If they had to do so, we would have fewer of these professionals available to our communities. So, in a sense, the emergence of wandmakers in this time signals the resurgence of magical practitioners, and vice versa; the professional wandmaker makes it possible for more people with talent to practice magic.

Whether you are a druid, a witch, a ceremonial magician, or any other sort of wizard, I am sure that you will find much in this book to ponder, as well as the inspiration to try wandmaking yourself.

PART ONE

The Wand and the Wizard

You ask deep questions,
Mr. Potter. Wandlore is a complex
and mysterious branch of magic.

— Mr. Ollivander in
Harry Potter and the Deathly Hallows by J. K. Rowling

A Little History of Wands

$\mathcal{T}$HE MAGIC WAND is the iconic instrument of the wizard. By "wizard" I mean mages of all kinds—witches, sorcerers, druids, and adepts of the mysteries. We all know them from fiction, films, and video games. If there is a fairy godmother or a sorcerer's apprentice, we expect there must be a magic wand too. Sometimes wizards like Gandalf or Merlin appear with a walking staff, but this too is a wand, for the word simply means "a rod." Size doesn't matter. Real-life mages also use wands. In the East, Taoist wizards and Zen masters convey their power through staves. The druids of old Irish myth and legend wielded wands to conjure magical fogs, to transform adversaries (or themselves) into pigs, to foresee the future, or to recover lost information.

The druids were the wizards of the ancient Celts. Today's druids also employ wands in their ritual work, healing, and meditations. Ceremonial mages have revived the ancient mysteries and employ many types of wands in their lodges. While magic and wizards were driven underground in Western culture in the Age of Enlightenment (the 1700s), these old traditions continued to be revived; in the past three hundred years, druidry, witchcraft, and hermeticism have become once again living and growing spiritual traditions. They all share an understanding of the visionary imagination and the many spiritual dimensions of existence. They also all share the use of wands to perform magic. In druidry today, the wand symbolizes individual spiritual inspiration, the *awen* of the bards. Awen is a Welsh word meaning "poetic inspiration," but it is also a living force, a transformative energy directed by the will of the enchanter.

Across many cultures and historical epochs, the wand has been an instrument for conveying a mage's will. At its simplest, the wand is a branch, more or less straight, used for pointing and

In the Greek pantheon, Mercury (right) was Hermes, the messenger of the gods and wielder of a magic wand; he evolved into the figure of Hermes Trismegistus (above), the "thrice-great" Hermes who is the legendary founder of the Hermetic magical tradition.

directing the intentions of the mage outward into the world of manifestation. Some wands are made of metal and crystal, bone, or even clay, and some ceremonial magic traditions, such as the Hermetic Order of the Golden Dawn, use several quite elaborate wands for specific purposes, offices, or rituals. However, it is the simple stick from which magic wands developed. For the druids, each type of tree had special powers, and druids today are beginning to reclaim the ancient understanding of the tree spirits, or dryads.

The twentieth-century Czech magus Franz Bardon wrote of the symbolic nature of wands and the ability of the wizard to apply them to different purposes. A wand is always first an instrument of will, that power through which a wizard influences the higher spheres. Different wands may be dedicated to particular purposes: one to influence other people, animals, plants, and objects; another to cure people suffering from diseases or other misfortunes; and perhaps another to evoke spirits, intelligences, or daemons (Bardon, *The Practice of Magical Evocation,* 41).

Wands direct the will outward from the mage into the world. The upright staff of the itinerant sage, by contrast, draws power from the earth and the sky with the staff and the wizard as the conduit. A small wand has the virtue of being easily concealed. The staff is usefully concealed in having practical value as a walking stick. A rod may be used for herding animals, and it is also the traveler's most practical weapon. Buddhist monks have used a staff with jingling metal rings on the bronze headpiece to announce their arrival in a village and to warn small creatures out of the way lest they be inadvertently stepped on. Taoist wizards use staves as a martial arts weapon and as a walking stick. The staff is an archetypal symbol of the wise old wanderer full of hidden powers. Nowadays, in Western cities, it would be pretty eccentric to walk with a staff, but it is still a good tool for the open road and wilderness track, and many druids today adopt them as part of their ritual accoutrements. Wands, by contrast, are mostly used in private ceremonies and spell weaving.

Did the wand derive from the wizard's staff, or vice versa, or did each evolve independently from a common source in the royal scepter? At its most primal level, the magic wand, along with the club, is derived from the mystery of the male phallus, a symbol of life and generativity but also a symbol of self-assertion and will. A royal scepter or a marshal's baton symbolizes the authority to command or lead others. One can easily see the mage's wand and its purpose at any orchestra concert in the conductor and his or her baton.

Joe Lantiere, in his lavishly illustrated history of "mystical rods of power," traces many details of the magic wand and its relatives. He mentions the talking sticks, dance sticks, rain sticks, and rattles of the shamans and tribal medicine men. There is also the caduceus of Hermes, messenger of the Greek gods and a patron of magic, and the staff of Asklepios, each twined with snakes. Mr. Lantiere notes the connection between the serpent-twined staff, or wand, and the human spinal cord with its coiled "kundalini serpent energy." He cites Manly Hall when saying, "The staff is symbolical of the spinal column of man, and this is the true wand of the magicians; for it is through the power within this column that miracles are performed" (Lantiere, *The Magician's Wand*, 43).

Similarly, W. Y. Evans-Wentz describes the silver branch of the bards and its link to the world of Faerie, that realm of the otherworlds replete with magical power:

> Manannan of the Tuatha Dé Danann, as a god-messenger from the invisible realm bearing the apple-branch of silver is, in externals though not in other ways, like Hermes, the god-messenger from the spiritual realm of the gods bearing his wand of two intertwined serpents. In modern fairy-lore this divine branch or wand is the magic wand of fairies; or where messengers like old men guide mortals to an underworld it is a staff or cane with which they strike the rock hiding the secret entrance (Evans-Wentz, *The Fairy-Faith in Celtic Countries*, 343).

Joseph Peterson, in his web article "The Magic Wand," speculates that one origin of magic wands may have been the ceremonial bundle of twigs carried by Persian Zoroastrian priests (the original "magi"). This bundle is called a baresman, or barsom. It was traditionally made of tamarisk twigs and functioned as a bridge of souls between the realm of mortal life and the realm of the spirits. It was a conduit of power and communication from spirits to human beings. Admitting no scholarly authority on ancient Persia, I would note on the face of it that the bundle of twigs and the name *barsom* is remarkably similar to the witch's *besom*, or broom. Was the witch's broom descended from this Eastern fire cultus, the combination of a wizard's staff and the magus's sacred bundle of twigs?

Peterson also notes that the Roman flamen, also a priest of fire, used similar bundles of twigs, and this is even more likely to be a direct borrowing from Zoroastrian practice. Hans Dieter Betz has included in his collection *The Greek Magical Papyri in Translation* a spell to summon a familiar spirit in which, at one point, the mage shakes a branch of myrtle to salute the goddess Selene (Betz, 5). This branch would appear to be one with leaves still on it. In another operation (to summon a spirit of prophecy), we find twigs of laurel used: "Take twelve laurel twigs; make a garland of seven sprigs, and bind the remaining five together and hold them in your right hand while you pray" (ibid., 13). The laurel branches have leaves on them and the leaves are inscribed with special magical ink. So, the practices are not quite like the more modern use of wands, yet we may say the magical papyri provide us with documentary evidence that wizards in the Hellenistic Age used the magical properties of branches taken from particular trees. Myrtle is considered to be sacred to the goddess Selene; laurel to Apollo.

We find other wands in myths that are sources for our modern wands. One wand user, the Greek god Hermes (Roman Mercury), has long been linked to the passage between earth and the higher realms. The staff or rod of Hermes has become associated with the caduceus, a baton entwined with two snakes mating. Originally, the Latin word *caduceus* came from Greek *kerykeion*, from *keryx*, a herald. The term *kerykeion skeptron*, meaning "herald's wand," was abbreviated to *kerykeion* and then in Latin became *caduceus* (Friedlander, *The Golden Wand of Medicine*, 5). Greek *skeptron* is the root of our English word *scepter*. The caduceus of Mercury-Hermes has come to be associated with healing and the medical profession due to its similarity to the rod topped with a brazen serpent employed in the Bible by Moses to work healing magic. It has also been mixed up with the wand of Asklepios, a Greek demigod closely associated with medicine and healing. Asklepios used a wand that is usually depicted as a rough branch with a single snake spiraling around it (ibid., 6).

The association of Mercury and wands shows the wand used not for healing but for magic. Herald of the gods, Hermes-Mercury is lord of communication; magic is, after all, a form of communication. We even call an act of magic a *spell*, which is the Old English word for "word" as in *gospel* ("good word") or the verb *spelling*. To cast a spell is to cast forth a word or series of words. But the significance of the ophidian wand—the wand with snakes—bears a closer look.

An example of a serpentine wand, this one
with a crystal tip and a pommel stone.

Snakes and Wands

SERPENTS ARE POWERFUL symbolic animals in virtually every culture. The serpent symbolizes the fire of life and the will to live. Their resemblance to the phallus makes them ripe to being viewed as fertility symbols; their ability to shed their skin makes them the ideal animal symbol for immortality. When one dies, one "sheds the skin" of the body, and the serpent does just that yet lives on. So, it should be no surprise that the snake symbolizes healing, but it clearly also symbolizes knowledge and wisdom—the knowledge of immortality at the very least, which has always been itself emblematical of all knowledge. Witness the serpent in the Garden of Eden, the original educator and initiator.

But what is the significance of two serpents intertwined? One answer is that the twin snakes represent twin helical energies bound together; this might be interpreted today as the double helix of DNA. It can also be interpreted to mean the energies of yin and yang or the forces of order and chaos, creativity and destruction, light and dark—or all of the above. Friedlander tells us:

> According to mythology, Hermes threw his magic wand between two fighting snakes. They stopped their fighting and entwined his wand. Some have interpreted the entwined snakes as copulating, so Hermes was considered to have brought love out of hostility (ibid., 16).

The symbol of two entwined snakes resembles the figure eight, the emblem of infinity. The forces indicated by the figure eight are indeed infinite as well as eternal. It is no coincidence that the kundalini energy—that life force that the yogis describe as running up one's spinal column—is also symbolized as a serpent. The serpent lies coiled and still, then rises up and strikes. The snake's behavior is a good metaphor for the action of building up magical potential and then releasing it with the triggering incantation or gesture, all of which points us to the essence of magic and the wand itself—the will.

The most basic hidden secret of magic is that the wizard must go within him- or herself, inside the mind, and there, encountering Hermes, lord of communication, be led into the otherworlds. These otherworlds, as they are often called in Celtic legends, are the higher planes of our existence, especially the astral plane and the mental plane. If Hermes, the divine psychopomp, leads us to those worlds, then our consciousness becomes capable of magical action.

The caduceus

Fire and Will

*T*HE POWER WE call the will (Latin *voluntas*) is the direction of one's intentions to manifest changes in the higher planes and so bring about change in the material world; this power to transform matter is the essence of elemental fire. In the system of magical elements, fire comprises all energy and, by extension, what scientists call electromagnetic energy, thermal energy, and force fields of various kinds, as well as emanations of spirit, desire, passionate attraction (or repulsion), love, anger, aggression, and devotion. These things, which psychologists call emotions, may be considered in a magical view of the world to be palpable forces projected outward from one's astral being. It is this quality of extension that is evoked in the linear shape of the wand.

If the wizard's staff is like the spinal column linking heaven and earth. A wand is the pointing finger of a child, the thrusting phallus, the beat of the maestro's baton, the command of the king's scepter, the pushing up of the new green shoot, the index finger that signifies the number one: single-mindedness and directed intention. The wand, staff of office, marshal's baton, and so forth, are all instruments of profound transformation, symbols that transform their bearer into a person of authority and will.

In the Western magical tradition, fire is one of four elements, the building blocks of the cosmos. These are not the elements of the periodic table used by chemists; they are the four essences identified by ancient natural philosophers and medieval alchemists. They are organizing forces underlying the material world, not matter itself. However, the four alchemical elements are manifest in the physical states of matter; that is, solid (earth), liquid (water), gas (air), and plasma (fire). But each has many more manifestations on the higher planes.

Elemental fire, we may say, is life itself, and wood embodies this conceptual fire because it comes from a living being. That is one reason a wizard's wand is most often made of wood. This is especially notable in the druid tradition, in which druid wands are usually described in terms of particular sacred trees: a wand of ash, birch, hazel, or oak. The old druids performed the wonders of transformation by borrowing the power of the trees, and those following the druid path today still do. The method is somewhat similar to the medieval Kabbalist or Solomonic mage borrowing the powers of daemons; however, there is a significant qualitative difference.

Medieval magi worked with a theory that daemons and the dead could be commanded by means of the names of God; their reasoning being that the damned were under complete control of the Creator and so did not have free will of their own if the divine names were used. Druids operate in a completely different cosmology. There are no damned spirits, though there are mischievous creatures and many divinities. Trees, like all other living creatures, are free within their natures, so the druid mage does not command them with god names. For druids, the spirit of a tree is one of the many kinds of spirits that animate the worlds. They are part of an ecology of spirit, as we might say, in which one species is not more important than another, but all are valued equally, and the soul—or individual consciousness—may manifest in different forms within different lifetimes. Nor are rocks and minerals excluded from the many species of spirit entity. Different species are animate or intelligent in differing ways, but spirit is continuous throughout the cosmos.

The ubiquity of spirit in nature means that the material and the spiritual are not radically separate. The magical properties of trees and their wood are practical—just as practical as the material properties of wood considered by the carpenter or builder. Both kinds of properties are an intrinsic part of the tree for those with the eyes of ethereal perception open. A bridge-builder does not need to command alder wood to resist rot when submerged in water, nor does a wizard need to command a wand of alder to aid in seership and oracular crossings between worlds; it's just the right wood for the job. What spiritual affinity must be created between wizard and wand is done not through a hierarchy of spiritual authority but through the affinity of kinship and love, and through an understanding of the material and spiritual elements. It is a relationship of willed co-creation, not authority and service.

Creation and the Elements

WITHIN MAGIC, FOUR elements compose material existence. These four are air, fire, water, and earth. A fifth element, aether, is also included in the system, but this quintessence is, in fact, of a different order altogether. Quintessence is that spiritual substance from which air, fire, water, and earth are made. The four elements are symbolized by an equal-armed cross within a circle, or by a square. The four plus one that is the great mystery is symbolized by the pentagram with its five points.

Each element manifests in five different planes of existence, what we might call five dimensions of one reality. Those planes are sometimes called worlds because they are inhabited by living entities. The planes are commonly named material, astral, mental, archetypal, and divine. The part of reality that we perceive with our ordinary physical senses is the material plane of existence, but we also exist in and can learn to sense the other planes. The classic work on this subject was written by Theosophist and Freemason C. W. Leadbeater and titled *Man Visible and Invisible*. Each of us exists simultaneously in all four worlds, even if we are unaware of it. You can think of them as dimensions of one reality. Understanding this magical cosmology underlies all magical work, including the art of wandmaking.

The element of fire is where we will begin, and it manifests in the astral world as intention, will, desire, and action. Wandmaking is itself an act of intention and will. As such, it involves both the fiery principles of creation and extension and the watery principles of destruction, restriction, and flow. The creation of a wand in wood involves removing some of the material used and altering it by the exercise of restriction into the desired shape and material configuration. Moreover, the magical creation of a wand involves the expression of the wandmaker's emotions, or his or her feelings, through the material medium, and this too combines water and fire—the force that draws heart to heart and the force that gives the union movement and purpose. It creates a material (earth) embodiment of ideas (air), will (fire), and relationship (water). The caressing hands of the maker imbue the wand with magical power and awaken the sleeping dryad spirit in the wood (aether or spirit). The act of crafting a wand is, like most magic, fundamentally an act of love and passion applied to the higher dimensions of the physical implement.

A wand may be simple and elegant, knobbly and overtly branchlike, or it may be elaborately carved with sigils, runes, and totem animals. But at bottom it is the wood itself and the wandmaker's mindfulness that must give it the qualities that prepare it to be taken up by its owner and used as a magical instrument. The wakening and drawing forth of the tree's spirit, or dryad, occurs not only in the final act of enchanting the wand but throughout the process of its making as the wandmaker pours into it his or her own spirit.

Some among the cognoscenti say that a druid or witch must make his or her own wand. Some suggest that the use of iron tools of any sort detracts from the wand's energy, so a flint should be employed to better connect us to the Stone Age past. Such rules can certainly be followed for those who accept their premises. While steel tools naturally give many trees the willies because they are so often mutilated and killed by humans wielding such implements, I do not believe there is anything inherently detrimental in steel or iron. Indeed, iron is one of the magical alchemical metals sacred to Mars. Metallurgy is an art that lies at the root of magic and alchemy. It was practiced by the ancient Celts and the Tuatha Dé Danann to a very high degree of refinement.[1] A sharpened steel blade is a truly magical thing.

There is no doubt that the use of one's own hands in quiet contemplation at a slow, human pace brings a deeper communication with the spirit of the wood and allows love and attention to be lavished upon it with hand tools and ancient craft. The object for the wandmaker should never be to "save labor" or to produce a wand quickly. One should feel free and unrushed, and let the moon turn through her phases as the work proceeds.

Nothing embodies elemental fire better than the tree striving upward in the dense forest, triumphing over its crowding neighbors to dominate the canopy and aspire to the light—all the while being home and food to many animals, birds, and insects. Thus, it is to the tree spirits that we must turn to see inside the workings of a magic wand.

---

1   See Mircea Eliade, *The Forge and the Crucible*.

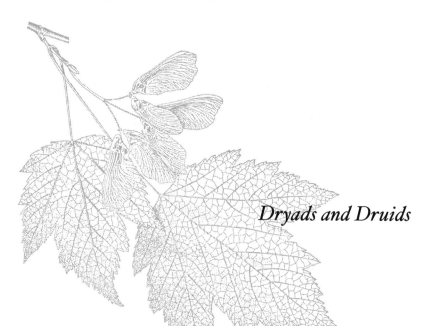

Dryads and Druids

*T*HE DRYAD IS the spirit of the tree—its essential pattern, or psyche. It is a living being linked to the tree and growing with it, but it is also a transtemporal and transspatial creature, living in the astral dimension as much as in the material world. This is the same way I would describe the human soul or the spirit of any living being. Commonly, spirits are thought to be some sort of substance that inhabits a physical body and leaves it on the moment of death. Neither of these statements is quite accurate, as I see it. The spirit does not live in a body like a person lives in a house; it *emanates* the body, which is to say that the spirit is causally connected to the body and able to exist without it.

Moreover, death does not completely separate the spirit from its emanation in matter any more than life confines the spirit to the body. In the case of humans, we note that consciousness is gone, but in many traditional cultures it is understood that the spirit lingers for some time. This is even more the case with trees because their bodies decay so slowly and because their consciousness is so much more diffuse than that of a spirit in human form, where indeed very slight disruptions in the delicate chemistry of the brain can wreak havoc on the psyche.

So, generally speaking, when a branch falls off a tree or is pruned, the dryad spirit is still in the wood. It is not really accurate to speak of "parts" of a spirit, but one might consider the spirit of the wand to be part of the tree's psyche. If a part of the physical tree breaks off, the spirit in that part remains and is like a piece of broken holograph in which the whole picture will be in each fragment. So, the dryad does not so much divide as it is reproduced in miniature when the break occurs. The spirit always remains to some degree until after the wood decays, but it may be asleep. In a sound branch, the spirit can be awakened by enchantment when the branch is crafted into a wand.

In some types of tree—oak and ebony come particularly to mind—there is a clear presence and consciousness in the wood that interacts with the wandmaker from the very start of the work. Such consciousness will often cause a branch to be cast in one's path and call out quite unmistakably to one who is aware. Other trees are much more shy, and their spirits may be hard to wake up in the enchantment process.

Orthodox modern botanists do not accord consciousness to trees.[2] Yet, among the Fay and many modern druids, trees are considered to have spirit, mind, and consciousness, as well as will and emotions (all of which are collected in the word *psyche*). Trees have a larger proportion of feeling and intuition than intellect in their psyches (to use our human terms). They do not reason the way we do, but they do ponder, brood, and feel. If a druid (or other magical person) touches them and makes contact with their dryad spirit, some trees at first seem sluggish and hard to reach. Other trees respond immediately to such attention with the same kind of reaction many of us would have if suddenly touched by the mind or gentle hand of another being. Some seem surprised, and who can blame them when for hundreds of years the touch of a human hand has most often been a prelude to violent death? Fortunately for us, trees have a very long and deep race-memory that goes back to before humans became so numerous and so destructive. Trees do not hold human emotions like hatred or revenge or even fear, though they can register pain and distress or anxiety.

It is somewhat misleading to anthropomorphize dryads. They share many spiritual (and, for that matter, biological) qualities with us, but they do not think or live like human beings. In its present incarnation, a tree is fixed in one place, its mobility limited to the dance of leaves and the relentless reaching of root and branch. It has an intimate relationship with the elements that we can hardly imagine—especially to the wind and sun. Much of a tree's attention is directed into the ground through its roots and outward into the air through its branches and leaves. Deciduous trees drop their leaves and grow new ones; many drop seeds or flowers. They carry on both symbiotic and hostile relationships to insects, mammals, and birds. They are physically intertwined above and below with their neighbors, especially in a forest, where one often gets the sense of one vast being rather than a collection of individuals.

---

2   But for the contrary view, see Peter Tompkins and Christopher Bird, *The Secret Life of Plants* (Harper and Row, 1973).

There is a great deal of activity in trees but it is the sort that, in humans, remains largely unconscious. We too produce seeds and eggs, grow hair and nails and new skin, circulate our sap, and throughout childhood our whole body is growing. Even in adulthood the body changes shape, and our skin is replaced every seven years. But trees have very different bodies, and their spirits are diffused throughout their bodies without the distracting, narrow focus of a brain structured by language. They do not even have a nervous system. Thus trees, unlike humans, have never suffered from the dichotomy of mind and body, yet they can sense, feel, and communicate.

If a tree's consciousness focuses on different parts of its body, it is on the roots, the trunk, and the branches in seasonal cycles of growth and withdrawal. The leaves are the most sensitive organs of trees, but the bark is also very sensitive, flowing with tree-blood underneath, much like our skin. It is perhaps significant, however, that a tree's "skin" is not sloughed off and renewed like ours, but quite the opposite: it grows thick, hard, and cracked, like a protective shell. Even in such species as the paper birch, whose tissue-thin white bark is peeled by humans to make baskets and canoes, there is quite a different quality to this "skin." It is not quite the sensitive and supple organ we humans enjoy but is still a medium of sensation.

I associate many of the trees and their wood with one of the four elements (earth, air, fire, water). Some of the old Celtic and English treelore also makes such associations. Alder, for example, is considered a watery tree, in part because of its ability to be immersed in water without rotting. Willow is likewise considered watery because it so often grows near water. Moreover, willow is associated with the moon, which itself is linked to elemental water because of its influence over the seas and women's menstrual cycles. Oak is associated in many traditions with the sun and with lightning. The associations of trees with elements and deities are drawn from many sources, including my own intuition. You can make your own judgment based upon individual experience quite as well as I have done, and you will find that other wizards will differ in their associations. The matter of associations between trees and constellations or planets will benefit from more organized research as modern wizardry continues to mature.

It is important to note that while many trees can be found to have sympathies with the philosophical elements, dryads themselves are not "elemental spirits" as such. Elementals, as they are usually called, are beings that embody one of the four elements. Their traditional names are salamanders (for fire), nymphs (for water), gnomes (for earth), and sylphs (for air). Dryads, by contrast, embody the "fifth element" recognized in the Taoist system of elements:

wood. Dryads are representative of all of the four elements combined into a quintessence that is a living organism.

Trees draw water and minerals from the earth, and light from the fire of the sun; they breathe the air and exhale oxygen, which is the chemical medium of terrestrial fire. Moreover, their dried bodies are the chief fuel for human fires, and as charcoal they hold the secret for smelting metals and forging steel. As ash or decayed wood, trees become the earth element in soil. Trees are the pinnacle of the plant kingdom, filled with nobility, grandeur, and wisdom that comes from a long life in one place. We are indebted to them in ways that are often not realized. In the gift of oxygen, wood, and paper, trees have made human civilization possible. They are thus, we may say, the midwives of all intelligent life and human creativity.

So, what about druids then? I am a druid, so I write from that standpoint. Many books have been published on druidry over the past twenty years, but still it may be necessary to address the question of what a druid is. Druids are not, of course, dryads, even though some etymologists note the similarity between these words derived from Gaulish and Greek, respectively. Druids are notoriously difficult to define. Ask four druids for a definition, and you will get five different answers. Here's mine: a druid is a wizard, a wise one, in the Celtic tradition. Druid wisdom is rooted in the clear, conscious apprehension of all the elements in one's being and in the close attention to nature. For a druid, deity is immanent in the natural world.

The term *druid* has been linked with two other distinct classes of mage in the Celtic traditions: the ovate, who is a healer and seer, and the bard, who is a lore-master, poet, and enchanter. In many druid organizations today, ovates and bards are considered to be druids, even though the highest grade of the order are called "druids" as a title. In reality, apart from organized orders, anyone who feels called to the druid path may call him- or herself a druid. Moreover, there is nothing preventing today's druids from studying Hermeticism, Kabbalah, witchcraft, or ceremonial magic. Throughout this book, I use the terms *druid*, *mage*, *witch*, and *wizard* interchangeably, without reference to any particular religious point of view.

A druid begins magical training by becoming deeply aware of the four elements, and then, as an ovate, cultivating the fifth element. This study leads finally to an integration of all five elements into a transcendent being that comprehends spirit, the living combination of all five elements into a conscious structure. The druid's sentience goes beyond the merely physical, emotional, or intellectual so that the ego-consciousness becomes a tool, not a limitation, and the whole self is aware of all its parts working together in the subtle dance of existence. This level of self-awareness is beyond that of most human beings. It is very like the awareness of the trees.

However, dryads lack one thing the druid has, which is language. Human language is unique to humans. Other sapient beings—such as elves, dwarves, giants, and the many other denizens of Faerie—share this power of language, and to a degree are both limited by it and can use it transcendently. If the ego, as the center of consciousness, does not transcend language, it is limited to those thoughts that can be expressed in the languages it knows. There are few languages, even in Faerie, that can express the plenitude of spiritual being. But all language arises from the use of symbols, and that is another fundamental aspect of magic.

In the practice of wandmaking, one would do well to first seek out this state of being, this higher sentience of the mage. It is the first necessary step to conscious communication with dryads, as well as the first step to enchantment.

A fancy wand with goddess handle, carved acorn point,
and what I call a "flame tree" in the middle.

Conversations with Trees

MODERN DRUIDS, IMAGINING how their ancient forebears may have felt in their sacred groves, work to develop a special rapport with the dryads, or tree spirits. One way to do this is to meditate with one's back up against the trunk of a tree. Seated or standing, enter into a meditative state and listen. The only way to hear a tree communicate with you is to listen with your whole being. Your ears don't have any more to do with it than your liver.

"Becoming the Tree" Meditation[3]

- Let go of any expectations.

- Feel your deep breathing; slow it down.

- Wave away the chatter of your mind as you might wave away an annoying fly.

- Imagine that you are the tree.

- Imagine that your spinal column is the trunk of the tree.

- Imagine that your legs and feet are its roots, extending deep into the moist, dark soil.

---

3   Though too long to quote here, I can recommend the tree meditations found on page 150 of Mellie Uyldert's book *The Psychic Garden*. See also "Expanding the Sphere of Sensation to the Vegetable Kingdom" in Zalewski, 142.

- Your head becomes the crown of the tree and your eyes, its many leaves.

- See through these leaves, not through your limited eyes.

- Your awareness extends in all directions equally.

- You no longer have a "face" or a "back," and your attention is raised up to the sun and the air, downward to the soil and water.

- Spend some time feeling what it is to be the tree. Then listen for what the tree may tell you.

- If you feel moved to do so, ask the tree a question or express your feelings for it.

- Words may form in your mind out of what the tree communicates. If not, don't worry; be aware of feelings, emotions, or symbols that may occur within your mind.

- When the time feels right to return to your own body, feel your tree-consciousness recede and your human mind return to its body, its orientation, its skin and bones.

- Open your eyes, and focus on your breathing for a time.

- Touch the ground around you to re-establish yourself firmly back in your ordinary awareness. You will retain the memory of what your heart has learned.

- Whether or not you feel that the communication was successful, thank the tree for its blessings and its presence. Honor it and leave a small gift in the soil at its base—a bit of tobacco or other sacred herb, a pebble, a coin, or some water thoughtfully given.

- Pay attention to your dreams after this encounter.

- Write down what you experienced—perhaps as a poem, a song, or an image, symbol, or drawing, or express it in music or paint.

Cultivate a new attitude toward trees. In our modern mechanized culture in the West, we too often walk past the trees around us without even noticing. To the city dweller, trees may be merely a kind of decoration or, at best, a source of shade adding value to one's property. To the farmer, the trees may be windbreaks or timber lots, appearing in the imagination only as so many dollars of income when they are mature enough to cut into lumber. In a culture of clear-cutting forests that all too often assumes nature to be nothing more than "natural resources," we lose the love of trees as they are, inspirational through beauty, not reason.

If you desire to follow the druid way or that of any other nature religion, if your hope is to converse with dryads, you must first of all tend to your attitudes, your consciousness, and your awareness at the deepest level. You will have to cast off programming that has been poured into your head all your life from preachers, teachers, television, radio, and movies. All of these cultural institutions replay the same messages: humans are privileged, humans are chosen, nature is something to manipulate and "improve"—something to conquer. Animals, trees, much less the grass and the weeds and the bacteria in your own gut, are regarded as mere objects of study and scientific tinkering, not as noble and autonomous beings, as our benefactors and ancestors. "Machines are the true source of glory and self-esteem," say all the television commercials. In today's Western culture, technology and chemistry are still preached as the way to salvation, the way to paradise. Yet public attitudes have changed much in the past hundred years. If you are drawn to the druid way, chances are you already love trees and the wild.

Loving Nature

*H*AVING FIRST BECOME druid-wise, what does the wandmaker need to do next in order to pursue the art of making magical instruments of wood? First, greet the trees around you. Touch the delicate leaves of the saplings. Lay a hand on the rough bark of the old ones, and offer them your respect, love, and humility. The ancient Greeks, who invented the name *dryad* (and also *hamadryad*) for tree spirits, must have known a thing or two about the trees in their early, more shamanic days. By the classical era, when dryads were depicted as elusive female spirits, the picture seems to have been filtered through an anthropomorphic literary imagination that was no longer quite in touch with the more-than-human world on its own terms.

Yet the gesture of anthropomorphism is a way to acknowledge that tree spirits are the equals of spirits in human form. The dryad moves the earth and breaks boulders; it offers up its branchings to the nests of eagle, raven, and wren; it bears with gentle patience the depredations of squirrels and beetles, knowing that the body is the manifestation of life and food for the next generation. The druid must cultivate a dryad wisdom, honoring the body for what it is, neither romanticizing it nor deriding it as a source of sin. We eat; we are eaten. We take; we give abundantly from the source of our life. Spirit goes on, leaving the body as a gift to the worms, the insects, and the soil.

Before all else, a wandmaker must love the trees. If a wandmaker has no personal connection and affinity with the trees and their dryad spirits, then he or she is still caught up in the web of Western modernity and its objectification of everything nonhuman. Making wands is not like making furniture legs or wheel spokes. Magic wands are not merely utilitarian objects that use the physical properties of the wood for strength, elasticity, or durability; nor should they be merely pretty theatrical props. Magic wands are more like offspring.

Woodworkers in general often do have much knowledge about the material properties of woods, and this kind of knowledge does come into wandmaking. In wandcraft, one does well to understand about the different grains of woods and the different stains and finishes that might be appropriate for cherry but not for oak. Linden is easier to carve than sinewy cedar. Yet such material concerns are only one layer of wandmaking as an art. So, let us turn to the first elemental aspect of wandmaking: fire and the spirits of the trees.

PART TWO
Fire

Tejas is inner radiance, the subtle energy of fire, through which we digest impressions and thoughts. Tejas, fed through visual impressions, is the essence of the heat we absorb through food as well as sunlight ... It governs the development of higher perceptual qualities. Tejas, at the deepest levels of consciousness, holds the accumulated insight of our will and spiritual aspirations.

www.yogatherapy-om.com

The flaming tree motif

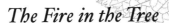

The Fire in the Tree

$\mathcal{F}$IRE IS THE element of will or the transforming force of desire, and trees exemplify this force perfectly as they reach ever sunward, striving for the light yet firmly rooted in the life-giving earth. Wandcraft begins with the trees, and the first step in making a wand is choosing the wood. Sometimes it is best to let the wood choose you. Walk in the forest or down the city sidewalk and watch for a branch that may be cast in your path. Let your intuition guide you to consider whether you want a straight wand or one that is bent and knobbly, as many branches are. Test it with your hands to see if it breaks. Peel away some bark it to see if it is rotten or worm-riddled. To become a wand, a branch must be sound and strong and preferably not too long separated from the tree. Give thought to the length and diameter too, for when the bark is removed, the branch may be considerably slimmer than it first appears. This will be especially true of trees such as oak and elm, which have thick bark. A branch between three-quarters of an inch and two inches in diameter is best.

If you desire a wand of a particular type of wood, it may be preferable to cut a branch. Sometimes when one finds a branch on the ground it is hard to tell what kind of tree it comes from. Some among the wise insist that a wand must be cut from a living tree. I do not think that is necessary; so-called deadwood is not dead in the spiritual sense, and the dryad in it can be awakened just as with a branch cut green. If you do cut a branch, do so with care and consideration for the tree. Talk to the tree first, and let it know what you are going to do. Don't be hasty. Cut close to the trunk in a clean cut that will be least likely to attract disease and will heal quickly. Cut a branch that needs to be pruned.

In the well-known medieval grimoire *The Key of Solomon the King*, the author suggests that a wand branch must be "virgin" wood—that is, of only one year's growth—and cut, moreover, in a single stroke with a "virgin" knife. As most branches grow very slowly and do not grow in one year to be more than twigs, I fail to see how this tradition came about unless the wands in question were extremely thin and whippy. One interpretation of the tree's virginity is that it was not yet old enough to have flowered. Possibly this was mixed up with a suggestion that the wizard meditate upon the branch for the cycle of one year before cutting it.

That would make sense because it would ensure that the aspirant took the time to get to know the tree in question. The wait would pour the wizard's will and intent into the branch before it was ever cut. Personally, I don't have the patience for that. If one is pruning a tree for its health and growth or if one's neighbors are pruning their trees, it is perfectly acceptable to take branches acquired in this way for a wand—if they call to you for that purpose. You will do well to sincerely thank the tree and tell it what you will use the branches for. Scott Cunningham, in his *Magical Herbalism*, instructs the witch to use a ritual knife to cut a branch. Mr. Cunningham advises that one take a purification bath, dress in "clean, plain clothes or a robe," and then walk thrice around the tree clockwise, pointing one's knife at the tree and saying:

> *O Great Tree,*
>
> *O Strong Tree,*
>
> *I ask thee to give me of your wood to further me in the magical art of herbalism;*
>
> *Thou shalt grow strong by my stroke; stronger and taller,*
>
> *O Great Tree!*[4]

After cutting a branch "tenderly, whispering your thanks to the tree," tie a "red bow around the trunk or bury an offering of bread, wine, or a precious stone at its base" (Cunningham, *Magical Herbalism*, 7). A coin, a bit of fertilizer, or simply water can also make a good offering.

The idea of cutting with a single stroke of a knife might work if you are dealing with the yearling twig, but for a branch of the size usually considered big enough to carve into a wand, the idea seems whimsical. It reminds me of the heroic tales of warriors who behead their

---

4   This promise strikes me as a bit disingenuous unless the mage plans to make a gift of a growing spell to the tree after the wand is fashioned, which wouldn't be a bad idea.

enemies with one stroke of the sword. There is something poetic about the image. Kosher butchers kill with a single swift stroke. I'll grant that a sharp and stout sword, bill, or machete can cut through a one-inch branch in one go; it isn't impossible. However, it is the symbolic meaning that counts—the *singularity* of the gesture. One stroke symbolizes the focused will. I recommend focusing your will while employing a sharp pruning saw for as many strokes as it takes.

I've read very wise writers who have suggested that one should warn the tree and wait at least a day before cutting the branch so that the tree can withdraw its sap from the branch. I have never seen an example of such a thing happening. Others insist that the branch must be green and alive. From a practical standpoint, green wood ensures a healthy branch, free of decay, but at the same time, green wood needs to dry and cure before it can be carved (unless you can learn that trick of getting the tree to withdraw its sap on command).

Wood that has already dried, especially "deadwood" still on the tree, seems most desirable to me because it is less likely to crack and split as it cures further, and it is doing the tree a service to remove such a limb, which can often serve as the entry point for disease as it rots. I have made fine wands either way—with wood harvested green and full of sweet-smelling sap or dried. Some woods, such as pine or spruce, have so much sticky sap underneath the bark that they may need to be set aside to cure and dry for a considerable time before attempting to remove the bark.

Each type of wood has a distinct character, grain, texture, and color. The bark of some woods—such as oak, cherry, or beech—is so lovely that one is tempted to leave it on, at least in part. If this appeals to you, consider your design carefully. The style of wand I will be describing in this book really demands a certain amount of carving to form the reservoir and the point. However, it is possible to leave the bark on the handle or part of the shaft of your wand.

Some trees have very distinct magical proclivities, but any of these woods can be used to make a fine wand, useful for any magical purpose. It is, after all, the wizard, not the wand, who makes the magic. The choosing of a particular wood for your wand is more a matter of personalities. How do you respond to a given type of wood or tree? What associations does the tree have for you? Or is there a particular type of magical action you intend to do with this wand—healing, for example, or protection?

This chapter describes the trees with which I have had the most experience. The trees are divided into four groups, each group corresponding to an element. These assignments stem from my own research and identify the dominant elemental essence in the tree's character and power. All wands can employ any of the elements to perform magical work. In each entry, you will find the elemental correspondences and connections to divine spirits of each wood. These associations are not always clear or consistently rational, being the stuff of myth and the magical arts. Some associations with other deities are also given, as well as lore from the work of various writers on the Celtic ogham signary, or tree alphabet of the bards. The common English name of the tree is given. In addition, I have included associations of the trees with the constellations of the zodiac and the modern Pagan system of eight seasonal festivals.[5]

The matter of Celtic festivals, calendars, and astrology is complex, and little scholarly work on these topics has been done, or at any rate brought to the view of the general public. The result of this void is that many writers have adopted and elaborated on the tree calendar invented by the poet Robert Graves in his book *The White Goddess*. The accuracy of Graves' interpretations of Old Irish and Welsh poetry has been pretty thoroughly discredited by scholars in those fields, yet the popularity of the book among occultists has resulted in an uncritical acceptance of its system. My own linkages between trees, constellations, and festivals is largely my own original work and also should not be mistaken for ancient Celtic lore.[6] It may be hard to see the thread connecting the various magical properties or predilections of the trees. To aid that understanding, I have also included for each tree a keyword that is the root, as it were, of the tree's particular magic. Any tree can be used for any magic, but you will appreciate that some trees have energy that is well suited to particular kinds and applications of magic.

Finally, I will note that this book is not a field guide. To learn to identify different species of tree, you will want to pick up the Peterson Field Guide to trees for your area—or another well-illustrated guide; look for one with photographs of leaves and bark. I use the guide *Eastern Trees* by George A. Petrides.

Now, to the trees!

5   This chapter is not intended by any means to be comprehensive. I heartily recommend Jacqueline Memory Paterson's compendious *Tree Wisdom* for much more detailed information about the biology, uses, folklore, and magical applications of all of these trees and their wood. See also Hageneder, Mountfort, and Blamires.

6   On the matter of research into astrology actually practiced by the Celts and what we do or do not know about the topic, see Ellis, "Early Irish Astrology" and O'Dubhain, Bayley, and Clouter; for an example of an elaboration of Graves, see Helena Paterson's *Celtic Moon Signs*.

Trees of Elemental Earth

Rowan • Elder • Ash • Juniper • Maple
Elm • Blackthorn & Plum • Ebony

An example of a rowan wand, top, and
an ash wand with a beehive pommel, below.

Rowan

KEY: *Quickening*

Also called mountain ash, quicken tree, and quickbeam for its powers of bestowing and enhancing life, rowan may be assigned to the constellation Capricorn and the beginnings of the return of the light at the winter solstice. Rowan unites fire and earth, a union that symbolizes the bridging between the world of ordinary reality and the astral world, accessible through magic and imagination. The earthy element is combined with elemental fire by the smith, even in winter's darkness. This combination of elements is also characteristic of the spiritual energy of the rowan tree, as seen in her fiery red-orange berries. Fire is the element of the magical will and is also the underlying essence of all crafts—the power of the human mind to transform raw materials into works of art.

The Celtic Govannon, lord of architecture and metalwork, is among the divinities of myth whose qualities rowan conveys. The Greek god Hephaestus also personifies this power, and in the Irish tradition so also do Goibniu, the smith and builder, and the Lady Brighid, triple goddess of fire made manifest in poetry, healing, and smithcraft. All three of Brighid's arts derive from elemental fire: in poetry, through the fire and light of poetic inspiration and passion; in healing, as the life force manifested in the warmth required for life in all warm-blooded creatures; and in smithcraft, we see how the heat of the forge transforms metals, and in so doing transforms human culture. Smelting metals may indeed be seen as one of the first magical arts (see Eliade, *The Forge and the Crucible*).

The goat of Capricorn also links the rowan to the Greco-Roman god Sylvanus or Pan, spirit of forests, half goat and half man. Capricorn is the sign the sun enters at the winter solstice, the longest night of the year. The orange berries of rowan trees are said to be the seeds of the reborn sun at this time of year. I think of the goat as the animal that waits on mountaintops for the sun's return. I also imagine the forge of Brighid containing the fire of the sun during the darkness of winter. She banks her coals through the night in order to bring back the warmth and life in spring at her festival of Imbolc. In Britain and Ireland at that time, the first lambs are born and the snowdrops appear.

The rowan's flowers and berries bear the pentagram, symbol of the five elements and five senses. The pentagram's use as a sign of protection lends rowan its traditional value as a tree of protection. Also called witchen or witchbane, the rowan has been considered the enemy of all evil witchery and protects against one being carried off to Faerie against one's will. That is, it offers some stability to the psyche that prevents one from spontaneously traveling to otherworlds under the influence of other entities. A tree of astral vision and protection that is particularly good for warding off evil spirits, rowan also is said to avert storms and lightning, and to bring peace.

Rowan is associated with serpents, dragons, and sacred places, and also with the ley lines or dragon lines of earth energy that are sometimes considered to be related to fairy paths. The dragon embodies primal energy, a strong force of creativity and natural flow that cannot be slain or tamed. For the wizard, dragon energy is considered natural, not supernatural, and a part of the power of the earth itself that is sometimes likened to the chi meridians in the human body, so well known now through traditional Chinese medicine. Dragon energy is drawn into harmony when we enter into partnership with it through the erection of standing stones at intersections of the dragon lines or by directing it in a wand or staff. Rowan's power is doubled by the inclusion of a dragon-scale core when it is fashioned as a wand.

Fine grained and creamy smooth, rowan wood is a delight to carve. It is especially suited for magic invoking form and order, ritual, growth, fertility, protection, rebirth, women's autonomy, poetry, metalwork, stone carving, weaving and spinning, geomancy, and work with ley lines.

Elder

KEY: *Regenerating*

The elder is another tree of abundant fruit. Elderberries are food for both humans and animals, and magically this means fertility and life in general. I associate elder with the constellation Taurus and its astrological ruler Venus, divine spirit of love, attraction, seduction, and coupling. The elder, by virtue of this bovine link, may be connected to the Irish cow goddess Boann of the Tuatha Dé Danann. It is a tree of birth, prosperity, and victory.

Jacqueline Paterson notes that the Hyldemoer, or "Elder Mother," was considered to be a spirit indwelling in the elder tree, who "worked strong earth magic" (Paterson, *Tree Wisdom*, 279). "No forester of old would touch elder, let alone cut it, before asking the Elder Mother's permission three times over, and even then he was still in dread of her possible wrath ... Certain North American tribes also believe that elder is the mother of the human race" (ibid., 279).

Elder is a famous witch tree—that is, one of the trees that witches were supposed to turn themselves into. It was considered to be one of the trees that could act as a conduit to the Faerie realm, especially if a person laid down under one and fell asleep, seduced by the fragrance of its flowers. Elder branches have traditionally been used in funeral pyres and were placed in the ground with burials (ibid., 289). Elder was said to have been used for the handles of witches' broomsticks.

The negative, deathly, and vengeful associations with the tree are perhaps overstated by medieval and Renaissance writers, when our ancestors were generally more fearful of forests and paranoid about malevolent witches. Paterson considers that elder is actually a healing tree associated with life itself, partly because of its medicinal properties and partly because it "regrew damaged branches and rooted from any part of itself. Thus [illustrating] the regenerative power of life" (ibid., 283). The power of life and regeneration is also the power of the Taurean bull, and like the bull, elder is both death and life.

The pith at the core of elder branches makes it well suited for the sort of design that includes a crystal point and a reservoir pommel stone or an inclusion in the center if the pith is removed. Some wand designs include a magnetized wire running through the center, and elder is a good choice in that case. Because this structure makes elder branches good for musical pipes, the wood is naturally suited to all sorts of enchantment through the association of music and song (chant). It is also particularly suited for healing and is an excellent choice for a wand of protection.

Ash

KEY: *Journeying*

The mighty ash with its many-fingered leaves is sacred to the constellation Virgo, the realm of the unmarried goddesses like Artemis (Roman Diana), who is the sister of Apollo. Virgo's traditional planetary ruler is Mercury—that same Roman god of intellect, method, and reason who is patron of magic. In the Greek pantheon, Mercury was Hermes, the messenger of the gods and wielder of a magic wand. He evolved into the figure of Hermes Trismegistus, the "thrice-great" Hermes who is the legendary founder of the Hermetic magical tradition.

The reasons for associating ash and Hermes have more to do with the quality of craft than with any mythological linkage. Hermes was represented as the god who taught human beings all the arts. Among the Irish divinities, Lugh Lámfada, the Samildánach—master of all crafts and arts—corresponds best to Hermes/Mercury. In Welsh legend, it is Gwydion, the trickster nephew of Math ap Mathonwy, who fulfills Hermes' role as trickster and divine mage. His son Llew is cognate with Irish Lugh, but the latter has different parents, and his story is also different. In the Irish myth, it is Lugh's possession of a magical spear that saves the Tuatha Dé Danann at the Second Battle of Moytura. Ash was a common wood for spear shafts; perhaps the shaft of this spear was made of ash wood.

The number of the ash tree is nine (thrice three), seen in the nine worlds of Norse Yggdrasil, the world tree or Tree of Life from which all the worlds spring. In this respect, it is the pathway or bridge by means of which the wizard may travel among the nine worlds.[7] We may think of the tree symbolically as Faerie or the astral dimension and its many worlds. Beneath Yggdrasil, the three Norns or Fates control the lives of gods and men. A dragon lives in the roots of the world ash and an eagle in its branches; the goat of Odin feeds upon the leaves and turns that food into ambrosia, the drink of the gods that provides immortality. Hanging upside down on the ash tree, Odin drank of the spring of destiny at its roots and the runes were revealed to him.

Tradition holds the ash also to be sacred to the Welsh sea god Llyr. The seas in myths are often the way to the otherworlds. The sea is changeable, ever in motion, questing, guiding, concealing, and revealing. Ash partakes of that primordial energy signified in Celtic cosmology by the sea. It is the medium in which all potential lies, the cauldron of creation.

Across Europe, the ash spear is a symbol of divine power. Poseidon, Odin, and Thor each wield a spear of ash, symbolic of an irresistible magical will and invincible protection. The Greek goddess Nemesis carries an ash wand as a symbol of divine justice. With it, she ensures that fortune (good or ill) is shared among all people and not only by the few. Nemesis is also called "Nemesis of the rain-making ash," identified as Adrasteia, daughter of the sea god Oceanus. The ocean—the water encircling the world in the Greek cosmology—symbolizes limitation and circumference. It shapes the boundary of the earth above and below.

Thus, the ash tree resonates with water and with earth—the two elements of the archetypal feminine. Ash is the consummate wood of spiritual growth and fecundity, independent and intellectual women, and female sovereignty. It is a wood of balance and the marriage of opposites. So generally magical is the ash that it is the wood often used for Yule logs, Maypoles, and, in some traditions, witches' brooms. Thus the phallic spear shaft or pole unites the masculine and feminine archetypal powers.

---

7   The Norse worlds or *heimar,* "homelands," are Alfheim, Asgard, Jotunheimr, Midgard, Muspelheim, Nithavellir, Niflheim, Svartalfheim, and Vanaheimr. In English, Alfheim is often named Elfhame or Elvenhome.

Prized for its straight and prominent grain and elasticity, ash wood makes a bold and sturdy wand. It is well suited for shamanic magic, traveling between worlds, protection, and the search for knowledge, as well as for magic to enhance one's skills at any art or craft. It is suited to the magic of wells and caves. Also, working with plant roots, the magic of female sovereignty, and—because of its links to water—weather working and dowsing. Ash's combination of earth and water make it ideal for healing magic. This may seem strange in the light of the association of ash with the spear of Lugh, but actually it is perfectly congruent. The act of killing in war is the inverse of healing. What can give life also can take life, and this is true of both earth and water. A body comes from the solid matter of earth, and to dust, ashes, or compost the body returns at death. Water is the source of life, and yet living things can drown in it. How especially aware of this last fact were the Irish fisher folk, who risked their lives on the sea. The spear also symbolizes moving straight toward a goal and hitting it. Thus we may see the key concept of pathways at work in ash.

Juniper
KEY: *Transforming*

Juniper is sacred to the Morrigan, "great queen" of the Tuatha Dé Danann or Fair Folk, and also to the Cailleach, the "hooded one." Both are dark forms of the Great Mother, goddesses of death and rebirth. Juniper is a tree of darkness and yet is evergreen. Its berries can be medicinal or poisonous. It evokes the season of Samhuinn, the waning of the year as winter begins and the natural world retreats into cold, darkness, and dormancy. For the vegetable world, as for humans in an earlier age (before central heating and electric lights), winter is a time of inward turning, contemplation, meditation, and dreaming. It is a return to the womb of the sheltered home and the huddled family fire, which either led to wintery death or rebirth in the spring.

Juniper manifests yin, the dark female power, mystery of the womb, and power of shadow that is the complement of light. We may also visualize the vast, dark depths of caverns and ocean—those places of darkness that swallow the dead. Juniper amplifies the power of seduction (in Latin, literally "to draw aside"). Seduction, in its broadest magical sense, is drawing aside the curtain of matter to reveal the spiritual being beneath. In this case, it is the seduction of the Great Mother, the irresistible psychic hold upon a person's emotional being, which results in the death of the person's ego and its submersion into the object of desire. Juniper is a tree of the *geas* and of fate.[8] A geas is a powerful binding spell that binds its subject to a particular task or restriction. Frequently in Irish legends, the playing out of a geas laid upon a hero reminds one of the playing out of fate in the Greek tragedies.

The Brothers Grimm retold the tale of "The Juniper Tree," in which a mother's spirit is manifested magically in a juniper that guides and magically helps the mother's daughter. In that tale we see combined death, the mother, and magical aid. Juniper wands are well suited to magic involving transformation and transition, the crossing of otherworldly thresholds, and the fundamental process of death and rebirth, not only in terms of reincarnation but in the symbolic sense contained in all mystery schools. To be fully human, wizards—and indeed all humans—must die to their merely material existence in order to be reborn with a spiritual perception of the higher dimensions of their own being.

Juniper is a soft wood with a coarse grain that polishes up beautifully. It is light and tough, supple, and emanates the power of transformation.

Maple

KEY: *Changing*

Maple is sacred to the autumnal equinox because of its fiery autumnal colors—a bold celebration of the season and the cycle of death and rebirth. Poised on the equinox, it is linked to both Libra and Virgo, air and earth. In North America, especially in its northern forests, the maple is a dominant tree with many varieties, including the sugar maple from which maple syrup is made. As such, it is associated with the life-giving sap of the trees, providing food and sweetness for those who treat it with respect and care. The autumnal equinox is also known in druid lore as the feast of Mabon, dedicated to the son-consort of the Great Mother. In the Welsh myths, Mabon, son of Modron (literally, "the son of the mother"), represents the power of the sun when it is imprisoned within the darkness of winter.

The dying-god motif is also to be found in the tale of John Barleycorn, who is sacrificed at the corn harvest and feeds the tribe, then is reborn in spring. Again we can find the pattern in the story of Gwion Bach, who by chance tastes Cerridwen's brew of wisdom and is pursued by her until, after many transformations, the goddess eats him. He is reborn from her womb, but Cerridwen still wishes to consign him to the darkness, so she puts him in a bag and throws

---

8   Pronounced as English "geese"; plural *geasa*.

him in the ocean. He is nevertheless reborn again and named Taliesin, "Shining Brow," by the nobleman who fishes him out of the water. The great poet is the reborn sun ever escaping the darkness of winter. This is, once more, the magic of the great rebirth, but maple also embodies the transcendent power of beauty. Maple represents both this power and the hope given by the brilliant red, yellow, and orange of its autumn leaves.

The maple certainly contains the power of the reborn sun, but it is most deeply a tree of the goddess Cerridwen herself. Sometimes the name Cerridwen is translated as "the bent one" or the "bowed one" and is thought to be an epithet for the moon. This goddess of wisdom and transformation, ambition, passion, life, and death may be compared to the Roman Minerva or the Greek Athena, all embodying a woman's power imbued with knowledge, wisdom, and magic. Minerva was born from the head of Jupiter, not from a mother's womb. She is woman as maiden, unruled by a husband; the powerful and mature wise virgin; patroness of art, words, music, magic, and war. This kind of virginity is not the Christian sexual sort (a woman who has never had sex with a man); rather, it is the woman of any age who is independent of a male sexual partner and not sexually active—so maiden or crone, as distinct from mother.

Maple is a strong wood, sometimes rebellious and tough, sometimes more gentle. It has a beautiful, smooth grain. It is hard yet excellent for carving. Maple is well suited to spells of control, finding, binding, transformation, creation, revolution, rebirth, poetry, beauty, harvest, healing, and abundance.

Elm

KEY: *Containing*

One of the tallest ancient forest trees, graceful in its chalice shape, limbs bowing down to the earth, elm is sacred to the Great Goddess in her form as Wise Grandmother. She is the Kabbalist's Binah, "understanding," who is associated with Saturn and limitation of created forms. Among the Celtic divinities, elm is sacred to Dana (Donn, in Cymric), the mother of all the gods and goddesses who gives her name to the Tuatha Dé Danann. One of elm's nicknames is elven, for its connection to the elves (the English or Germanic name for the people of the hollow hills). As such, elm is associated with burial mounds and with the doorways to Faerie. In recent times, many American and English elms have been killed off by Dutch elm disease. The tree has come to symbolize and embody the struggle of nature against humanity's destruction of the old forests. Elm's spirit is majestic and expansive, rooted and wise.

Elm is coarse grained, and staining brings out the grain pattern beautifully. It is a tough, hard wood. Elm is well suited to earth magic and the invocation of the Great Mother, healing, fertility, gardening, rebirth, destiny, understanding, binding, passage from one life (or phase of life) to another, metamorphosis, and endurance.

Blackthorn & Plum
KEY: *Blocking*

Blackthorn and plum are both members of the *Prunus* genus and so have similar properties. Blackthorn is one of the trees assigned to the Irish ogham few[9] Straif. Both blackthorn and plum resonate strongly with elemental earth. In European folklore, blackthorn is particularly associated with the Faerie Folk and Faerie mounds as a protective, densely thorned thicket or hedge tree. Sacred to the war goddesses, blackthorn and plum are nevertheless fruitwoods and so possess the power of fertility, fruitfulness, and abundance. Their thorns evoke protection and the setting of boundaries. The combination of fruit and thorns hints at forbidden pleasures.

Plum wood is extremely hard and ill tempered. It is a good substitute for blackthorn in regions where that Celtic sacred tree is unavailable. Blackthorn has a darker character and is considered by some to be hazardous to cut because of its associations with the Fair Folk. It embodies the spirit of the Irish dark goddess Babh, crow goddess of battle, winter, and protection, in whom we may see similarities to the witchy Welsh Cerridwen, protecting her potion-pot of wisdom. According to Susa Morgan Black, the blackthorn tree is "esoterically known as both the Mother of the Woods and the Dark Crone of the Woods."

Since the time of the Celts, folklore has given blackthorn a sinister reputation. The stories of witches using the thorns to prick and impale curse dolls may or may not be true, but they certainly *could* be used for such a purpose. I never like to recommend that anyone cast curses. Fantasy novels, movies, and games have rather trivialized the whole business of cursing, suggesting that such spells can be used as a quick self-defense and just as quickly undone. In real magic, curses are nursed over time, often generate unpleasant backlash or unintended side effects, and take time to bear their dark and bitter fruit. They are also sometimes extremely hard to undo. Like most destructive forces, once the explosion has been triggered, its energy

---

9   The letters of the ogham signary are called *fews,* meaning "branches" (see appendix I).

cannot be taken back. More benign defensive and protective spells are well suited to the nature of blackthorn and plum, and more practical for the mage. These woods are also, as you might have guessed, well suited to communication and collaboration with the Fair Folk, yet such relationships must be approached with care.

I do not recommend blackthorn or plum to the novice mage. They are not trees that submit easily to being told what to do, and their characters are distinctly shadowy and dark. Handling a thorn wand requires a mage who has fully mastered his or her own shadow and feels confident in relationship to the dark goddesses.

When polished, plum and blackthorn wood take a smooth luster but are very hard to carve. They are excellent wand woods for the creative artist overcoming barriers, keeping people or disturbances at bay, and evoking toughness, persistence, patience, and protection. Plum and blackthorn are also suited for the divining of precious metals or minerals, due to their closeness to the hollow hills.

Ebony
KEY: *Dominating*

The tropical wood ebony is a powerful wand wood, often jet black in color but also brown or even mottled with creamy streaks. Ebony is extremely hard and dense, making a heavy wand charged with power. In Africa and Indonesia, ebony is a traditional carving wood despite the difficulty of working with it, and when polished it produces a superb medium for dark moon magic. From working with this wood, I've come to associate it with elemental earth, even though the moon is usually linked to the element of water. Hecate, that powerful and mysterious Greek goddess of the dark moon, resides alongside Hades in the underworld. The magic of darkness is earth magic precisely because of the absence of the moon's light.

Ebony is certainly a wood of darkness but not necessarily of black magic or the dark arts. It has powers to conceal or reveal secrets, to heal, and to draw upon the powers of the "dark" gods and goddesses—such as Greek Circe, Hecate, Hades/Pluto, Celtic Cerridwen, and Arawn, lord of the otherworld. Access to the realm of Hades or Arawn is not access to a place of evil, it is access to the realm of the ancestors. Those souls not alive in the sunshine world ruled by Zeus and the Olympians dwell in this mirror-image world. Put in Taoist terms, the "normal" world is yang and the otherworld is yin. The wizard who seeks to interact with the denizens of that world will be greatly aided by a wand of ebony.

Ebony is also a wood of dragon energies, and takes a dragon-scale core with its black fire very well. Its shiny black surface is alluring and seductive, and no doubt the wood is particularly suited to magic of seduction, for good or ill. Consider Circe, the enchantress who imprisoned the Greek hero Odysseus as her sex slave and turned his crew into pigs.

The energy here is the aggressive and assertive side of male and female sexuality. That is, the energy is masculine in the archetypal sense of being active, aggressive, and dominant. This energy applies to more than sex. It may be used to penetrate any problem to its core and take control of it, dominating as a leader, not just as an evil dictator. It is the dark, shadow part of the soul that holds all the energy we must suppress in our daylight social roles. This energy is a strong source of the kind of dominance in which a leader takes aside another person to persuade that person to go along with the will of the leader.

Trees of Elemental Air

Hawthorn • Hazel • Lilac • Cedar
Apple • Linden • Yew • Walnut

An example of a hazel wand stylized in the unicorn-horn fashion,
top, and a yew wand with a crystal-embedded fork, below.

Hawthorn
KEY: *Guarding*

Hawthorn or whitethorn is sacred to the constellation Aquarius and to the white hart of Arthurian romance who leads the adventurer into the otherworld through the ancient darkness of the forest. Hawthorn's vibration is that of the Green Man, personification of the wild and of the union of human, animal, and vegetable fertility. We see the same union in the figure of Cernunnos, the antlered stag god, and the antlered caps of prehistoric shamans. The donning of antlers unites man and beast, the upper and lower worlds, and spirit and body.

With its twisted branches and sharp thorns, hawthorn is a tree of defense, and it holds the power of lightning, the Promethean fire stolen from Zeus. Loremasters say it can detect the presence of magic because it is a tree through which magical powers enter the manifest world from beyond. Thus it is highly suited to projecting powers over other kinds of magic—counter jinxes and counter curses, but also controlling the accuracy of all spells. Hawthorn is well suited for magic of protection and for strengthening one's magical powers generally, as well as spells of control, warding, sending, detection, concealment, weatherworking, and protection against lightning and evil spirits. Its association with Bealtaine through its white blossoms in May makes hawthorn a particularly good wood for Bealtaine rituals that celebrate the rebirth of the Green Man and the renewal of fertility in the earth.

Hazel
KEY: *Understanding*

Hazel is the tree of the White Goddess, the Queen of Heaven. It conveys the energy of the constellation Libra. For me, the goddess of stars is Welsh Arianrhod, whose name means "the silver wheel." Some scholars believe this name refers to the moon, but unlike Cerridwen, who represents the thin crescent or the dark of the moon, Arianrhod is the goddess of the full moon. She is the miraculous virgin mother who gives birth to Dylan and Llew in the fourth book of the Mabinogion (these children are, respectively, the sea and the sun). Arianrhod's story reminds me of Venus and Aphrodite in Roman and Greek myth, for she is a goddess of attraction and female beauty. She is also a virgin goddess like Greek Athena and Artemis. This goddess may rule love, but she is not a male plaything or seductress; quite the contrary. It is she whose power controls men, and it is to her that a man comes for his name and his arms, symbolizing all that makes him a man. Arianrhod is manifest in all forms of attraction, particularly those hard to resist, and in the pride of beautiful women to choose their own man or none at all.

Arianrhod, sister of Gwydion, the god of magic and cunning, is said to reside in the constellation Corona Borealis. Beyond the moon's bright face, I think that her power is also that of the greater silver wheel of the galaxy, the spiraling power of gravity itself, the force of attraction that binds the worlds together and determines the relationships between and among bodies.

Arianrhod is not usually interpreted to be a goddess of love. Indeed, in her story, she is very insistent on her virginity. However, as mentioned before, these stories show signs of revision by the monks who wrote them down during the medieval Christian era. Pre-Christian ideas about virginity were more complex than not having your hymen broken. In Latin, the word *virgin* meant merely that a woman was not married and so not controlled or owned by a husband. *Virgo* in Latin meant an unmarried woman and implied one who was whole and undefiled, which is the real issue when it comes to virgin goddesses. The goddess Sophia, "wisdom," was considered to be a virgin in this sense.

Arianrhod embodies this sacred freedom, and so does the hazel. She does not want to marry and insists upon her own sovereignty. But the story of the miraculous birth of Llew and Dylan does implicate her in the power of reproduction, and in fact puts her in the same league as the blessed Virgin Mary. The story represents her parthenogenesis as due to Gwydion's trickery, but the actual cause is a mystery—the primal mystery of the womb.

Hazel is a tree in which this spirit of female autonomy and power dwells. Arianrhod is the goddess not so much of carnal love but of the enchanting power of imperious female beauty to inspire emotion. We must consider this on the level of the divine powers. Arianrhod is also the teacher of enchanters and poets. All worthy wizards and bards are summoned to her table. In the Celtic legends, hazelnuts feed the salmon of wisdom in the deep pool of Segais, otherworld source of the River Boyne in Ireland. This watery association is important to remember in hazel. The well of Segais is surrounded by the nine hazels of inspiration. The hazelnuts ripen and fall into the pool, where the salmon eats them. She cracks their shells, which stain the waters of the well purple. The empty shells float off down the five streams that flow from the well to give poetic inspiration—what druids call awen. The five streams are the five senses through which humans perceive the world. The story of the Boyne is a primordial creation myth much like those associated with Eden and the rivers that flowed out of it. The well at the center of creation is also the heart chakra—center of love and attraction.

Hazel wood is close-grained, white, and takes detailed carving beautifully. It is well suited to magic of wisdom, beauty, charm, love, stars, navigation, summoning, attraction, and creativity. Its strong associations with the sidhe, or Celtic Faeries, make it ideal for communication and collaboration with them in a much lighter and more cerebral character than that of blackthorn and even hawthorn.

Lilac
KEY: *Imagining*

Evoking the energy of the constellation Gemini in the zodiac, lilac wood carries the power of spring. The intoxicating scent of its flowers in springtime exemplifies the magic of air. It is the power of mental ecstasy, inspiration, awen. Gemini is ruled by Mercury, whose domain is writing, speech, song, reason, enchantment, and travel. In the Welsh myths, it is Gwydion who is like the Roman Mercury, the mage-trickster whose chief power is wit. His role as communicator and guide of souls makes the mercurial Gwydion the patron of all who walk between the worlds. Air is the element of communication, both verbal and nonverbal, through the senses of sight, hearing, and smell. It is a masculine element in the sense of being actively assertive. You can see this if you consider the strength of wind. Wind can destroy, it can bring fertility in the rains, and it carries the seeds and pollen of many plants. Air manifests in lilac as charm, wit, cleverness, learning, knowledge, and reason—all powers that are intimately involved in spoken and written language. Lilac flowers demonstrate that this wit can be intoxicating in its scent.

Lilac wood is close-grained, creamy, and smooth, excellent for carving intricate interlace patterns. It is well suited to magic of union, attraction, intellectual enhancement of sexual pleasure, cultivation of creative bliss, intellectual pursuits, imagination, information, mental power, creation of harmony, travel, illusion, detection, verbal wit, writing, charm, and work with the Fair Folk.

Cedar
KEY: *Cleansing*

The cedar tree is sacred to the cross-quarter feast of Imbolc (February 1), the feast of Brighid (Bride, Brigid, Brigit, Brigantia), goddess of poetry, healing, and smithcraft. These three arts may be assigned to the elements—poetry to air, healing to water, and smithcraft to both fire and earth. Thus Bride envelopes complete wholeness, the entire universe—not surprising for the daughter of the Dagda. That great Father God is the patron of druids, and his daughter (or three daughters, as some say) masters the three principal arts of the bards, seers, and druids. Bards work enchantment in the art of poetry and music; the seers (or ovates) used their sixth sense to practice healing; and druids delve deeper into the alchemy of the cosmos, symbolized by smithcraft.

Cedar is applicable to all the magical arts. It is especially powerful for clearing negativity from an area prior to magical work. The tree is also called arborvitae, "tree of life." Its bright-grained, soft wood is especially suited to preservation of sacred places, forests, and groves; dedication of sacred space for worship and magic; and bringing light out of darkness. This spiritual light is the source of magic and is well applied to healing, smithcraft, metallurgy, the making of jewelry, poetic inspiration and enchantment through poetry, and for healing, whether through energy work or the use of herbs.

Apple
KEY: *Singing*

Apple is sacred to the feast of Lughnasadh (Lúnasa), the Celtic goddess Rhiannon, and the god Lugh. The link in the realm of time between apple and Lughnasadh (August 1) is a matter of the tree's life cycle. The apple fruits are ready to harvest after August. The Lady Rhiannon, like Romano-British Epona, is associated with horses. She was honored by cavalry soldiers and knights during the Roman occupation of Britain. Rhiannon is also portrayed as a queen of the otherworld, a Faerie bride who comes to take Pwyll, King of Dyfed, as her husband. The apple is an otherworldly tree, its fruit the food of the gods. Another name for the otherworld is Avalon, the land of apples, to which King Arthur was taken after being mortally wounded. So, we may expect apple wood to be particularly attuned to travel between worlds.

The core of the apple fruit in cross-section is a pentagram, a five-pointed star. This symbol is traditionally associated with the five senses or the four elements with the addition of the fifth—quintessence. The pentagram is also considered a symbol of protection and blessing. The theme of passage between the worlds and the ability to perform enchantment is reiterated in the story of the silver bough. Celtic bards are described in legend as carrying apple branches laden with silver bells as a symbol of their office and magical power. The mythical Silver Bough of Apple provided entry to Faerie and may be considered the epitome of the apple wand.

In Old Ireland, there was a marvelous silver bough, which, like the golden bough of Virgil, served as a doorway into the otherworld of the gods. Some say it was the property of Manannan MacLir, others that it belonged to Lugh. Cut from a mystic apple tree, the silver branch gave forth magical music that none might resist. The apples it bore, dangling like bells, served the sojourner for food while in the land of the gods. Cormac MacAirt, High King of Ireland, was lured to the Summerland one day when he encountered a young man holding a wondrous branch of silver that had nine golden apples dangling from it. When the youth shook the branch, the apples touched and made sweet music like bells so that he who heard it forgot his sorrows and cares.[10]

Thus are apple wands especially suited to opening the doorways into otherworlds and spells to do with travel, deception (or the unmasking of it), illumination, love, harmony, beauty, harvest, abundance, magic of rescue and recovery, and the defeat of dark, devouring powers. Apple evokes poetic inspiration and the power to enchant through words and music. It brings the otherworlds into this world.

Linden

KEY: *Attracting*

The linden, also called basswood and lime-tree, is the tree perhaps most sacred to the power of love. There are many Celtic heroines who exemplify this power, which the Romans gave principally to Venus—Dierdre, for example, whose beauty was so peerless. But the Irish deity of love is male, and his name is Aengus Og.

The linden tree's flowers look like shooting stars, and its flowers have an intoxicating perfume in summer. Linden wood is laden with the power of attraction that underlies love, infatuation, musical harmony, and the very fabric of the cosmos in such forces as magnetism, adhesion, and gravity. It is a very lightweight, airy, and smooth wood, excellent for carving. Its fibrous wood was used by Native Americans to make strong ropes, something that is also symbolic of its power to attract, hold, and bind. Linden is especially suited to spells of creation and transmutation, illumination, love, attraction, binding, obligation, healing wounds,

---

10 Adapted from Lewis Spence, *The Magic Arts in Celtic Britain.*

enhancement of beauty, peace, and acts of enchantment generally. It is particularly ill suited for cursing or any magic that aims at division or separation.[11]

Yew
KEY: *Remembering*

Yew is sacred to the Celtic god Arawn, the gray lord of the dead and master of possibility, and also to the Morrigan, the Great Queen Maeve. In several guises, she is the goddess overseeing the death of heroes, the lifeblood, and the doorway death presents between the worlds. We may also think of the Greek god Hermes' office as psychopomp (guide of souls), leading the souls of the dead into the new world of the afterlife, or of Hades, brother of Zeus and lord of the underworld. The evergreen yew is attuned to travel between the worlds—changes of state between life now and life with our ancestors. This is why yew trees appear in so many British and Irish churchyards beside the graves. Yew's toxic berries give further associations with death and shamanic trance.[12] In druid orders, the yew is considered the tree of the ovate—the seer, diviner, and healer—who works with the ancestors.

Yew is especially suited to spells of transformation, illusion, astral travel, mediumism, and necromancy; the conjuration of helpful spirits, guides, and ancestors; and also spells to bestow knowledge, eloquence, or persuasion. Obviously, a yew wand is also well suited to spells related to death and grieving.

Walnut
KEY: *Illuminating*

Sacred to the lord of winds and lightning, walnut partakes of both air and fire. It is perhaps the consummate wood for weather magic. It is not clear who among the Celtic divinities can be clearly called the spirit of the sky, storm, and wind. In Gaul he was called Taranis, lord of

---

11 Many love spells of the classical age took the form of binding spells, but linden is not well suited to the magic of the so-called curse tablets that aim to divide one lover from another to the advantage of the spellcaster (or the client). See David Ogden's "Binding Spells: Curse Tablets and Voodoo Dolls in the Greek and Roman Worlds" in Ankarloo and Clark.

12 I do not recommend using yew berries in potions for voyages to the otherworlds unless you want to make the voyages permanent, which I also do not recommend.

thunder. Jupiter and Zeus are the Roman and Greek gods, as is Jehovah of the Bible and Indra in the Vedic pantheon of India. Many gods and goddesses are associated with the heavens as either sky, storm, or sun deities.

In the Irish pantheon, I am inclined to look to the Dagda to fill this role. Portrayed in some stories as a buffoon, the Dagda's main claim to fame is that he can produce and consume vast amounts of porridge. His magic cauldron could supply endless quantities of food to feed an army. In addition, the Dagda was known for his long club, an instrument that caused the Romans to equate him with Hercules. We may also interpret his club as a wand or a wizard's staff, for the Dagda was known as the god of druids—that is, workers of magic.

If we read these images mythopoetically, we can say that the cauldron of plenty is the universe itself, the dome of heaven, a universe of limitless abundance. The Dagda's miraculous appetite is a symbol of his omnipotence. The rod or staff is the lightning bolt that comes from the clouds, the source of fresh water and successful agriculture, and the storm winds that refresh the air.

It is this elemental power of air and abundance that we find within the walnut tree. The shape of the walnut tree's nut connects it magically to the head. It looks like a brain when opened, right down to the left and right hemispheres. So, walnut is attuned to the crown chakra, to mysticism, and to one's Holy Guardian Angel, as Abra-Melin the Mage calls it. This is to say that walnut's power includes the ability to open one to the fullest dimensions of one's being. If we look to Jupiter, we find that the sky father governs all forms of expansion and increase: expansion of wealth, horizons, the mind, the feelings.

Walnut wood ranges from light to very dark brown in color and is easy to carve. In a wand, it is especially suited for wind and weather magic; spells of expansion, vortices, and enhancement of the powers of breath; and spells to conjure or avert lightning, hurricanes, or cyclones. It's also good for spells of teleportation, astral travel, and inspiration.

Trees of Elemental Fire

Oak • Holly • Redwood &
Sequoia • Cherry • Beech

An example of an oak wand with Futhark rune
leaves, top, and a cherry wand, below.

Oak

KEY: *Opening*

The most powerful and sacred of druid trees, oak resonates with the constellation Leo by virtue of its solar associations in folklore. It holds the power to draw lightning or the bolt of inspiration. The sun, which rules Leo, is the source of life and light. Psychologically, the sun is the center of the self, as it is of the solar system. Oak symbolizes all solar heroes, those who venture out from their homelands to achieve great deeds and bring home wondrous treasures after voyaging into the underworld. There are a number of Celtic divinities who are called solar deities by scholars. Lugh and Ogma Sunface are two, but Brighid is also sometimes considered a solar goddess. Hu and Arthur are also numbered among the supreme solar deities in Celtic lore, but perhaps the most primal is Bel or Belenos, who is often considered to be the primal spirit of fire. In the Greek and Roman pantheon, the sun is Apollo, who is also the divine spirit of law, healing, and beauty.

Oak traditionally has provided not only one of the most durable woods for construction and fuel but also the acorn on which our ancestors fed their pigs. Oak is one of the longest-lived trees, thus embodying great wisdom as well as strength. The word *druid* is thought to derive from the Old Celtic words for *oak* and *wisdom*. As the wizard wood, there is no more magical wood for wandmaking, and it is especially noted for enhancing the endurance of spells against time and counter-spells. The acorn resembles a helmeted head and so relates to the crown chakra, the seat of spiritual power and wisdom. Acorns also often resemble the head of the penis and so are an embodiment of fertility in all its forms. The symbolic union of wisdom and fertility is one of the remarkable qualities of oak trees.

Natural branches of oak are often twisted and gnarly and have thick, rough bark and a coarse, dark grain that can be tough to carve and does not easily carry detailed figural carving on a small scale. Oak can also be hard to harvest, as deadwood will cling high in an oak's crown for a very long time before a wind comes along strong enough to break it loose. Oak is a hard and heavy wood, especially suited to the magic of leadership, wise rule, personal sovereignty, authority, power, protection, sealing or opening doors, endurance, and the invocation of wisdom, fertility, and abundance.

Holly

KEY: *Penetrating*

Holly and oak form a pair in the lore of the Celts, for each represents half of the year. The story was told how the Holly King and the Oak King would battle each other to determine who was stronger twice a year. At midsummer, when the oaks are in full leaf, they dominate the forests, and the smaller holly trees are lost in the abundance of the Oak King's splendor. But after the sun turns again southward, starting its waning journey, the Holly King grows stronger each day. As an evergreen tree, holly remains green and bold when the oak leaves begin to fall, and at the winter solstice, the Holly King has triumphed. The oaks stand naked and apparently dead while the holly trees now show their red berries upon their spear-sharp leaves.[13] As the winter solstice passes, however, the cycle comes round again and the sun wanes hotter each day, traveling further north until the oaks begin to leaf out again and by midsummer are ruling the forests once more.

This story is one of the things that links Arthur, the solar king, to the oak—*Rex Quandam et Futurus*, the Once and Future King. This makes the holly a darker figure, not evil, but the natural complement to the sun king. Some among the wise associate this dark king with the Greek Hades, who rules the underworld of shades and who abducted Persephone and brought on the grief of her mother, Demeter. The despair of Demeter, the earth mother, caused all living things to die and winter to descend upon the earth.

Despite this association with winter and the underworld, holly is one of the most fiery of woods from the standpoint of the alchemical elements. The Gaelic word *tinne,* used for the holly ogham few, means "fire."

If we consider the holly king to be Hades, then he corresponds to Arawn in the Welsh pantheon. He does not rule over a dark world but a world that is the opposite of our reality. When it is winter in our world, it is summer in the otherworlds. So, we find that what seemed a sinister figure is really just the sun in another guise—the sun as it exists in the otherworlds, in our unconscious soul.

Holly, by its mythical associations to Arawn and Hades, is a powerful protective wood, good against evil spirits, poisons, angry elementals, and lightning. It is also particularly good for averting fear and so allowing courage to emerge. It is also associated with dream magic and

---

13 It is actually the female holly trees that bear the red berries in fall and winter, so perhaps it should be the Holly Queen.

eternal life, and is well suited for any magic dealing with the overthrow of old authorities and success in business, hunting, or quests. Its energy moves us to progress to a new stage of development. Holly wood is very fine-grained, hard, and smooth, and almost ivory in color if it is not stained. It is a truly exquisite wood for wands.

Redwood & Sequoia
KEY: *Aspiring*

The giant redwood is among the most magnificent of all conifers. As an evergreen, redwood is the embodiment of life and the assertive striving upward to the sky. Redwood is associated with the constellation Sagittarius, the archer or centaur. It is also associated with the stag god Cernunnos, the Wild Man, and with the hunted stag of summer, king of the forest, and the white hart, who guides souls through the realms of Abred (the world of forms) and across the boundaries between worlds.

The key factor in redwood, besides its fiery color, is the extraordinary age and durability of these trees. Redwoods can grow to over 300 feet tall and 20 feet in diameter at their base. They are truly giants. They are also enormously old. The ancient sequoias of the North American West Coast are older than human history. They have two ways of reproducing—the ordinary sexual way involving seeds and also cloning. Because of this, a whole series of genetically identical trees can proceed from one seed. Some of the trees alive today may be the last in a line of clones extending back twenty or thirty thousand years.[14] Magically, this means that redwoods have born the secret fire, concentrating it for ages. Used for a wand, redwood is ideally suited for any magic that aims at protection, survival, endurance, persistence, restoration of self, and communication with ancestors. Beyond even ancestors, redwood wands open the wizard to communication with the prehistoric and ancient roots of the earth herself.

Another natural quality of the giant redwoods that has magical implications is their dependence on the coastal fogs of the Pacific Northwest. Redwoods are so tall that their circulation systems can barely pump water to the top limbs, so they have developed the ability to absorb water directly into their needles from the fogs. This characteristic makes a redwood wand ideal for raising druidic fogs. These magical fogs are famous in the ancient Irish tales, where they are used to bewilder and defeat enemy armies or ships. However, fog has a more benevolent

---

14 See the Trees of Mystery website at http://www.treesofmystery.net/sequoia.htm.

quality too—it masks the present world of illusions and opens doorways into the otherworlds. It brings water and green to all plant life. Water mist and water vapor are the stuff of clouds, and the water cycle of cloud, fog, and rain, with evaporation, is the very life's breath of the earth.

Thus, wands crafted from redwood can offer the deepest power of the earth's living presence, personified in Greek myth as the goddess Gaia. The fire of the redwood is the fire of life at its very core.

Because of the tree's size, redwood has a very broad and beautiful grain, is quite lightweight and soft, and has a dark red color without the need of any stain. Because it is a soft wood, the fibers tear easily, so it is not well suited to detailed carving. It is better to keep the form simple and let the beauty of the wood itself come forth without adornment. Besides those qualities already mentioned, redwood is excellent for drawing down power from heaven to earth and for spells of religious seeking and discipline, mystical union with nature and wild animals, hunting magic, the martial arts as spiritual discipline, and spells for wisdom and experience.

Cherry
KEY: *Desiring*

The cherry tree, like the holly, is sacred to the spirit of the hunt and of protection; in classical astrology that quality is the spirit of Mars. Called Ares by the Greeks and often identified with Teutates among the Celtic tribes, Mars should not be thought of as strictly a god of war. Such divinities served as patrons of the warrior class in a society. This type of social class does not represent the sort of military organizations of modern states. At a more fundamental level, the warrior class in tribal societies are the protectors of the tribe; in many ways, they are the ideal of manhood. This is the spirit of cherry wood.

It is notable that in Japanese culture the cherry tree is associated with love because of its blossoms, delicate perfume, and red fruit. This may at first seem like a contradiction, but the matter will be clearer if we remember that Ares was the lover of Aphrodite—not her husband, who was Hephaestus, the divine smith, a solid working craftsman. Mars is her *lover*. The union of opposites in the two deities of female love and male assertive strength exemplifies the union of all assertive and receptive forms of action. This is the love of sexual attraction, a force that draws a woman to a man because of his confidence and daring, and a force likewise that draws in the man to a woman. It is the force of desire. Cherry wands partake of this quality of sexual attraction, which provides them with a powerful spiritual polarity. This tension of polarized forces, which are opposites but also powerfully attractive to each other, enhances the fundamental dynamic nature of all magical actions.

Cherry wood is red in hue; like blood, it darkens with age and exposure to sunlight. It is imbued with the power of making and doing, achievement, and self-assertion over obstacles and critics. The cherry fruit is magically linked to the root chakra and so to sexual love—the life force of attraction and renewal. Cherry wands are especially well suited to invocations and blessings of sacred fires, as well as to spells of finding, hunting, conflict, war, competition, communion with animals, unification of groups or tribes, mating, the balance of assertive and receptive forces, and the amplification of magical will generally. Cherry wood can also make a very powerful healing wand for injuries of body or soul sustained in conflict, loss, or from the breakup of a passionate attachment.

Beech
KEY: *Learning*

The stately beech is another tree sacred to the sun. The leaves of the beech turn on their stalks to face the sun. It can thus be considered sacred to Greek Apollo and to Celtic Lugh, Ogma, and Belenos, each of whom is associated with the brilliance of the sun. The sun represents the deep source of all life and beauty at the center of the planetary system. It is a symbol of the Self, the deep center of the human psyche. The beech nut, like the oak's acorn, is a food source eaten by humans and their pigs. Jacqueline Memory Paterson calls beech "Mother of the Woods" for its nurturing qualities, but the beech nut may also be food for thought. The tree is most intimately associated in Celtic tradition with wisdom and books. In several Germanic languages, the word for *beech tree* and *book* are very similar, and legend has it that the beech was the first wood upon which words were written.

This legend links the beech tree to the gods of writing, thought, and wisdom—Egyptian Thoth, Greek Hermes, and Roman Mercury. In the Celtic pantheon, Ogma, the inventor of the ogham signary, is considered to be god of eloquence and persuasion. In Welsh legend, it is Gwydion, the trickster mage, who may be likened to this power of language and solar brilliance. For language is the root of wisdom and the root of magic; both are founded in communication and its power to illuminate the mind.

Beech is a beautifully grained wood, golden in color, and it takes fine carving well. It is well suited to all forms of solar and positive magic and to the enhancement of creativity, learning, and the search for information. The wizard seeking magical books and learning will wish to employ a beech wand.

Trees of Elemental Water

Alder • Chestnut • Spruce, Pine &
Fir • Birch • Willow • Poplar

An example of a feminine willow wand with crystal point,
moonstone pommel, and stylized willow leaves; the crescent moon
and willow ogham accentuate its use for divination and balance.

Alder

KEY: *Preserving*

Soft and easily carved, alder is a superb wand wood, sacred to the constellation Pisces, the fishes. Alder is famous in bridge building for its ability to resist rotting when submerged in water. It was used in Scotland to build *crannochs*, fortified villages floating on alder logs in lochs and connected to the land by a defensible bridgework. Most of Venice, Italy, is built on alder pilings. Alder is symbolically a wood of bridging, crossing over, and connection to other worlds, both in its use to make bridges crossing waters and in its use submerged in water. Water was the element most thoroughly connected to the Celtic otherworld of Faerie. The alder has been revered because its sap turns red when exposed to air, thus giving it the appearance of blood.[15] This characteristic is also the source of considerable negative folklore, suggesting that alder is dangerous. Paul Kendall speculates that this negative press might be because alder woods were boggy and treacherous, as well as filled with boggarts and bandits hiding out:

> When Deirdre of the Sorrows of Irish mythology eloped with Naoise, son of Usna, they fled from Ulster to Alba (Scotland) to escape the wrath of King Conchobhar mac Nessa, to whom Deirdre had been betrothed. They hid from the king's pursuing warriors in the alder woods of Glen Etibhe, where they eventually settled, and themes of hiding and secrecy connected with alder recur elsewhere in Celtic lore (Kendall, "Mythology and Folklore of the Alder").

Alder is also associated with the Celtic god Bran the Blessed, and so also with ravens, immortality, and oracular powers. Like birch, alder is sacred to bards and musicians because it is an excellent wood for making pipes and whistles (Paterson, 247). Thus, alder makes an excellent water wand and is especially suited to oracular magic, seership, dreamwork, and spells for preservation, concealment, crossing, emotional bridges, and bridging the worlds. It is also well suited to magic of music and enchantment, and spells against flooding or to protect from water damage or drowning.

---

15 I have come across loremasters who consider alder to be a fiery wood because of this blood-red color, suggesting that its fiery nature explains why it endures in water. That, to my mind, seems unsatisfactory. By the same logic, we would say that salamanders (the fire elementals, not the amphibians) are of the element of water because they endure in fire.

Chestnut

KEY: *Producing*

Like the oak, the chestnut is a tree of abundant food. Though I ascribe it to the element of water, it is also a wood with strong sky energies. Its nuts are prolifically feminine in their fertility. Among the ancient Greeks, the chestnut tree was known to have originated in Lydia (in western Asia Minor) before it was brought to Europe. Though a tree of southern, warm climes, it has flourished in England. In North America, both the American chestnut and also the horse chestnut also flourished, and indeed chestnuts were the dominant climax forest trees of eastern North America until the introduction of chestnut blight, a fungus that originated in China. This blight almost wiped out the American chestnut. The American Chestnut Foundation is one group that has worked to breed blight-resistant American chestnut trees, which have been reintroduced into the forests their ancestors once ruled. This history of devastation and survival serves not only as botanical history but also as myth. Mythically, the chestnut is considered a tree of Zeus because its nuts were called the "acorns of Zeus." I suspect this is a punning reference to Zeus's testicles, as his seed was so prolifically planted throughout the world by his many love affairs. The tree actually bears an energy and character of the Great Mother, Gaia, whose husband, Ouranos, was castrated by his son Kronos (Zeus's father). The testicles of Ouranos fell into the sea and created Aphrodite from their *aphros*—Greek for "sea foam."

Such a complex testicular genealogy is speculation and applied mythopoetic logic. However, the chestnut dryads have led me to believe that the chestnut tree embodies the fertile womb of the Great Mother in her form as both earth and ocean. Since we are land animals, we often speak of Mother Earth and the fertility of the soil, yet Mother Sea is a figure deeply submerged in the collective unconscious of humanity. Born so prematurely (compared to other mammals), humans come from the womb utterly helpless and remain so for years. We have a strong subconscious memory of life in the warm, dark, watery depths. Paleontologists maintain that the first life forms on earth (Gaia's first children) emerged in the sea. Indeed, life forms did not climb out of the sea for millions of years. Can a tree embody such vast prehistory?

Consider Aphrodite in a larger context: the chestnut tree and her nuts have been compared to "the acorns of Zeus" and his grandfather's "acorns" as a primal seed implanted in the sea to bloom into the goddess of sexual reproduction and sexual desire. The emergence of sexual reproduction into the plant and animal kingdoms is a crucial turning point in the evolution of life on earth. The chestnut tree's reproductive organs illustrate the complexity and diversity of sex among trees. It bears male, pollen-bearing flowers and also bisexual flowers that are male at the extremities and female at the base, where the flowers cluster and transform into chestnuts. The seeds themselves are delicate and must be protected from moisture and frost, so the husk that forms around the nut is extra protective—not only waterproof but covered in spikes. This gives chestnut wood strongly protective energies, especially potent when used to protect children and families. A wand of chestnut wood draws upon the power of Aphrodite and also her mother, the sea.

Chestnut is linked magically to the constellation Cancer, presiding over midsummer, the highest festival of the Fair Folk. The Celtic deity I associate with chestnut is Manannan Mac-Lir, the Irish lord of the sea. Likewise, we may point to the many ladies of the lake in Welsh legend, and to the goddess Dana, who is linked by some Celtic scholars to the Danube River, from which the people of Danu were thought to originate. As Donn, she appears in the Welsh Mabinogion as the Great Mother, progenitor of many deities.

The House of Donn descends from this mother goddess and includes Gwydion, god of knowledge; his sister Arianrhod, goddess of the stars and moon; Govannan, the smith god; and Llew Llaw Gyffes, the solar god born of Arianrhod and raised by Gwydion. The other divine house in Welsh legend is the House of Llyr, which includes, besides that sea god, Manawyddan, the cognate of the Irish Manannan MacLir. Read the full stories in the Mabinogion (see Ford), but my point here is that both of the divine houses of Wales descend from water divinities. One is the goddess of the Great River, and the other is the god of the sea.[16] In Greek, Roman, and Celtic thought, the sea or ocean is personified by male deities, while rivers, springs, and lakes are the realm of goddesses. Greek legends call these sea and water women naiads and the water elementals undines.

A chestnut wand is perfect for the magic of water, including the protection of waters, purification, and travel by water. Its power is the power of reflection, making a chestnut wand most effective for magic of introspection, meditation, or indeed of gestation either literal or figurative. It is a wand wood also unquestionably suited to any magic of fertility, abundance, nurturance, and creativity, as well as concealment, emotional balance, and cleansing ritual spaces. Finally, a chestnut wand is well suited for magic having to do with relationships, especially that of mother and child.

16 It is worth noting that when Arianrhod gives birth to Dylan, her first son unites the line of the river with the sea, just as we may observe all rivers flow to the sea.

Spruce, Pine & Fir

KEY: *Turning*

Spruce trees are sacred to the winter solstice, which is a holy day marked by meditation, chants, and the ceremonial burning of a spruce log on the hearth or in a clearing. Participants in the ritual are invited to cast scrolls into the bonfire bearing their wishes for the coming cycle of light. Spruce is a genus that in the Latin nomenclature is called *Abies*. It is a member of the Pinaceae, or Pine, family of conifers.

Spruce, pine, and fir may all be used for wands but require some conditioning on account of their pitch, the fragrant, sticky sap. These three sisters of the Pinaceae are all evergreen trees, and so they are the trees of winter, of the dark half of the year, when the boughs of deciduous trees are bare. This darkness is not to be equated with evil but rather with gestation and the realm of Annwn, the underworld from which all things are manifested into the world of forms. Annwn is considered to be a dangerous place, ruled by the god Arawn; he is not a god that is usually invoked by wizards unless they wish to enter his realm. He is easily compared to Hades in the Greek myths, the ruler of a land of shades—both the shades of those who lived in our world and died, and also the shadows of beings yet to be born into our world. In Celtic myth, this is the otherworld and is not always depicted as dark. In fact, it is simply the other side of our world, and its denizens only seem like shades when viewed from this side. Spruce, pine, and fir are likewise sacred to the powerful enchantresses and goddesses Cerridwen and Hecate, who are often depicted as witches in post-Christian versions of their stories.

The story of Cerridwen and her magic cauldron of inspiration, the source of magic in our world, is a fascinating tale. In it, the goddess brews up wisdom by taking one of the salmon of wisdom from the pool of Segais, where they feed on hazelnuts (the ultimate source of wisdom). The goddess is a master of transformation, shapeshifting from one animal into another.

Spruce, pine, and fir partake of this power of transformation and passage easily from one world to another. They are well suited to all manner of cleansing with their clean scent, and also to magic in pursuit of wisdom or purification. The branches of spruce, pine, and fir are among the trees used for witches' brooms, to sweep out a circle or a house spiritually and to serve as the instrument of a witch's night flights through the astral realms. Such flights were, traditionally, not to do mischief but to battle against the forces of evil that threatened a community (see Ginzburg, *Night Battles*).

Birch

KEY: *Beginning*

In Celtic ogham lore, birch is the tree of beginnings; it is the first letter in the Irish ogham signary. As such, it is sometimes accorded to the time of Samhuinn as the beginning of the Celtic sacred year, or to the winter solstice if that is taken as the beginning of a new cycle of waxing sunlight. I myself attribute birch to the vernal equinox as the beginning of spring. In the Celtic ogham, birch is accorded prestige as the first tree, one of the trees that emerges early to establish a new forest, a harbinger of youth and springtime. It is a tree of beginnings in general and so is the symbolic tree of the bards, the first grade of the druid order. The bards are accorded first honor as the singers of the creation epics, those who sing the worlds into existence. The bard is not first in the sense of an apprentice druid; bards and poets were among the highest ranks of Celtic society, rivaling kings. The grade of bard is first in the sense that its arts are foundational to all further magical study. The bard learns memory, grace, language, and the entire lore of his or her people. By itself, that is a great accomplishment. It is also the foundation of imaginal power, upon which one can build the magical and healing arts and all philosophy.

Birch is also a wood with great powers to purify and discipline, to create the new forest in service to the great trees that will come after, such as the oak, ash, and maple. Birch groves bespeak a young forest, and so birch is linked to youth and all things that are the foundations of things to come. Yet, we should recall that individual birch trees can live quite long lives compared to the fleeting human lifespan, and a few become quite ancient in their power. A birch wand is especially suited to magic of new beginnings, spells of youth and fresh starts, bardic enchantment, creativity, procreation, birth, renewal and rebirth, purification, and spells for discipline and service.

Willow

KEY: *Weaving*

Sacred to the moon, willow may be associated with the many goddesses of the moon, including Diana, Selene, Artemis, Circe, Hecate, and Cerridwen. Willow is distinctly a wood of the water element, often growing at water's edge, and so it is good for dowsing and other forms of seership. Willow has been used for rain-making, funerary rites, love spells, easing childbirth, fertility, healing, and spells of glamour and bewitchment. Willow osiers have been used since earliest times to make wickerwork. Paul Kendall remarks,

> Before the advent of plastics, willow was widely used to make a variety of containers, from general basketry to specialised applications such as lobster pots and beehives. A sixth-century basket discovered by archaeologists on Shetland, and apparently made of willow, used the same weaving techniques as those still practiced in Scotland. (Kendall, "Mythology and Folklore of the Willow")

Kendall also notes that willow wood was used in making the sound boxes of harps. It is a remarkably flexible wood and regenerates quickly when coppiced, demonstrating its powers of healing and rebirth. Its bark is widely known as a pain reliever, the source of the main ingredient in aspirin, salicylic acid (from the Latin *Salix*, the genus of willow). As the consummate witch wood, willow invokes and guides change, relationships, ovulation, menstruation, menopause, and female rites of passage, as well as magical weaving and needlework. It is the perfect wood for the ritual of "drawing down the moon" and is suited to magic of the dark moon and night acts of concealment, secrecy, and germination, as well as magic of the full moon (and any other moon phase, for that matter). As a water wood, willow is the wood of choice for stir wands used in potion making. As apple embodies harmony, willow embodies melody and combination, weaving together diverse strands of reality into containers of magic.

Poplar
KEY: *Feeling*

Poplar, popple, cottonwood, and aspen are all names for the genus *Populus*. Though these trees differ in size and appearance to a degree, they may be treated together, much as the wandmaker treats the oaks as a single type. The slender quaking aspen seems shy and timid, while the towering cottonwood is a gentle giant full of old wisdom drawn from the watery depths of the land. In the Great Plains of North America, the cottonwood often marks out those lakes and rivers that are like oases in the vast grasslands. The wood of these trees is soft and pliable. The leaves are heart shaped and quivering and lighter on the bottom than the top, so that the sunlight or moonlight flickers on them in the smallest breeze.

All the poplar trees have the character of deep emotional sensitivity. They are the trees of empathy and feeling, quintessentially the water element in this aspect. Water, alchemically speaking, is the element of feeling and relatedness—emotional connection that draws from energies that are unconscious and more powerful than the rational, conscious mind. Water is manifest in the human soul in such feelings as love, attraction, revulsion, hatred, and fear—positive and negative emotions, as we call them, but all responses that we feel subliminally, out of the reach of our rational mind. The power of attraction between two people, whether sexual or as friends, or even as blood relations—all these forms of attraction are triggered by such subtle senses as the sense of body language, the language of the eyes, and the sense of humor. This astral ability valued by druids is called empathy, the ability to feel what another person feels, and to form a connection with them on that deep, subconscious level.

Because this magical ability is so seldom understood, except by psychologists, it may not be out of place to take a moment here under the poplar trees to consider it more closely. Our emotional life is almost entirely unconscious. The ability to examine one's emotions and articulate them in words or art is rare and, in the end, these are only acts of interpretation. The emotions and emotional structures of the soul, as we call the unconscious mind, cannot be translated fully into words or even art. They truly exist as emotional energy in the body, mind, and soul.

The arts of music, dance, and song are the best media in which to achieve emotional expression because they do not actually attempt to articulate feelings in words. The art of dance, especially, takes the emotions and translates them into movement, which acknowledges that emotional energy originates in the body, not the mind. Magical philosophers sometimes locate the place of the emotions in a distinct body—the astral body, which is distinct from, though completely symbiotic with, the material body. Dance is an extension of all the many instinctive ways we express emotions and feelings in movement—sex, violence, tender touch, facial expressions, body language in general. Here we may find a reflection in the dancing motion of the poplar leaves.

What is the difference between "feeling" and "emotion"? I use these two terms following the distinction made by Dr. Carl Jung. On the one hand, the distinction is between the raw power that rises up inside our bodies and our unconscious minds (emotions) and, on the other hand, the establishment of relationships and connections through those embodied reactions (feelings). Dr. Jung, writing in the first half of the twentieth century, identified the "feeling function" of the psyche as that capacity to evaluate subjectively and to form a personal relationship to others—other people and other things like ideas, animals, or trees. Feeling is the establishment of relationship. Emotion is deeper, the aquifer from which wells up the power of connection. We experience this kind of relatedness before we rationalize it.

In those relationships that have rational (or, as we would say, practical) origins, such as business relationships or casual acquaintances (not exactly rational but random), we build a formal relationship on top of feelings that emerge from our emotional unconscious. This is why business relationships or acquaintanceships can become complicated and confused by unconscious emotions such as attraction or repulsion.

All of this has to do with poplar trees and wands made from their wood because it is this tree that draws its magic from the deepest wells of the unconscious mind, from the fundamental polarities of attraction and repulsion. I attribute these emotions to the goddess Arianrhod of Welsh myth, the goddess of stars manifest in those fundamental forces of the cosmos. The emotions of attraction and repulsion are at their root the same forces that give us magnetism and gravity in the material plane of existence, the fundamental forces of celestial mechanics (though I tend to think "mechanics" is a misleading word that oversimplifies by limiting our understanding to the analogy of machinery). Moreover, Arianrhod is the mother of Dylan, the Welsh lord of the sea.

Thus, poplar is the tree of joy and sorrow, feeling, and emotion; all of this is complicated and elusive. It is inherently hard to grasp rationally, and this makes the poplar trees and their magic something that ultimately must be felt, not explained. The bark of the poplar is gray, like the shadow realm of Annwn, the unconscious otherworld. The aspen's bark is thin skinned, while the cottonwood, when mature, has bark that is tremendously thick and spongy. I believe the finest application for poplar wood is in a wand for delicate sensitivity to emotions and feelings, or for protection of the emotions and feelings.

This means that a poplar wand serves best not to project the mage's will but to project the mage's deep emotions. Above all other wand woods, poplar connects on an emotional level, projecting emotion, creating feelings, and also sensing these patterns in others or in oneself. Enchantments to create love, attraction, repulsion, or fear are all perfectly suited to poplar wood. Protection spells that work on an emotional level are also well suited to this wood. For example, while holly might serve well to create a protective spell that repulses harm on a physical level, and hawthorn may serve well to create a protection spell that works on the imagination and conscious mind of he who would do harm, the poplar wand is the one to pick for a protection spell that actually inspires fear, self-doubt, or panic in a person, and so drives away or overmasters the person. Conversely, poplar wands are well suited to dissolve fear, self-doubt, panic, and other emotional problems. Additionally, poplar is well disposed to magic of emotional and relational healing. Poplar is the wand of the goddess Psyche and the sea gods Poseidon and Proteus.

Trees of Life

*T*HE TREES OF earth, fire, air, and water included in this section are just a few among thousands of species of woody plants. All trees are all magical and sacred to those who choose to observe, respect, and become intimate with them. The systemization of trees and their wood into an ogham (a web of connections) acknowledges the magical and spiritual qualities of trees and their connection to the qualities of our own lives and spirits. Nigel Pennick describes trees this way in the introduction to his book *Ogham and Coelbren*:

> Trees are a Celtic metaphor of human consciousness, overtly so in the Welsh language. The trees of the natural, uncut forest parallel the inner, tameless part of the human soul: they are deep symbols of natural wildness...Such wildness should never be considered to be a state of being out of control. Rather it represents innate naturalness that exists in balanced harmony with natural principles (1).

Wizards are sensitive to such connections and the "wildness" that is essential to life and health. Wilderness in nature is the unconscious mind and vice versa. Moreover, the wise understand that while there are connections that exist physically in ecological systems and historical relationships, there are also connections that are made by subtle similarities and deep metaphors. These are the imaginal connections employed in the art of magic. They form what I call the spiritual ecology within nature. These interweavings are elemental fire of will expressed in the vegetable kingdom—the fire of life in the trees.

PART THREE
Wind

Fair laughs the morn, and soft the zephyr blows;
While proudly riding o'er the azure realm
In gallant trim the gilded vessel goes,
Youth on the prow, and Pleasure at the helm;
Regardless of the sweeping whirlwind.

From *The Bard* by Thomas Gray

Wandmaking Style

*T*HERE ARE FOUR great winds. The north wind, Boreas, brings intuitions and perceptions through the senses. The west wind, Zephyrus, brings feelings and connections among souls, or relatedness. The south wind, Notos, brings inspirations, intuitions, and sparks of genius that ignite passion and action. The east wind, Euros, brings thought and innovation, reasoned decision, and evaluation according to intellectual standards. Under the heading of elemental air—the winds—I place those aspects of wandmaking that engage the mind and imagination. Under this elemental heading, we shall consider matters of design, aesthetic judgment, practical reason, and creative inspiration, for the mind engages with wood to fashion a wand as much as the hand does.

There are many styles of wizardry and many styles of wand. The mind of the wandmaker must be the mind of a wizard. That is, one must understand magic and the uses of wands in order to design and create a tool that will faithfully express and perform the mage's purposes. The wandmaker does well to understand a thing or two about many magical traditions and schools of thought if he or she is to make wands for others, for every tradition uses wands differently and employs its own symbols.

From a design standpoint, there are infinite varieties and possibilities within the basic elongated form of the wand. Some mages give more attention to the type of wood used in a wand. Others focus more on the symbolic structure and decoration of the wand. Still others leave out the wood and focus on the shape, constructing wands made of metal or a combination of metal and crystal. The two extremes of simplicity are the plain branch and the crystal point used each by itself as a wand. The extreme of sophistication has no limit, and a few wandmakers produce fantastical works of art. The wandmaking tradition in which I am myself trained uses wood, stone, and crystal, along with etheric magical cores taken from astral creatures; each of these components is given detailed treatment in this book. Here, we will consider how they combine first in the mind of the wandmaker, intellectually, into a design as a whole. While in the realm of air, you will need a sharp pencil for a magical implement.

When you choose a stick or find one gifted to you from a tree, it may have knots, it may be forked, it will quite probably have branchlets and twigs, and it will most likely still have the bark on it. All of these features may be left largely alone or may be altered. In addition to the simple-fancy spectrum, there is the organic-artistic spectrum. At one end of this design spectrum are unadorned branches. Further on are organic wands of a shamanistic sort, complete with bark, sometimes scarcely altered from their natural appearance or with the addition of leather wrappings, sinew, feathers tied on, beads, antlers, skulls, and that sort of thing. (For one example of the use of thread and beads, see the oak and lapis lazuli pocket wand in the color section.)

One sometimes thinks that the ancient druidical wands were simple branches or staves. However, in the old Irish tales, "druid wands" seem to be a particular tool associated with druids. The fabled silver branch of the bards, for example, was an apple branch with silver apple-bells hung upon it, rung to announce to the assembled listeners that the bard was coming and to settle in for a song and a tale.

Usually we think of a magic wand as something fashioned and created, a human artifact easily distinguished from a plain stick. The basis of its power may be the spirit of the tree from which it came, but like a fine piece of handmade furniture, the wand is a human artifact intended to be kept, guarded, and cherished as a tool—perhaps for generations. By being made as a human artifact, the wand accumulates the power of its user over time.

The techniques of woodworking that I will discuss in the present chapter are drawn in many ways from the making of hand tools and furniture. One removes the bark from the branch, for example, in order to more carefully preserve the wood and bring out the beauty of its inner structure, grain, and color. But apart from such practical considerations, the wandmaker works the wood as a craftsperson because this is part of the magic of turning a stick into a wand. The art of woodcarving is a kind of transformative magic, each stroke of the blade sculpting and drawing out the wand that lies within the wood, just as Michelangelo chiseled away the marble that was not David until the marvelous figure emerged.

Further to the artistic end of the spectrum of wand design is what I call the classical style of wand. A classical wand is symmetrical and somewhat architectural in style, like a tapered Greek column. This style of wand is more than just a straight, plain dowel painted black and white like the wand of a stage magician; it usually has a handle and a shaft (the long, tapering bit) and is distinguished by elegant coves and beads, as one finds on turned table legs. For the classical style of wand, all the turner's art can be employed to create elegant and alluring shapes with perfect circular symmetry. Since the release of the film versions of the Harry Potter novels, many woodturners have turned out beautiful examples of this classical style.

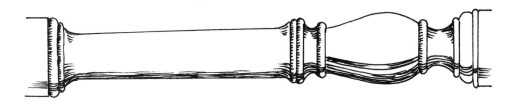

Coves and beads are the concave and convex shapes characteristic of turned table legs and spindles.

The classic holly wand shown in the color section illustrates what I call the classical style. The lignum vitae wand illustrated below was based on one made by wandmaker Tom Melin, one of many wandmakers who have applied their lathe skills to the art of wandmaking. While marketed to Harry Potter fans, this type of wand is perfectly capable of enchantment and use in magic. The use of a lathe creates perfect symmetry of form. It is because of this symmetry that I call this style "classical."

The lignum vitae wand, an example of a classical wand.

However beautiful the result, consider that to get this kind of perfect symmetry, one must use a lathe or other kind of powered rotary tool, and that such creations usually require milled wood stock. Milled wood is the sort you get from the lumberyard or specialty wood store. It has been cut into dowels or squared boards in various sizes by a machine. Natural branches generally have too many knots and irregularities in their grain to make good turning stock. These technological objections may be addressed if one uses larger unmilled sections of a tree trunk or larger branch for the stock and a manual lathe powered by bow, wheel, or treadle. One can find instructions on the Internet from reenactors and craftspeople who have constructed lathes in the old (human-power) style.

It is also possible to imitate the coves and beads of turning with hand tools and a patient eye. This technique yields a design that takes advantage of the roundness of the cylindrical shaft while still preserving the quirks of a natural branch. Setting off the handle of the wand with coves and beads helps to differentiate the parts of a wand—which end is which—and to give a sense of proportion.

Parts of a Wand

ᴇVERY WANDMAKER HAS his or her own style. However, most wand designs have four parts, regardless of whether they are distinctly set off from each other. These four parts are:

- ☾ The point
- ☾ The shaft
- ☾ The handle
- ☾ The pommel or reservoir

The division into four is symbolic of the four cardinal directions and the four elements. These are, in turn, manifestations of the four primary powers of the human mind: thought, active desire, intuition, and feeling. Each power of the psyche corresponds to one of the parts of the wand, as shown in the accompanying table on page 83.

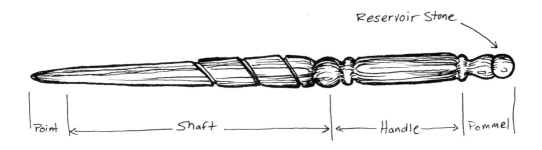

The Point

In doing magic, one generally points at or taps on the thing one wishes to influence or transform. This is the fundamental magical gesture of symbolic connection between the mage (the subject) and the target (the object). One can think of magic as energy or as the life force called *prana* by the yogis and *chi* by the Taoists. Alternatively, one can think of it as pure will and intention, but it is will that has made a connection to a target. This target may be a person, a thing, a place, or even a field of action. However one conceives of magic, it is something that is cast outward from the mage to make a connection, and the wand is the instrument of direction. It is an extension of the pointing finger—a very potent instrument in itself.

The projective end of the wand, opposite the handle and pommel, is the point. The inclusion of a crystal point on a wand emphasizes the projective power, but it is not something I believe to be strictly necessary in the design of a wand. The point may be a simple taper at the end of the shaft, or it may be highly ornamented. Some ceremonial wands are intended to be used more like scepters than pointers and include elaborate symbolic decoration such as, for example, the colorful wands of Golden Dawn magic used by the several officers of a temple in a particular degree setting. (You will find a photo of a Golden Dawn lotus wand on the color pages.)

In such wands, the point of the wand is the uppermost part and is often decorated with quite elaborate shapes or carvings, such as in the case of the lotus wand. The archetypal fairy godmother's wand has a star on top, and we see this sort of wand in toy shops or films like *The Wizard of Oz*, *Cinderella*, and *Sleeping Beauty*. Although presented somewhat fancifully in the movies, the star-tipped wand actually evokes a perfectly good symbol of the astral dimension of magic; *astral*, after all, means "of the stars."

In all cases, the point of a wand is the part that functions in the elemental realm of air. Through air, imagination, symbols, and thought, the druid, mage, or witch connects his or her inner will to the external world of forms. The wand can be thought of as the outer interface transmitting the power of intention.

The Shaft

The shaft is the part of the wand that may be longer or shorter and connects the point to the handle. As a wand grows longer in design, it moves toward being a staff or rod, intended to be carried in an upright, vertical way. The horizontal power of the wand, directing energy outward to a specific target, is shifted in a staff or rod of office to the flow of power from heaven to earth. As the shaft becomes longer, the upright rod of a marshal becomes a scepter. There is a close kinship between the sovereign will exercised by a wizard or sorcerer and the power of command symbolized by the scepter of a monarch or officer who serves a higher power.

The will or intention of a king is the archetype of human willpower. It is the archetype, not the material monarchy, that is of magical importance. Mortal kings or queens may have faults, but the ideal of the king is that of masculine responsibility and personal integrity—the manly strength that other persons of either gender recognize and honor. In a subordinate role, the rod serves not as a symbol of rulership but as a symbol of leadership—the ability to lead a person or group and to transmit the ultimate masculine energy. At its most fundamental, the rod is a phallic symbol of masculine sexual dominance.

However, the phallus is itself a symbol of the archetypal power of will. One can also think of the rods of office used by marshals who wield a baton (which is one French word for *wand*). Such batons are usually shorter than scepters to indicate that their power derives from the sovereign or master. Longer rods that reach the floor, such as those carried by the deacons and stewards in a Masonic lodge, symbolize greater authority that is still subordinate to the master. The greater length of the rod is used as a potential weapon or guiding rod, something like the crosier of a bishop or pope, which emulates the shepherd's crook. However, all of these examples are of the upright rod or staff. The magic wand held horizontally (or as one would wield a dagger) may be better compared to the shaft of a spear.

In Celtic legend, the spear of Nuada is one of the four hallows that the Tuatha Dé Danann brought to Ireland. The spear was one of those enchanted weapons that would do the fighting for its wielder, flying wherever it was directed. In fact, you couldn't get it to stop unless you kept its blade quenched in a cauldron of blood. In the medieval Grail romances, this magical spear became associated with the spear that was thrust into the side of Christ on the cross (to see if he was really dead or if he had just fainted). That spear symbolizes the reaper's scythe that brings about the sacred harvest of the dying and reborn god of the green world. The male power of the planted seed grows straight toward the sun and, when ripe, is cut down. The phallus becomes the plow and the human semen, the seed of the corn.

Consider the cultivation of corn (meaning wheat, barley, rye, maize, etc.). It is the principal power, skill, and knowledge that made human civilization possible. Reliable sources of food that were high in protein and could be stored to seed the next planting made the great ancient civilizations of Sumer, Egypt, Çatalhöyük, and Mohenjo-Daro possible. The power of the seed manifested in corn permitted the great shift from wandering hunter-gatherer tribes to settled communities composed of individuals who could specialize in skills other than those of basic survival. Remember this when you think of the masculine principle and the shaft of a wand, rod, or spear.

The Grail spear and Nuada's spear are the masculine complements to the Grail itself. The Grail, while elusive, is usually conceived to be a cup or chalice bearing Christ's blood. It is capable of miracles like those of the magic cauldrons in the Cymric and Irish legends of Bran, Cerridwen, and the Dagda. These cauldrons could, respectively, return the dead to life (or a semblance of life), give inspiration and knowledge, and feed armies with an endless supply of food. In these three cauldrons, we discover the vessel into which the seed of the masculine is placed—the womb of woman, which itself is a manifest symbol of the Earth Mother. While the wand represents the source of the seed, it is the cauldron that gestates the seed and multiplies it into new life.

Given all this, it is not surprising that the Grail became a part of Christian legend and iconography. The Blood of Christ gave eternal life and was the "staff of life" in the sense of the food of immortality, and symbolically drinking Christ's blood brought knowledge of God. The cauldron is likewise an important magical symbol for druid ovates. In rituals, the wand is inserted into the cauldron as a symbol of the union of the archetypal masculine and feminine.

In some tarot decks, the suit of wands is represented with spears or shafts like a quarterstaff. In fact, most tarot decks represent wands not as we should think of magic wands, but rather as clubs (as the suit is called in the mundane deck of playing cards), which is, in French, *baton*. The air and fire suits are identified with the masculine and are both weapons (sword and staff). The wand is a weapon of self-assertion and so is emblematic of the element of fire and the will. Swords are given to the element of air and represent not the will but the power of reason to analyze, dissect, and divide the world on all levels, including the division of peoples in enmity.

The blunt bludgeon is perhaps the true ancestor of the spear, the scepter, and the magic wand. It is probably one of the first weapons invented by our Stone Age ancestors to assert one's individual will over another using either force or the threat of force. Remember the magic wand's kinship with these instruments of death, for the human will is a dangerous thing that can be used for destruction as well as direction and creation. Yet, think of the club or the quarterstaff as an instrument of protection as well—one that may be used to restrain the rampant will of others where they, not we, err in surrendering to violent passions.

The Handle

The handle of a wand is of practical importance as a place to grip the wand, yet its basic functionality should not lead us to overlook its importance on a subtler level. I find that the texture of the handle, whether rough or smooth, is one of the most important sensual aspects of using a wand. When you pick up your wand, you feel its handle. This is where the wood makes direct contact with your skin with its warmth, its prana. Here it becomes an extension of the wizard's hand and so of his or her will. The handle of a wand is a good place to add intricate Celtic or Norse interlace designs. It is also a good place for figural carving, whether animals or a goddess figure.

The handle represents the element of earth in the wand's structure. Earth is the element of perception, the senses: touching, smelling, tasting, hearing, seeing, and other higher senses such as intuition, sense of direction, and sense of humor. The senses are in the body and the mind. The sense of intuition allows us to see into other dimensions to a greater or lesser degree. All of this perception is expressed through elemental earth, the body's material, electrical, and magnetic structures. We must grasp the fact that even the earth element exists in astral, mental, and archetypal forms.

The higher senses, we can say, are the physical senses extended into the astral realm. Prana, or chi, is that etheric energy that ties our bodies to our higher forms of existence—our astral, mental, and archetypal bodies, as mages say. Prana—the subtle life energy that flows in all living things—is the medium through which all magic is done. The handle of the wand touches the hand and especially the *lao gong* point in the center of the palm. The lao gong points are named thus by traditional Chinese medicine and martial arts that work by moving chi. *Lao gong* means "husband" but also means something like "moving the old man"—that is, moving the yang force, the active force of the cosmos. In Western Christian terms, we might say "moving the Holy Spirit"; in Jewish terms, perhaps "moving the will of the Lord." Secular druids might prefer to say "moving the Dagda."

If the symbolism of the design placed on the wand's handle is related to elemental earth, so much the better. Some representation of the Mother Goddess or a symbol of the weaving of the senses in matter is most appropriate.

The Pommel or Reservoir

If the point of the wand is air, the shaft is fire, and the handle is earth, then it will not surprise you to discover that the pommel of the wand embodies elemental water. The term *pommel* comes from the construction of swords and daggers. It is a knob of varying size and shape that balances the blade. The word comes from the French term for "apple" (*pomme*). If a stone or crystal is affixed to a branch as the pommel, its weight will serve a similar balancing purpose. However, the knob end of the handle also serves as the reservoir of power. The owner of the wand can fill this reservoir with his or her prana, building up a kind of battery for use in spellcasting or other magical work.

For this reason, the pommel is also referred to as the reservoir. As elemental water manifests in our power of feeling, our connection to the outer world, so the reservoir is the means by which the will of the wand wielder is connected to the outer world. The whole wand makes this connection of inner and outer worlds, of course, but the power of connection is anchored in the feelings accumulated in the wand's reservoir. Feelings are not thoughts; they are a sub-conscious and wordless connection through how we value others and how we value ourselves. This includes what we call beliefs, and so we should not express surprise that beliefs are seldom rational.

The pommel rests in the palm or against one's wrist, depending on how one holds the wand. The inclusion of a stone is very useful in this respect, especially to counterbalance a crystal in the point of the wand. However, there is also a symbolic purpose for the rounded end of the wand. The point is considered to be the masculine, or transmissive, end of a wand, so the law of polarities makes the other end the feminine, or receptive, containing pole.

Because of its gender, the pommel is rounded in shape. It may also be carved in a shape that suggests the power of the feminine and the wand wielder's soul, such as an egg, an acorn, a pine cone, a beehive, an apple, or some other appropriate shape suggesting the power of containing, gestating, and giving birth. The acorn is an interesting symbol because, depending on the type of oak, it can resemble a woman's breast or a man's uncircumcised penis and so serve as a sexual symbol in both ways, on pommel or point.

An acorn pommel

Another shape that I find suitable is a stupa shape, after the stepped temples of the Buddhist tradition. A round stupa shape is like a step pyramid, and the number of steps may also be symbolic of the four winds or the three worlds, for example. It is also a stylized female breast and so symbolizes the feminine power of containing and giving life.[17] Similar to this shape is the beehive, which has a continuous spiral from apex to base.

A beehive pommel

17 On stupas, see Govinda, *Psycho-Cosmic Symbolism of the Buddhist Stupa.*

This vine wand uses a crystal on both pommel and point.

If a crystal or a stone is used as a wand reservoir, the capacity to store etheric energies is even greater than in a carved knob. Why this is true has not been fully explained, but my sense is that it is due to the denser molecular structure of minerals as compared to the cell structure of wood. Each stores etheric energy in different ways, but the more dense the matter, the more interconnections there are among its molecules, and it is within the interstices of the atoms that the etheric energy resides. A crystalline structure is the ideal reservoir of this energy, so that quartz crystal or precious gemstones are excellent as reservoirs.

The prana, though essentially pure and devoid of intention or desire while in the reservoir, may be aided and colored by the powers of the stone. We shall take up the matter of stones and crystals in part four. All the parts of a wand add to its magic.

Table A: Parts of a Wand

PART	ELEMENT	DIRECTION	PSYCHIC POWER	MEANING
Point	Air	East	Thought	Thought as the invisible organizing principle that uses symbols to manifest the will
Shaft	Fire	South	Active desire or will	The force of personal intention and desire to shape action
Handle	Earth	North	Intuition	The physical and astral senses focused through the hand
Pommel	Water	West	Feeling	The force of emotions and subjective evaluation to create relationships

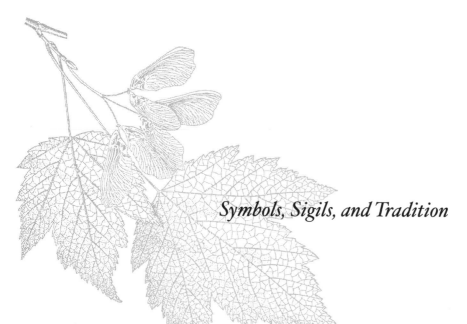

Symbols, Sigils, and Tradition

Carving symbols or inscriptions on a wand is essential for some wandmakers. The instructions for making the Solomonic wand in *The Greater Key of Solomon*, for example, detail the sigils and letters that are to be included thereon.

The Solomonic wand, bottom, has a bead dividing the shaft and handle, a spiral-shaped stupa pommel with two rings below it to symbolize "as above, so below," and five-petaled rosettes with decorative leaves on the handle; the Solomonic sigils in greater detail, top.

Each wizard develops his or her own particular set of symbols or names of divinities and then presents them in books as the best, or indeed the only, way to fashion a wand. For example, in the Solomonic tradition or the Enochian system of Dr. John Dee, the symbols and names are stipulated in minute detail. Divine or angelic names are used or else sigils that symbolize such supermaterial beings. Each angel has a particular area of spiritual authority in the medieval cosmology, and angelology can become as complicated as any modern corporate organizational chart. The essence of this kind of angel magic is that it invokes the aid of a spiritual being, an ethereal entity who may be trusted to act only for God's will or goodness.

The same is true when invoking daemons by name—except that you can bank on them being mischievous, rebellious, and malicious unless commanded using the divine names of the Supreme Being. Any mage who draws about her- or himself the mantle of divine authority can command pretty much all of creation. The fallen angels are considered to be bound to obey God now that they have been incarcerated in hell—at least that is one theory historically part of the Christian worldview.[18]

In a polytheistic cosmology, the particular divine power invoked will color the character of the wand. If it is the particular patron saint or deity of the wand's owner, the name or symbols can create a strong spiritual link between the wielder and the wand. A wand that is carved with symbols and images having to do with Cernunnos, the antlered god of the Gauls, will have quite a different character and energy than one carved with symbols of the British goddess Cerridwen, for example. What is necessary in all these cases is to understand the symbolic world of the particular system you are using. Mixing Kabbalistic names of angels with Celtic divine names could just create a confused mishmash unless you have actually done the work to create a system that fuses the two.

The objection to mixing, for example, Judeo-Christian archangels and Celtic Pagan gods comes from the Pagan side of the debate as much as from the Christian Hermeticists. The debate probably goes back to Ur, but we can see it active in many religious sects that are resistant to changing either their symbols or their interpretation of those symbols.

---

18 I do not mean to generalize about the worldview of Christians. Much has changed since the Middle Ages, and many Christians differ on the question of whether daemons exist or in what way they exist. However, the religion was built upon the cosmology of heaven, earth, and hell, and it is upon this worldview that angelic and daemonological magic generally depends.

Yet Christians, who originated as members of a Jewish sect, took Jewish symbols, books, and ideas, giving them new interpretations. The Gentile Christians in Greece and Asia Minor borrowed concepts from the Greek Hellenistic philosophers. Later, they borrowed and incorporated the Roman calendar and many Roman religious customs. When they came up against the druids, the church borrowed gods and goddesses from the Celts and turned them into saints.

The Celts themselves borrowed from those people they knew—the Greeks and Pagan Rome, and possibly the pre-Celtic megalithic cultures that preceded them in the British Isles, Iberia, and Ireland. Everybody seems to have borrowed from the Egyptians, the Chaldeans, and the Persians. In the twentieth century, many Western spiritual organizations (and individuals) borrowed ideas and symbols from Hinduism, Buddhism, and Taoism, who in turn had borrowed from each other centuries before. The idea of keeping a tradition perfect and unchanging belies this historical process of religious borrowing. Usually the borrowing occurs when an institution is young and just forming or when it encounters a larger, more powerful culture with a different religion. Once a religion has become the dominant force in a powerful culture, it tends to deny its prior borrowings and emphasize keeping the traditions static, letter-perfect, and unchanging.

Freemasonry and other mystery schools are also like this. In the seventeenth and eighteenth centuries, Freemasons borrowed from ancient mystery schools, Kabbalah, alchemy, the Bible, Pythagoras, and the stonemasons' guilds. But by the nineteenth century, the leaders of Craft Masonry had become increasingly concerned about the standardization of rituals and customs among the lodges and about keeping the ritual letter-perfect so it could be passed from one generation to the next intact.

Interestingly, at the same time this ossification occurred in the mainstream of Freemasonry, splinter groups broke away—most prominent among them being the Hermetic Order of the Golden Dawn and the Ancient Druid Order. In their turn, these groups had many offspring during the twentieth century, including Wicca, which carries on some Masonic forms. Various sects of Wiccans now are notorious for arguing over keeping the tradition pure. Druids, for the most part without rules and without a holy book (such as the Masonic *Constitutions* or Gerald Gardner's *Book of Shadows*), have escaped this trap. Though one can find dogmatic druids, some of whom insist that modern druidry must be based on the latest archaeological theories. It's a new twist on dogmatism: clinging to an ever-changing scholarly present rather than an unchanging tradition.

But magic is not religion, and the use of symbols and traditions in wandmaking may or may not stick to orthodoxy. Magic is more like science in this respect (like father, like son): magic consists of methods and techniques that must be tested as well as worked out theoretically. In science, as in magic, adopting other people's ideas, even if they come from another culture and speak a different language, is a necessary part of the advancement of knowledge worldwide.

A good example of the sort of cross-cultural fusion I am talking about is in Christian Kabbalistic magic, which had its origins in the Renaissance. Drawing upon the Hellenistic syncretism of the early Christian period, Renaissance philosophers created correspondences between the planets and the Kabbalistic sephiroth, or spheres of manifestation. The fusion of these two systems brought together Greco-Roman gods and goddesses (for whom the planets were named) with Judaic angels and God names. It also merged astrology, a system of divination going back to Babylon, with Kabbalah, which is a system of Jewish mysticism.

Later, this Hermetic-Kabbalistic system was also integrated with tarot and its symbols, and with Egyptian divinities to form the Golden Dawn school of magic. The twenty-two paths connecting the ten sephiroth of the Tree of Life in Kabbalah have been associated with the twenty-two greater trumps of the tarot. It is this Kabbalistic-Hermetic system that has formed the mainstream of the Western magical tradition during the Christian era. The idea behind such syncretic synthesis is that all magical systems ought to be true at some level and may be related to each other in correspondences.

For the past two centuries, druid orders have sought a native Celtic wisdom (or pre-Christian Indo-European wisdom) prior to and distinct from the Judeo-Christian systems of the medieval and Renaissance periods. Even Egypt, long considered the repository of the most ancient wisdom about magic and spiritual powers of life and death, is largely excluded from a system that seeks to restore the native religion and magic of the pre-Christian Celts. This endeavor has introduced new symbols and correspondences into the Western magical tradition.

This history of magic and its various currents is worth considering when designing your own wand and your own personal symbols. The important thing is to make sure that any combination of symbols you use makes sense to you on a deep level and is not just a superficial concoction of things you have pulled out of books. That sort of random mixture is just as dangerous as if you randomly combined a collection of herbs into a potion and drank it. It is generally not recommended by anyone that you carve the sigils or names of divine or angelic beings if you have no knowledge of them. Seek communion with them in meditation before deciding to include such beings' names on your wand.

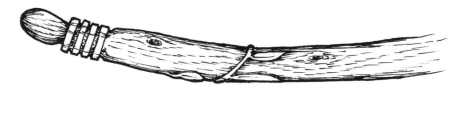

In this four winds motif (above, top), each ring symbolizes the fourth part of the circle of the sky and land; that is, north, south, east, and west winds, or the whole cosmos. In the Faerie wand below it, made of a twisted hawthorn branch, designs include a seven-pointed Faerie star, a Faerie seen from the back with a triquetra in her hands pointing toward the wand's tip, and crystal points in both tip and pommel.

A wolf's head holding the crystal point is a powerful symbol of the wolf energy joined to the power of the crystal, above, and an owl is carved into this handle, right.

The best sigils are the ones you create yourself. However, there are also traditional sources. Raven Grimassi has published some traditional Italian witch symbols, many suitable for wands—for example, sigils of manifestation or transformation, protection, and magic in general (see wand on page 96).

Carving symbols in a wand is not the same as making a talisman or bind rune. You do not (probably) want to inscribe specific spells onto the body of the wand. If you do so, this logically limits the wand to the casting of that particular spell, so it is best not to get too specific. A wand is meant to be a general-purpose tool.

On the other hand, many wizards do have different wands for different sorts of magic—a walnut wand for weatherworking, for example, or a birch wand for performing bardic initiations or magic seeking artistic inspiration.

In addition to such magical symbols and sigils, there is a whole range of other artistic and naturalistic symbolism that can be incorporated into a wand. I often carve my wands with vines and leaves, especially oak leaves and acorns, which are particularly symbolic of wisdom and life for druids. The carver can also use the leaves of other sacred trees, particularly the leaves of the tree from whose wood the wand is made.

Beads and coves, as mentioned earlier, are part of the vocabulary of wooden table or chair legs and spokes. In the context of a magical cosmology, various numbers of beads or coves can represent, for example, the four winds or the three worlds of druidry, the four worlds of Kabbalah, the seven planets, the ten sephiroth, etc. The four winds motif is one that I have borrowed from the designs of Native American peace pipes.

Another whole realm of design for wands is in the carved animal or deity. Representations of gods or goddesses in human form or various animal totems and spirit guides may all be included for their special significance to the owner of the wand.

An owl carved on the handle of a wand uses the wisdom and silence of the spirit owl to draw power from the hand of the mage who wields that wand. The owl also ties this wand to Minerva, Roman warrior goddess of intellect and wisdom.

Such carved wands are clearly much different from the simple turned style of the classical wand. The layers of symbolism imbue such a wand with much greater power and permit the user to bond to it much more personally. The personality of the wand itself derives from the dryad, the inclusion of stones or crystals, the symbols carved in the wood, and the magical core, as we shall consider in subsequent chapters.

Inscriptions

BEYOND SYMBOLS, SHOULD a wand include words and sentences? Runes or oghams can be included for their individual symbolic meaning or they can be used to actually spell out a name or phrase. In the latter case, you get the symbolic meaning of each individual rune incorporated into the name or phrase. For instance, let's take the GUARD bind rune. The mage could be calling upon not merely the command word *guard* but also upon the meanings assigned to each letter of the word. If you open your mind to the meanings provided in the opposite table and synthesize them into a single series of energies, you can see how the individual letter meanings reinforce and define the power of guarding that is evoked.

This ash wood wand has guard *written in Futhark runes and a snake coiling around the handle, mirroring the spiraling pommel.*

G (ᚷ)	Gebo. Gift. Exchange of gifts, union of two forces, contract.
U (ᚢ)	Uruz. Wild ox. The primal formative power.
A (ᚨ)	Ansuz, the original name of Odin. The God rune. Inspiration, the source of the god within, magical incantation.
R (ᚱ)	Raidho. Wheel. The circle of the sun and the flow of circular forces.
D (ᛞ)	Dagaz. Daylight. Awakening of the light within yourself. Odin. Opening the portals between worlds.

You can inscribe anything on a wand, but here are a few ideas:

- ☾ A meaningful blessing

- ☾ An aphorism

- ☾ A verse of poetry

- ☾ A dedication to the wielder of the wand

- ☾ The names of gods and goddesses

- ☾ The name of the wand's owner

- ☾ The rune or ogham few associated with the type of tree used

- ☾ The sigil or seal of one's guardian angel

- ☾ The name of a great mythic hero

- ☾ The name of the wand itself

This last practice is traditional for enchanted weapons. Archaeologists have found magical swords and other items inscribed with their names. However, when it comes to a magic wand, I feel it is better to keep the wand's name secret. The name is a key link between the wand and its owner, and writing the wand's name on the body of the wand in such a way that anyone could read it is a bit like leaving your car keys in the ignition.

Similarly, inscribing your own name on the wand is potentially limiting. It is not like putting your name on the label inside your jacket; it has magical repercussions. Today you might feel that you are attached to a particular name, but after your next initiation you may find yourself going by a different name. If you keep your magical name secret and devote it only to magical work, it won't do to have it written on your wand for all to see unless you keep your wand completely secret as well.

On a practical level, inscriptions can be carved in various ways. One way that I find appealing is to carve a helical ribbon winding up the shaft of the wand. Give this ribbon enough width so that you can carve your runes, ogham fews, or letters on it. Another approach is to write your inscription on ringed panels that run around the circumference of the handle or shaft of the wand. The simplest method, and one found in the Solomonic wand, is to write the inscription straight out in a line from the pommel of the wand to its point (see illustration on page 84). In any case, when you have an inscription that runs down the length of the wand (straight or in a spiral), make it read from handle to point. That is the direction you want power to flow. For similar reasons, you probably want your spiral helix spiraling up the wand sunwise rather than widdershins.

A small V-tool (see part five on carving tools) is the best choice for carving inscriptions in most woods. In the case of soft woods such as cedar, redwood, or birch, you might prefer to use a wood-burning tool. Pyrography, as it is called, is a fine art and requires considerable practice and a steady hand. In soft woods, where the grain is likely to tear even with the sharpest V-tool, pyrography can be a good option. It has the added advantage of giving nice, dark letters and introducing the element of fire into the wand's creation.

An age-old way to introduce the fire element into an inscription is to ink the carved runes or inscription in red ink or stain. One very appealing method for inscriptions is to ink or paint in the carvings with gold or silver paint. Paints can be found with gold or silver suspended in them. Against a dark finish such letters or sigils can be particularly striking. Gold invokes the power of the sun, while silver invokes the power of the moon and the stars.

Another design question that the wandmaker must consider is what alphabet and language to use in an inscription. Norse runes? Irish oghams? British Coelbren? Theban letters? Enochian? Greek or Roman letters? English or another modern language? Any of these are perfectly fine, and the choice depends only upon the desires of the wand's owner or creator. Using magical alphabets such as Theban or Enochian, or even Irish oghams, is likely to carry with it a certain symbolic power tied to its particular magical system or culture (see appendix I, magical alphabets, and in the next section).

Finally, it need hardly be said: keep it short. Unless you are creating a large wand, a talking stick, or some other ceremonial piece, a long inscription or one that is overly complicated will seem cluttered. Brevity is the soul of magic as well as wit.

This Egyptian wand includes an ankh, lapis lazuli pommel stone, a scarab holding a carved bead to represent the sun, and the following inscription in hieroglyphics: "words of power speaketh the goddess."

This elven wand has text in elvish runes on a ribbon around the shaft; the pommel is lotuslike, reflecting the spiraling lotus leaves on the handle.

This oak wand has oak leaves and acorns and the ogham few for "oak" inscribed on its shaft.

Letters and Etheric Correspondences

$\mathcal{W}$HILE THERE ARE many magical alphabets, each of which may carry a current of the art quite appropriate to particular wands and particular mages, I will not attempt to cover them all in this book.[19] Among Kabbalistic mages, the Hebrew alphabet is the basis for an extensive system of correspondences that forms the core of mainstream Western Hermeticism. By assigning number values to each letter of an alphabet, any word written using that alphabet may be converted to a number and then associated with any other word that adds to the same number.

In addition, Kabbalistic associations are made between Hebrew letters and the paths of the Tree of Life diagram, and so with tarot cards, planets, and astrological signs. The details of systems of etheric correspondences, as we may call them, is beyond the scope of this book. Many textbooks of magic in the Golden Dawn tradition go into the subject from a Kabbalistic point of view. I can recommend DuQuette (*Chicken Qabalah*), Regardie (*Golden Dawn*), and the Wikipedia article on "Gematria."

In the druid tradition, such webs of association and symbols are called an ogham. As with the Hebrew alphabetic system, ogham associations are organized using the Irish ogham signary. This set of signs was used as an alphabet, but it is thought to have originated from simple tally marks (see table on page 228). The ogham letters are made by cross-hatching over a central line (called the *droim*). They look like tally marks and could be very subtly hidden if a bard wished a message to be secret. As a druid, I find special power in the Irish ogham signs because

---

19 For quite a full treatment, see Pennick, *Magical Alphabets*.

their first association is with the trees. The oghams form a kind of code used especially by the bards. Moreover, each ogham is an element in a larger system of interrelated codes, so that one coded meaning may imply one of the others associated with the same sign.

A tree ogham shows how each letter, or few, corresponds to a tree. A fort ogham links each letter to a fortress or castle. A hill ogham does the same with hills or mountains. Each tree has many meanings (as described in part two), and each hill is the site of an important event and story. Each castle likewise alludes to a whole story, and so forth. Hill, castle, and tree may all be linked together through the ogham few for, say, birch. There are lake oghams, animal oghams, and many more. It is thought that the whole collection of oghams were the structure upon which the ancient bards hung the poetry and history, and even natural history, of their tribes.

There is still much scholarly debate and many differences of opinion among druids about the meanings to be attached to the Irish ogham signary. Much of the focus has been placed upon the so-called tree calendar, as created by Robert Graves' work with the Welsh ogham poems. Whole systems of divination have been developed out of the very small amount of obscure information we have about the ancient oghams. However, because different students of ogham disagree on many points, even the attributions of signs to particular trees will differ from one book to the next. These contradictions are not errors; rather, they reflect the genuine ambiguities in the primary source materials and are sometimes an attempt to adjust the system where it seems to have become corrupted over the many centuries of tradition.[20]

Recent works by Mountfort and Thorsson take up the primary source material, the ogham poems and attempt to interpret their meaning directly. Ellison has likewise made a careful effort to compile some of the old ogham poems into a comprehensive collection for the use of modern druids.

For the wandmaker, it is a good idea to study the oghams and the trees they represent. The tree lore itself is useful to anyone working in wood. However, as a practical matter, one is usually not called upon to do more than inscribe a god name or motto onto a wand using ogham fews. The magical properties of the signs and their divinatory uses are not often relevant to the work at hand.

One important fact to remember when making an ogham inscription is that historically the ogham fews were written from bottom to top. The central line, or stem, is sometimes

20 See particularly Colin and Liz Murray's *Celtic Tree Oracle*, a set of ogham cards with instructions for use as a divinatory system similar to tarot. See also Carr-Gomm and Worthington, *Druidcraft Tarot*; Blamires; Mountfort; Peterson; and Thorsson.

decorated with a spiral at the base in order to clearly mark which end is up—a matter of considerable import in the Irish ogham system because the first and second sequences are simply the reverse of each other.

Although traditionally ogham inscriptions are carved on the straight edge of a stone, it is also quite permissible to make the central stem of the ogham line curved, in which the *droim,* or center line, spirals around the shaft of the wand. There are, of course, an infinite number of possible adaptations of oghams or runes to wand inscriptions .

In sum, the main principle of wand design is harmony. Not only should the wandmaker strive for beauty in a material sense, but also a complete, harmonious, and intentional combination of magical forces—wood, stone, symbols, and magical core—all embodying the imagination.

This ogham inscription on the left says imbas, *the Irish word for poetic inspiration. On the wand below, the pommel is shaped like a stupa to suggest a flame or torch, the crescent with flame hearkens to the Aradia teachings, the symbols are from the Grimassi book, and the Theban inscription says* strength.

PART FOUR
Stone

*The gems and crystals and veins of precious ore
glint in the polished walls; and the light glows
through folded marbles, shell-like, translucent...
There are columns of white and saffron and dawn-
rose...fluted and twisted into dreamlike forms...
wings, ropes, curtains fine as frozen clouds...*

Gimli, son of Glóin, in
The Two Towers by J. R. R. Tolkien

The Mineral Kingdom

$\mathcal{W}$HILE THE ORIGINAL wands of the druids may have been simple branches, today many wizards and witches like to include stones and crystals in their wands. Wizardwork with rocks and crystals is as ancient as any part of the magical art. In this part of the book, we will examine the role of minerals and metals in wandmaking. While crystals and stones are not necessary in a wand, they definitely deepen its character and power.

The folklore regarding the magical properties of stones goes back to the beginnings of history and beyond. In his book *The Forge and the Crucible*, Mircea Eliade suggests that the birth of alchemy may be located in the discovery of meteoric iron and the processes of smelting metals. Skill with making iron, bronze, and other alloys must have seemed truly magical and wondrous when first discovered. Turning rocks from the mine into copper metal must have been as amazing as the later idea of alchemists transforming lead into gold. Metals and other minerals are the manifestation of the earth element in the material plane. However, like all entities, they exist on the ethereal and astral dimensions as well. It is the ethereal and astral bodies of minerals that concern the mage most—the powers to interface and influence the ethereal and astral dimensions of the cosmos generally and one's own life and being in particular.

Stones and Crystals as Reservoirs

$\mathcal{A}$S DESCRIBED IN part three, most magic wands have a four-part structure consisting of the point, shaft, handle, and pommel. This structure may be simplified or elaborated. In all cases, however, the wand has two ends—one you hold and one you point. Wands that are well balanced are prized in much the same way as a well-balanced sword or knife. But the sort of balance desired depends on how the wand is to be used. As with a blade, if one desires a weapon that turns quickly in the hand so that the tip may be brandished with speed and agility, then the pommel end of the wand ought to be heavier and a bit larger than the point. The weight of the wand will then rest in the palm and not be inclined to flip out of the hand in the midst of commanding a recalcitrant spirit or spellcasting with a flamboyant gesture.

Balance can be accomplished in many woods by making the pommel larger in diameter than the rest of the wand. Alternatively, a rounded or ovoid stone or crystal may be affixed to the handle's end to serve as a pommel. The pommel, or reservoir, symbolizes the feminine polarity—what Bardon calls "magnetism"—so it is logical to employ the feminine element of earth in this part of the wand. Such a reservoir stone is a symbolic womb or cosmic egg containing the whole cosmos in potential. The rounded shape is important but does not need to be cut perfectly into a sphere or egg shape.

Not all minerals are equally good for holding a magical charge, but those who have made stones their particular study generally consider that all stones have their own energies and virtues. Some of the wise in stonelore consider that stones have a masculine or feminine polarity, so it would be logical to choose stones that are particularly feminine in temperament. However, it seems to be true that the stone's gender—if one can call it that—is often a characteristic of the individual stone, not its mineralogical type. For example, regardless of type, stones with holes in the middle or of rounded shape have a feminine polarity. Similarly, lingam stones, which are long and cylindrical, have a masculine energy by virtue of their phallic shape.

The terms *masculine* and *feminine*, in this context, are not referring to animal or vegetable sexuality, so a masculine stone's power is a deeper power that underlies human and animal sexual intercourse and desire—no sex, just the archetypal force that sex expresses. Other ways to name the fundamental polarities are, for example, solar and lunar, assertive and receptive, emissive and absorptive, or the ever-popular Taoist terms yang and yin. In the Taoist terms, yang is associated with male and yin with female, but the characters for these terms literally mean "the sunny side of the mountain" and "the shadowy side of the mountain." Light is the direct emission of energy, while darkness is the receptive state into which the light flows.

While every mineral may be judged yang or yin, from the wandmaker's point of view, there are some practical limitations. In order to serve as a reservoir stone, a mineral needs to be relatively hard. Many minerals are too soft to be durable under the circumstances of daily use in the field. A stone may also be impractical due to its shape or size. The more irregular the shape, the more difficult it is to carve out the end grain of a branch to fit it perfectly, and it must be approximately one-half to one inch in diameter to fit the size of the wand's handle.

The Crystal Point

THE USE OF a crystal or cut-stone point in a wand as a focus is a practice derived from the use of crystals in healing work, especially with regard to the chakras. Crystals are valued for their ability to focus energy and cleanse or unblock the flows in the astral and ethereal bodies. A crystal is a naturally pointed translucent structure. Lapidaries also cut stones into the shape of a crystal point. Either type can be used effectively in a wand. Such points are used in massage and acupressure treatments as well. Many crystals are powerful fluid condensers. The term *fluid condenser* refers to a medium through which spiritual "fluid" can be "condensed," or strengthened, and stored much as a pressurized tank is used to store propane gas. As such, they can be thought of as focusing or intensifying the flow of magical energy from the wand. The use of the term *focus* should not be confused here with the meaning of the word in optics. The crystal point does not act as a lens or a reflector. In magical terminology, the meaning is metaphoric—as when we say that our attention is focused. It is more closely parallel to the use of the term in geometry, where the points from which an ellipse are inscribed are called foci and a circle is an ellipse with one focus.

A quartz crystal point tip

The most frequent choice for a crystal point is clear quartz. Others varieties of quartz—such as smoky quartz, rutilated quartz, tourmalinated quartz, rose quartz, and the crystals amethyst, citrine, and so forth—each have their peculiar qualities that will be added to the energies passing through them. Inclusion of a citrine crystal, for example, can lend an overall solar quality to the energy transmitted by the wand. There is not likely to be anything negative in that, unless your purpose is to use the wand to draw down the energy of the moon. The wand will still work, of course, governed by your will, but it will not be as suitable as, for example, milky quartz would be. A few combinations might prove downright contradictory, such as using a wand with an amethyst point to cast a spell of intoxication over someone, but such conflicts are very specific.

From a practical standpoint, if a crystal point is to be included, it is good to balance it with a reservoir stone. In such cases, the choice of crystal and stone may strive for harmony or it may strive for the balance of polarities. If the latter is the case, one might, for example, balance a clear quartz point with a reservoir stone of jet or black obsidian. If harmony between the two minerals is sought, a combination such as moonstone in the pommel with milky quartz in the point could serve to provide a harmonious feminine energy. A point of cut lapis lazuli might be harmonized with a pommel stone of carnelian, the former having an abundance of essential air and the latter of essential fire. Both air and fire are masculine, so in this example, a harmonious balance of masculine energies is given to the wand.

The Magical Properties of Stones

WITHIN THE FOLLOWING section, you will find profiles of the stones and crystals most commonly used in wandmaking. You will find a description of the stone and a summary of its magical properties, according to my own findings and according to folklore. The bibliography will lead you to excellent volumes treating mineral magic in much more detail (see Fernie, Gienger, Melody, and Twintrees). You will find further information about how to set stones and crystals into wands in part five. It is worth noting that some magical properties of stones have to do with their color, while other properties depend on other characteristics (see table B, colors of magic, on page 121).

What exactly will you be introducing into your wand when you include a particular stone or crystal? Each has its own energy and temperament and will give your wand qualities suitable to particular magical outcomes. These qualities will not prevent the wand from being used for other purposes but will tend to give it an aptness for certain types of magic, such as healing spells, love spells, or protection spells.

One must use one's intuition when considering whether the magical properties of a stone will conflict with the properties of the wood that has been chosen for the wand. Finally, many of the stones have energetic links to particular constellations of the zodiac, and one must consider how they might interact with the stellar energies of the wood or the user of the wand. Many astrological considerations and individual circumstances come into play; in stone magic, the wandmakers must be adept in astrology. It might be wise to consult a professional astrologer on the matter. Each mineral below is described in terms of certain magical potentialities.[21] These are not necessarily automatic but are usefully brought out in magical workings. As with the wood, it would be wrong to believe that the stone will do the work for you without being directed by your will. At the same time, as with a branch, you must ask the spirit of the stone if it wants to be part of a wand.

Now, to the stones!

Agate

Agate is a type of quartz known as chalcedony with banded patterns of color. It has been attributed powers of protection, victory, attracting love, promoting fertility in crops, turning away lightning or evil spirits, finding buried treasure, curing insomnia, and giving pleasant dreams. Agate is said to reverse the energy flow of any chakra, thus removing blockages and illness. It gives strength to mind and body, increases balance, and is useful when sudden bursts of energy are needed. Several varieties of agate have additional properties as follows.

Moss Agate

Moss agate is green with bands in shades of blue and green. The Greek bard Orpheus said that to wear moss agate was to receive divine favor. The powers of eloquence and persuasion, fertility, magnetism, and eternal life are attributed to moss agate. It is associated with Taurus, Venus, and Gemini—Taurus, which is ruled by Venus because of its earthy healing energy and wealth-giving properties; Gemini in its power to magically seek out information. Moss agate is one of the most powerful healing stones. It protects and enhances the aura (the etheric body) and aids in opening the third eye, the brow chakra of the yogis. Moss agate is useful for meditation, scrying, astral travel, and speaking with spirit guides; it's also well suited for spells of wealth, happiness, long life, and actions to find friends. All these outcomes depend upon the careful manipulation of the delicate intertwined fibers of causality, of which the tendrils of moss are symbolic.

---

21   There is a good deal of difference between the lists of one mage and another regarding affinities between stones, trees, divinities, constellations, etc. To some extent, different wizards follow their own instincts and experiences. For one example that attempts to tabulate and collect the judgments expressed by ancient and medieval wizards, see Joseph Peterson, "The Magic Wand."

Tree Agate

This type of agate is usually white with black, brown, red, or green branchlike inclusions. Its white color radiates purity and light, while the treelike appearance of the branches emulates the many branchings of the paths of causation. This means that the stone itself will help with spells that adjust the branches of our choices and that direct circumstances along the lines of one's intention. Tree agate is one of my favorites for its implicit connection to the power of trees, and I call it "the druid's stone." It seems to me to be in harmony with the energies of the constellation Libra for the choices made and the balance of probability. It also draws upon Mercury, who is the guide of travelers. In terms of druidic divinities, tree agate is sacred to Gwydion, the trickster magician and traveler (see Ford, *Mabinogi*, the Fourth Branch).

Amber

The fossilized resin of ancient trees, amber is truly solidified sunlight. It cannot properly be called a stone, for its origins are organic. Its rarity and desirability as a semiprecious gem make it expensive, and there is hardly any substance more magical than amber. According to Bardon, amber is the best material to use as a fluid condenser. The ancients were aware of the electrical character of amber, which becomes charged with static electricity when rubbed with fur. Despite this apparent electrical quality, some mages consider it, magically speaking, a magnetic substance. It is probably better to think of amber as capable of condensing and storing up both magnetic and electrical fluids—that is, both yin *and* yang power.

Perhaps because of this dual gender, amber has long been considered capable of inspiring attraction and sensuality, thus making it useful in love spells. The yin-yang power of amber also makes it a protective stone, highly suitable to spells of protection, as it naturally creates a matrix of protection. Protection might at first glance seem the opposite of attraction, but in this case the protective matrix creates an ethos of attraction—a place of strength where sensual pleasures may be safely unleashed.

Amethyst

Amethyst is quartz that is purple or lilac in color, in most cases. It is traditionally noted to have the power to avert intoxication, a sympathetic association between purple and wine. This may be more broadly construed as protection from losing control of oneself or false infatuation with an idea or a person. It keeps your perceptions real. It is associated with the third eye, clairvoyance, prescience, and the ability to see through illusions.

Amethyst is also a stone recommended to men for attracting women. The logic of this seems to be one of similitude—that is, the crown chakra awareness and sensitivity to others makes a man attractive to women, generally speaking. This is a good example of how the magical properties may seem as if they promise the transformation of another person when, in fact, they perform the transformation upon the bearer of the stone. Amethyst is said to protect against evil sorcery and bring success and good luck. They are both effects that are, again, byproducts of the heightened spiritual senses.

The increase of hypersensory perception and intuition can enable one to avoid danger ("protection") and to sense the best course of action in accord with our desires ("luck"). A powerful healing crystal, amethyst is also said to calm mental disorders, purify the blood, and balance all chakras. The attachment to mental disorders comes through the crystal's association with the constellation Aquarius, an air sign that is strongly attuned to the mind and particularly the sense of being one with all humanity. The effect on blood is one of similitude based on the purple color and the aforementioned power of detoxification. Balancing all chakras is a wide power that derives from amethyst's connection to the crown chakra, which is the highest and so may be said to overlight all the others. This quality and its color also make amethyst most suitable for violet magic (see page 122).

Aventurine

A green type of quartz, sometimes called Indian jade, aventurine is a stone used to release anxieties, which inspires independence, positive attitudes, and good health. Linked strongly to elemental earth, it gives balance and calm. It is suited to spells of protection and good luck in gambling. It can enhance powers of creative visualization, writing, art, and music. Aventurine also is said to attract prosperity, love, and unexpected adventures or opportunities. Its color makes it suitable to spells of green magic (see page 121).

Bloodstone

Green with red flecks like blood, bloodstone is a form of chalcedony, an opaque green jasper. It is said to link the root and heart chakras, stimulating kundalini, the pranic flow along the spine that is the central driver of a human body's vital power. Bloodstone may guard one against deceptions and preserve health. It creates prosperity and abundance, and strengthens self-confidence. Bloodstone can lengthen life, give fame, aid invisibility, remove obstacles, control spirits, cause storms, and help in court cases. This wide range of magical virtues doubtless comes from bloodstone's association with blood and the fact that so much old magic was activated and sealed with blood. The use of blood may have been partly to tie the living to the spirits of the dead, through which many wizards of the classical period worked their magic. Bloodstone will enhance the power of any wand as well as lend its virtues to the wizard who carries it.

Calcite

Calcite is a soft stone, easily scratched but lustrous in green, pink, and many other colors, including the beautiful amber-colored honey calcite. The famous Carrara marble of Italy is composed of calcite. It helps clear negative energies from the environment and the body, intensifies mental and emotional clarity, and attracts love. A wizard desiring a wand to work spells in these areas will do well with a calcite reservoir. The choice of color will also enhance the stone's power in a particular direction—pink more toward love, yellow more toward thought.

Carnelian

Carnelian has always been prized. It is an orange or reddish form of chalcedony related to sard, bloodstone, and moss agate. Traditionally used to protect against the "evil eye," carnelian is also said to fulfill all desires. According to Agrippa, carnelian is sacred to Venus, the goddess of desire, so this makes sense. Carnelian speeds all manifestations, revitalizes and aligns the physical and spiritual bodies, strengthens concentration, increases the sense of self-worth, brings career success, and balances creative and organizational abilities.

The evil eye is a particular form of *maleficium* in which the look of a witch or wizard affects the target adversely. The adverse circumstances may come in a particular form—say, sudden ill health—or they may be more generalized (e.g., "bad luck"). "Fulfilling all desires" is one of those Faustian bargains that you might think would be good but which is likely to land you in hot water. However, that sort of magic is pretty typical of what many customers desire in a spell. Bear in mind that wishing for your every desire to be fulfilled is a wish that arises from a warped sense of one's own importance—very likely hubris, greed, or obsession are involved in such excessive desire. Even if a spell to that effect were done or the stone spirit willing to humor you, the result can almost be guaranteed to be other than you expect.

So, from that point of view, carnelian's power to fulfill desires and speed manifestations can be a very dangerous quality. You may get very fast manifestations (results), but they may be ones that turn out to be harmful for you or bad for someone else. This is most common in love spells in which the lover's desire is to capture and bind a particular person. Such a spell, if it is working against the will of the beloved, or if it involves him or her being unfaithful to a spouse, can yield tragedy as well as sexual attraction because the nature of the enchantment is illusory. It binds the will of another person, which can never be made to last forever, and regardless of the problem of impermanency, the thing is fundamentally the opposite of love in that it aims to take away the freedom of another person or cause them to act in a way that may very well be against his or her self-interest. So, *caveat encantor.*

Citrine

Citrine is a clear, pale yellow variety of quartz which can be used in rounded forms for reservoir stones and in crystal form as wand points. A highly solar stone, it is nevertheless connected to the constellation Scorpio (generally thought of as watery). It is used to protect against intoxication, evil thoughts, overindulgence, snakes, plagues, epidemics, and extreme sports. Citrine is useful for aligning one's ego with one's higher self and for giving clarity of thought. Citrine has the power to strengthen one's ability to deal with difficult karma—influences from other lives—and it opens channels of intuition. In these qualities, it is very suited to yellow magic, that of divination and rational understanding.

Citrine may also increase one's motivation and creative energy by means of this ability to align ego with the higher self. Citrine is also said to bring prosperity, but that is a common claim. In this case, it means that opening one's mind and spirit can draw prosperity as it draws motivation or self-confidence.

Protection against snakes is a problem in some parts of the world and pretty seldom needed in others. The general power here is protection against sudden misfortune of a physical nature—venom being placed in the same category as contagious bacteria or viruses. When the old witches say that citrine protects against "intoxication" and "overindulgence," that means that it prevents self-inflicted damage from excess. We can understand how these ideas are connected to the general theme of clarity of thought and intuition in that overindulgence in wine or food is a case of bad judgment and unclear thinking. Snakes and disease are dangers—poisons—from outside, while intoxication and overindulgence is self-inflicted. Overindulgence also includes use of recreational drugs to the point of self-detriment.

The ability to deal with karma is a complex matter. It is classified under spells of knowing because dealing with bad karma from another existence depends on knowing about it—that is, gaining knowledge and understanding of the source of the bad karma. Bad karma may be specific but often manifests as "bad luck" generally, and in this respect is another form of self-inflicted curse, quite similar to illness caused by intoxication or overindulgence.

Finally, the fact that citrine can help with these problems does not mean that you should carry around a citrine in your pocket and then go abuse yourself with chemicals or gluttony and think that you will be protected. If you think that's how magic works, you are being superstitious, not magical. In a wand, citrine lends its powers to enhance spells and enchantments devised to combat such tendencies—that is, the tendency to poor judgment stemming from one being too disconnected from one's higher self ("too bestial," as moralists used to say).

Fluorite

More soft and breakable than quartz, fluorite comes in a wide range of colors—green, purple, yellow, or colorless. Fluorite is connected to the constellations Pisces and Capricorn for two quite different reasons: Capricorn because it grounds excessive energy—mental, emotional, or nervous; Pisces because of its fluorescent quality (emitting light when exposed to ultraviolet wavelengths), which accords with the ability to enhance the senses of the etheric body. Because of this opening of the etheric senses, fluorite helps the consciousness of a mage to shift into the astral world. This makes it a powerful healing stone for all chakras and good for cleansing the aura. Enhancement of the ethereal senses also aids communication with fairies and nature spirits. Because it further helps open consciousness to the mental world, fluorite enhances the understanding of abstract concepts and of study in general, but also of meditation and dreaming. Included in a wand, it is an all-purpose amplifier of etheric energies.

Hematite

A dark iron-gray stone with a metallic luster, hematite exhibits a blood-red color when powdered. Sacred to Mars, hematite has been worn to gain favorable hearings or judgments, to win petitions before those in authority, and to protect warriors. Associated with Aries and

Aquarius, it energizes the etheric body and gives optimism, will, and courage. It repels negativity and gives strength to the physical and astral bodies.

Jade

Best known as apple green in color, jade can also be white, pink, yellow, black, gray, or brown. There are actually two different kinds of stone called jade: jadeite and nephrite. The stone under consideration here is jadeite, but nephrite also has its traditional and ceremonial uses in New Zealand and elsewhere. Jadeite has been long used in China; the translucent green variety is, pound for pound, the most expensive mineral in the world. Jade was also used in Olmec carvings. Associated with the constellations Aries, Gemini, and Libra, jade strengthens the heart, kidneys, and immune system. It increases fertility, cleanses etherically, balances the emotions, dispels negativity, and gives courage and wisdom. Green jade is famous for producing vivid and accurate precognitive dreams.

Jasper

A variety of chalcedony that is massive and fine grained, it may take many colors but is often red. When combined with hematite, it is called jaspillite. Bloodstone is a variety of jasper. Jasper is good for weatherworking (especially for bringing rain) and for curing snakebite. It helps in healing stomach ailments and can help balance all chakras, stabilize energy, and protect from negativity. It can drive away evil spirits, hallucinations, and nightmares, and is generally a grounding stone. It can build up steady energy for long periods of time. Jasper is sacred to Jupiter.

Lapis Lazuli

Lapis lazuli is not a single mineral but a felicitous combination of dark blue lazurite, hauynite, sodalite, diopside, white streaks of calcite, and specks of gold pyrite. Sacred to the Egyptian goddess Isis and associated with the throat chakra, it is useful for removing painful memories from the astral body. Lapis lazuli draws the energy of the planet Jupiter and is a stone of good fortune. It helps release tension and anxiety and increases mental clarity, creativity, and clairvoyance. Lapis lazuli helps overcome depression, aids communication with spirit guides, and enhances astral awareness.

Malachite

A relatively soft, dark green stone with swirls and stripes of lighter green, malachite's color comes from copper, and thus it carries the energy of Venus. I would also say it carries the energies of Minerva or Cerridwen, for this is the wise feminine as well as the nurturing and loving feminine. Reputed to confer the ability to understand animal languages, it is also valued as a protective stone, revitalizing to the body and mind. It repels evil spirits, inspires tolerance and flexibility, opens communication, and stabilizes energy. It is an excellent stone for creating through magical manifestation, for strengthening the intuition, and for the power of transformation. Malachite acts as a psychic mirror, reflecting the energy one projects into it and drawing one into other worlds in meditation.

Onyx

A type of chalcedony similar to agate, except that it has relatively straight rather than curved bands of color. Sacred to Saturn and earth, onyx balances male and female polarities, gives spiritual inspiration, and helps one to face past-life problems and transformational challenges. It protects against black magic, evil spirits, and aids communication with spirits. White onyx expands the imagination, while black onyx deflects negative energy.

Quartz Crystal

Perhaps the most generally powerful magical amplifier, quartz crystals are the most common stones for wand points. When rounded, they also make excellent reservoir stones. Amethyst, rose quartz, citrine, and aventurine all belong to the quartz family, but the so-called rock crystal is colorless and transparent. Chemically it is composed of a lattice of silica tetrahedra (SiO_4).[22] Geometrically, the tetrahedron is a polyhedron with four triangular faces. The mystical significance of the shape will not be lost on any student of sacred geometry (see Daud Sutton, *Platonic and Archimedean Solids*). Three is the number of the Divine, and four is the number of matter and the material world. So, the tetrahedron, as the union of three and four (composed of four triangles), symbolizes the union of the divine sphere with the material.

---

22 Silica is SiO_2 but when conjoined into tetrahedral form, the molecules share oxygen atoms, so it effectively becomes SiO_4.

Quartz crystals generate an electric charge when heated or placed under strain. Crystal balls are, of course, used for scrying. Ruled by the moon, quartz crystal is excellent for meditation and communication with spirit guides, telepathy, clairvoyance, and visualization. As a wand point, it serves to amplify the prana of the mage. As a reservoir stone, it collects and stores the same power.

Silicon is a particularly interesting atomic element, the second most common chemical element in the earth's crust. The most common is oxygen, so that silicon dioxide (silica) joins these two most common components of the planet's surface. Silicon is considered a metalloid and is found not only in quartz but in sand, making it the principal component of glass. It is also used by humans to make silicone plastics and silicon semiconductor chips for our electronic brains. Silicon is essential to plant life, especially the microscopic ocean algae called diatoms.

Diatoms are phytoplankton that have cell walls made of silica and are at the very base of the food chain, taking carbon dioxide from the air and oceans and converting it via photosynthesis into complex organic molecules. This means that all life on our planet depends upon diatoms to convert solar energy into the organic compounds from which all life forms are constructed in the material plane. Silicon is a crucial atomic element (an expression of the alchemical element earth). Magically it embodies the root power of bringing energy into material form—or, in other words, the production of prana in nature. This is what lies at the roots of quartz crystal's power.

Milky Quartz

Translucent white, this variety of quartz draws down the power of the moon to nurture and heal, especially feminine energies. It opens the doors of perception into the higher worlds and promotes good spirit guides for travel within the astral (lunar) sphere. Sacred to the Roman goddess Diana, the Greek Artemis, and the Celtic goddesses Arianrhod and Cerridwen, as well as the Egyptian Isis. Promotes all magic having to do with mothers and their children, home, family, emotions, moods, and feelings.

Rose Quartz

Rose quartz is called the "love stone" and aids in healing the emotions. It aids in the development of compassion and love, and it reduces stress and anxiety. It also enhances creativity and self-confidence through connection to the higher self. Rose quartz resonates specifically with the heart chakra.

Rutilated Quartz

Clear quartz containing thin threads (rutiles) of gold, titanium, or asbestos are called Venus hair or Thetis hair stones. The rutiles are said to augment the transmission power and energy of the quartz. Associated with the constellations Gemini and Taurus, rutilated quartz enhances life energy, increases clairvoyance, transmutes negative energy, aids in communication with one's higher self, and increases the efficacy of magic. It is especially enchanting when light falls through the rutile needles in the stone.

Smoky Quartz

Smoky quartz is a grayish-brown quartz that aids in discrimination. Very dark smoky quartz, called morion or cairngorm, is attuned to the root chakra. It also aids meditation by grounding and centering. It breaks up pranic blockages and resulting negativity. By virtue of its grounding properties, it frees the astral vision and so strengthens dream awareness and can help to contact nature spirits. It helps transform dreams into reality by bringing them into the material plane. Smoky quartz is thought to be a more powerful magical stone than clear quartz; however, I believe that its power is not quantitatively greater, but it is qualitatively more manifest on the material plane. It carries the energy of Pluto to break through blockages and counter spiritual adversaries.

Tourmalinated Quartz

Clear quartz with inclusions of black tourmaline is considered to have double the power of plain clear crystal. Attuned to the constellation Libra, tourmalinated quartz balances all extremes and is a powerful grounding and protective stone. The properties of quartz crystal are melded with those of tourmaline. The black inclusions are considered by metaphysicians to absorb negative energies, thereby removing them from the subject. Grief and other negative or traumatic emotions may be particularly addressed using tourmaline. Spells involving emotions and feelings in general (the watery element) are especially suited to this type of quartz, which carries the power of the moon and the constellation Cancer.

Rhodonite

A pink or rose-colored silicate of manganese with thin veins or patches of gray or black, rhodonite is a good stress reducer, calming the mind and enhancing the energy levels of both body and mind. It has the ability to deter unwanted interruptions on the physical or astral planes, and it aids in keeping one's temper and reaching one's maximum potential. The stone's pink color gives it some of the same qualities as rose quartz and pink tourmaline. It has been called "the rescue stone" because of its powers of emotional healing and love. *Rhodon* is the Greek word for "rose" and alludes to not only the coloration of the stone but its vibratory similarities to the flower. It has been known to warn a traveler of danger by quickening the heartbeat. Attuned to the heart and root chakras, rhodonite will serve especially well for magic that aims to reduce anxiety, protect, and forewarn. On a higher octave, this power to calm and balance the emotions can also assist magic of self-realization. Rhodonite channels the power of Isis and Minerva—goddesses of the calm, decisive mind coming to the rescue.

Serpentine

This striking green stone with light and dark hues and white or black speckles comes in twenty different varieties. It is actually a group of minerals. Chemically the serpentines are composed of iron and magnesium silicates. The Latin name *serpentinius* means "serpent stone" for its ostensible power to protect against snakebite. Serpentine is also thought to increase prudence and self-restraint. It has many of the same properties as green jade (see page 111). Its magical association with the serpent attunes this stone to indirect travel, quests, and the path of the wanderer who does not follow a direct, straight line. In a wand reservoir, serpentine is well suited to spells of protection while traveling or to bring the opportunity to travel, and also to spells that increase knowledge and wisdom in yourself or others.

Tiger's-Eye

A variety of chalcedony or quartz with silky chatoyancy, tiger's-eye is usually striped yellow and golden brown. Its beauty is created by the replacement of silica by crocodilite (blue asbestos). The name *asbestos* in Greek means "inextinguishable." Magically, tiger's-eye conveys the temperament of the tiger. Attuned to the constellation Leo, tiger's-eye is a powerful protective stone; in this case, protection comes through the inspiration of courage. The stone balances emotions and gives clear insight to free one from fears and anxieties. It grounds and centers the user and thereby also strengthens the will. Tiger's-eye is one of the many stones noted for bringing good luck; this manifests from the flow of increased self-confidence and clarity of vision to distinguish truth from falsehood and illusion. It is especially good for protection against the dark arts, or indeed for aggressive, assertive, or even predatory magic (not that I recommend it for those purposes). The assertive quality will be amplified if used as a cut point. As a pommel stone, it has more the quality of the tiger waiting to spring.

Turquoise

One of the most beautiful of stones, turquoise is named for the particular shade of blue favored by the Turkish decorative arts, especially porcelain and tile. It is suitable for a wand reservoir or may be found in rock shops cut into a point. Chemically it is a hydrous phosphate of copper and aluminum, so that in its structure it carries the powers of both of these metals. Copper is one of the basic alchemical metals, sacred to Venus, the goddess of love and attraction. The quality of attraction may be generalized into the power of conductivity, the power to conduct energies from one place to another or from one person to another.

Aluminum, though unknown to the alchemists as such, might be said to be poor man's silver. Geometrically, the crystalline structure of aluminum is called face-centered cubic, which alludes to the structure of the world, the cubic altar of the magus being another such use of this Platonic solid. Aluminum is also of interest because it is the most abundant metal in the earth's crust and the third most abundant chemical element after oxygen and silicon. It is very lightweight and so partakes of elemental air. Sky-blue turquoise melds the magical powers of Venus and Jupiter, the expansive sky father. It is also sacred to the Egyptian goddess Hathor, goddess of the Milky Way. Hathor was worshipped as a cow goddess, as was the Irish goddess Boann; Brighid was anciently associated with milk. Turquoise, by virtue of its sky-blue color, is exceptionally well suited for weatherworking and spells of expansion, attraction, and repulsion. It is naturally well suited to spells of love and prosperity. It has the power to build bridges between worlds and so is good for seeking knowledge and understanding. Turquoise is also a sacred stone to the Native peoples of the Southwestern United States, who often combine it with silver in jewelry. Although the blue form of turquoise is most famous, it also comes in a greenish variety that is well disposed to green magic dealing with plants and ecology.

Mineral Spirits

*T*HE PREVIOUS STONE descriptions have the term "sacred to" used in regard to stones. This means that particular divine beings (however you conceive of them) are expressed through the stones. More than one divinity may be so expressed without contradiction. In other words, any given stone is seldom sacred to only one deity. The metaphysical properties of stones derive simultaneously from their chemistry and their stories. These two ways of making meaning out of matter cannot be separated in magic. Alchemy is chemistry with the stories left in. Modern chemistry, however useful and marvelous, branched off from alchemy in the seventeenth century and discarded the mythos of matter in favor of an objectified understanding. Such a view is purely descriptive and uses the language of atoms, particles, and molecules. This molecular language is a form of poetry in itself. A magical description of minerals, by contrast, includes not only atomic poetry but all forms of poetry—metaphor, symbol, myth, and folklore.

Many of the descriptions in this book weave a lattice of such symbolic meanings and, as such, they should not be mistaken for science. A stone may exhibit certain properties magically for one user and not for another. Individual specimens of a particular stone may not exhibit the same powers as other specimens. Some specimens may also exhibit a higher overall magical vibration than others, and this can be sensed by the wizard or witch who understands how to read such qualities. Such "reading" is not scientific analysis, yet much may be revealed by a thorough study of the crystalline properties of minerals and chemical elements through the geometry of Pythagoras and Plato. It is beyond the scope of this book to elucidate this particular subject in detail, but my references to cubic and tetrahedral crystal forms may offer a hint in the right direction.

Many of the fine books on crystals and their uses in healing approach the subject of metaphysical properties through the method of intuition. That is, the authors of these books work closely with the spirits of the stones and through that intuitive communication determine the usefulness of their vibratory energies for human beings. It is worth noting that minerals, like trees, do not simply exist for human beings to employ. They are beings in themselves and have their own work to do within the ecology of the natural world. One may think of them as we do of healing herbs: useful in medicine or healing but also part of a much larger system of energies at work in all dimensions.

The druid way asks us to pay attention to the stone people as it does to the standing people (the trees). Stone spirits are much more long-sighted and slow than trees are, and it takes a good deal of patience to connect mentally to stone spirits. Traditionally, the spirits of elemental earth are called gnomes. However, in modern times that venerable name has become so associated with little plaster garden figures that it is a difficult term to reclaim for magic. The gnome in a stone or crystal is a creature of tremendously long memory with very little interest in humans because we move too hastily.

The wizard can speak to the stone, can touch its spirit with his or her mind and direct it to apply its talents to magical actions. It is possible that merely having a bit of lapis lazuli lying about will bring you good fortune, but it is far more likely that good fortune will be attracted when the human soul and the mineral spirit are joined in actively willing it to be so.

A stone or crystal incorporated by art into a wand becomes a part of the whole. The wand has one spirit, which melds and combines all its components. The gnome spirit, the dryad spirit, and the core animal spirit are all interlaced into an entity that unites the three kingdoms of the natural world—animal, vegetable, and mineral.

The Colors of Magic

WHEN CHOOSING STONES for a wand, and in the act of enchantment, you will want to pay attention to the colors used and their particular magical meanings. If you are painting any part of the wand in colors, then you should consider the significance of your color scheme as part of your design, relative to the purpose of the wand. The assignment of meanings to colors varies from one wizard to the next. It is the sort of thing that wizards and druids sit around arguing about in pubs.

You can find good guides to color symbolism in other books, particularly those on candle magic or general books of correspondences, but they will not always agree exactly. Which color you consider appropriate to wand enchantment depends on your intention for the wand. Each of the seven classical planets has a color associated with its energies, essentially making up the familiar rainbow spectrum. Some mages, such as Bonewits, Buckland, and Zell-Ravenheart, have associated colors with different types of magical practice, and many contemporary wizards think of magic as existing in a spectrum. The Hermetic Order of the Golden Dawn created an elaborate system of color correspondences (see Crowley and Skinner).

Consider the colors that follow and the type of magic with which they are associated as you choose your stones and crystals. You may also take color into account when enchanting the wand (see part five), using colored candles, altar cloths, and robes to gather together the magic of a particular frequency. White is a good all-purpose color of purity and magic. A healing wand dedicated to that frequency of the magical spectrum could be surrounded with blue and use a blue stone as its reservoir. Besides the outward, material symbols of your sanctum, you will want to include the color in your visualizations.

Do not be bound by these associations. They are not carved in stone. Or even wood. Nor are the associations here intended to be exhaustive. If you intuit some other association with a color, then go for that. The personal meaning it has for you will be the most powerful factor—not other people's systems.

Table B: Colors of Magic

COLOR	MAGIC TO DO WITH ...
Red	The body, blood, vigor, physical healing or disease, killing (in a military context especially), sexual attraction and urges, enthusiasm, love deeply felt in the body (from sexual intimacy or family ties of blood—e.g., mother love). Buckland places charity in this field—the strength that allows one to give of oneself. The root chakra.
Rose Pink	Relationships, love, peace, cooperation, social skills, compassion, empathy.
Orange	Material wealth and strength, mental ego strength, pride, self-confidence, courage, security, flamboyance, attraction of abundance, prosperity. Also, performance, drama, conjuring, entertainment, joy. Buckland also places encouragement, adaptability, stimulation, and kindness here. The belly chakra.
Golden	The color between orange and yellow—solar energies, masculine strength, wealth, leadership, beauty, vitality, life, and nobility. The solar plexus chakra.
Yellow	The mind and nervous system, thought, abstract ideas, logic, mathematics, learning, organizing ideas, theorizing. Also charm or charisma, persuasion, and applications of clairvoyance, clairaudience, and prescience. Divination also falls into the field of yellow magic, the logical and intuitive interpretation of words and symbols. Also, the solar plexus chakra.
Green	Agriculture, fertility, plants, herbs, trees, growth, creation. Also, in the United States, this color is connected to money spells because our money is green (or is our money green because of the magical resonance of the color?). Probably from this connection with money and fertility comes the use of green in luck spells. Growth, herbal magic, wortcunning, herbology. The heart chakra.
Blue	The field of emotions, feelings, relationships, astral perception, intuition, dreams, and meditation. Blue is also the color of emotional healing, mental health, meditation, tranquility, empathy and intuition, peace, and the throat chakra.

Indigo	Sky and weather, flight, and space travel, ocean voyages, astronomy, astrology, cosmology, and star magic of all kinds abide under the starry canopy of indigo magic. Zell-Ravenheart associates this with wizardry in general. It is the color of wizardry in its most fundamental sense, as the love of wisdom and philosophy. The brow chakra.
Violet	Cosmic consciousness and power, authority, intensity. Passionate love, ambition, sense of mission in life, ecstasy, epiphany. Violet is often employed in conjunction with other colors to intensify a spell. Zell-Ravenheart gives astronomy and the cosmology of astrophysics to violet. The crown chakra.
Ultraviolet	Also called "clear." Pure power, extremes, universals, sacred geometries, mathemagics. Mastery of death and resurrection. Sudden, radical transformations or changes; transfigurations. Theoretical and mathematical understanding of the cosmos in terms of numbers.
White	Self-purification and the ceremonial quest for light; the clarity of divine vision, enlightenment, truth, and blessing. That which contains all colors.
Brown	The animal world and its fertility, fecundity, health, and nurturance. Magic of animal husbandry, hunting, and animal familiars, guides, or guardian totems. Transformation into and of animals. Also used for spells involving homes and houses.
Black	Black is a favorite color of wizards and witches, but its associations with evil and negativity are still strong. It is the magic of the night, the deep cave, the deep ocean, and deep space—all places in which humans may easily perish, thus its association with death and fear. As a color, it is about domination, binding, revenge, deception, confinement, limitation, death, disease, cursing, brooding teenagers, and the Faustian search for unlimited power. Black magic also covers necromancy and magic performed with the use of blood sacrifices or dead bodies. The positive side of black magic is seduction, which is why it is considered the magic of monsters—vampires, werewolves, and so forth. Its methods may be employed in a defensive or preemptive manner. Binding and banishing can be used to combat the malefic actions of others. Black magic can be used for healing when disease is caused by malefic entities or curses. The color is used in magic to combat negative influences and symbolizes the occult, the hidden knowledge of the magical worlds.
Gray	Smokey and mysterious, matters of lore, books, the past, ancestors, what has been forgotten, and finding balance between light and dark, matters to do with the underworld and Lord Arawn (cognate with Greek Hades).

Walnut Pocket Wand
Close-up of the reservoir stone and four winds motif.

Wand with Four Winds Motif
This short pocket wand of black walnut was turned on a lathe and has a motif called four winds. You can see this motif used on Native American peace pipes. The reservoir is a large and very clear polished quartz crystal.

Apple Rose Quartz
Wand finished with clear varnish for a very shiny look.

Elm Wand
This elm wand was made from the boulevard elm that stood in front of our house. It was cut down because of Dutch elm disease. Note the two different colors of stain used, making handle and shaft dark and light, respectively.

Ogham Inscription Wand
An inscription in ogham letters spiraling around the shaft of the wand.

Black Beauty
A wand finished in three tones to set off the four parts of the wand.

An Organic Stone Setting
The pommel of my linden wand, showing the stone set in carved tongues of flame.

Lignum Vitae Owl Wand
This lignum vitae wand is sculpted with an owl for its handle, set with a turquoise reservoir stone and amber bead eyes.

Beech and Holly
Above, a classic holly wand and a more organic beech wand, each finished with nothing but Danish oil and wax.

Maple Stag Wand
On this maple wand, I left some branchlets on the handle end because they looked like a stag's antlers.

Ebony Three Heads
Black ebony carved with three Janus heads in a primitive style and inscribed with runes.

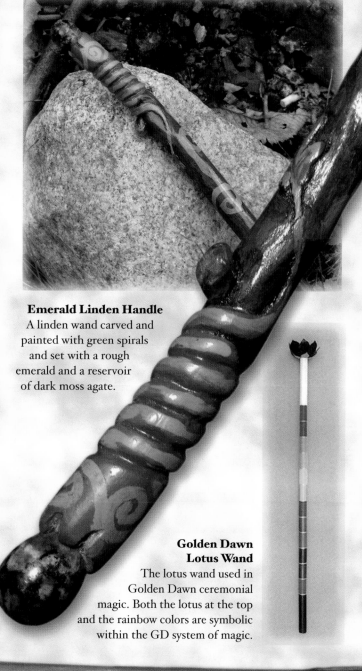

Emerald Linden Handle
A linden wand carved and painted with green spirals and set with a rough emerald and a reservoir of dark moss agate.

Hazel and Opal Air Wand
This is my own air wand, similar in design to the one shown in part five.

Bindrune on Holly
This bindrune is composed of three Norse runes: Tyr, Sol, and Ing. These combine into one sigil the names of the gods Tyr and Ing (Frey) with the sun. These three runes give the meanings of valor and justice transformed into the higher will.

Golden Dawn Lotus Wand
The lotus wand used in Golden Dawn ceremonial magic. Both the lotus at the top and the rainbow colors are symbolic within the GD system of magic.

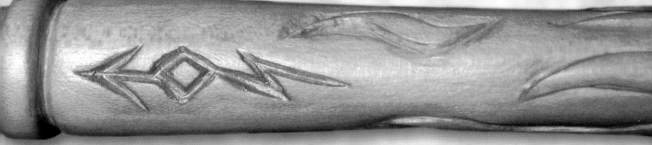

**Elvish Inscription
on a Ribbon**
The ribbon and letters spiral up the
shaft of the wand. The inscription
ribbon is done in Elvish script
and gone over with gold paint,
which sets off the letters well.

Classical Holly Wand Close-up of Handle
The pommel of the holly wand. I call
this shape the onion-dome shape.

The Finished Hazel Wand
Above, the handle of the wand from
part five with oak leaves and acorns,
and a moonstone reservoir.

Three Wands
Hazel, maple, and beech together
on my stone altar.

Forked Point
A forked point with a quartz
crystal point set in the crotch
to create three rays,
alluding to the three
rays of the druid
awen symbol.

Oak and Lapis Lazuli
This tiny pocket wand of oak with a lapis lazuli reservoir has
leather wrapping the stone and fancy beaded string frills.

Metals

THE INCLUSION OF precious metals in wands is something that can also be done, but it requires another whole set of talents. Gold or silver inlay are possibilities, to be sure, but very expensive ones. A less expensive and easier alternative to gold or silver inlay is to use gold or silver paint in carved designs. Fine paints containing suspensions of these precious metals can be purchased from art supply stores. You can even apply imitation or real gold leaf.

Many magi think of metals as having intrinsic magical properties. They do. However, when a mage says "intrinsic," he or she means something qualitatively different than when a chemist says it. Gold, for example, has the intrinsic material properties of its particular color, its density, and its malleability. But gold also has intrinsic *imaginal* qualities, and these are the ones that make it useful in a wand. Gold's magical qualities extend imaginally from some of its material qualities, but they create a web of associations that goes far beyond chemistry:

- ☾ Golden color and shine, light, the sun, life, reliability and regularity, radiates warmth, personality

- ☾ Beauty, good health, wholeness, healing powers

- ☾ Inspires desire to have it, also charisma, admiration of others

- ☾ As a ring, symbol of fidelity, eternity, unity, love, and devotion

- ☾ Heavy, impressive

‹ Rarity, wealth, high status, kingliness, rulership, greatness, magnanimity, power, protection

‹ Leo, lion, ego strength, physical strength, self-expression, masculine assertion, confidence, dominance

Gold and each planetary metal shares powers associated with its cultural significance and also powers derived from the planetary sphere it channels into planet Earth.

Besides surface ornamentation with metals, there are some wandmakers who like to make a wand with a metal core. The Hermetic Order of the Golden Dawn issued instructions on making a magnetized wand with a steel rod running through the center (see the Ciceros' *Secrets of a Golden Dawn Temple*). Being made from iron, steel is capable of holding magnetic force. The only way to make such an inclusion effectively with most wood is to cut the wood in half lengthwise, carve a recess on both halves, insert the magnetized rod, and then glue the halves back together. A copper wire is inserted by some wandmakers for its magical properties.

As a druid, I feel that it is important for a wand to be one solid piece of wood and not be cut apart and re-glued. However, for the purpose of inserting a magnetic core, an exception must be made. For some woods—such as walnut and poplar, which have soft, pithy cores—it is possible to use an awl or long drill to hollow out this core. The ends need to be sealed off with either solid plugs of wood or a pommel stone and a crystal point.

I do not use steel or iron as part of my wands—only in the carving tools. Iron is traditionally thought to disturb etheric bodies. It is for this reason that a steel blade is used for banishing ethereals and disturbing influences carried by the aether.[23] Some older schools of magic from the nineteenth and early twentieth centuries drew a connection between magnetism and etheric energy, and for this reason you will find that some writers on wands, such as Bardon, discuss polarities in terms of electrical and magnetic forces. Magister Bardon's ideas on wand-making are interesting in this respect.

---

23 Faerie Folk are known to be repelled by iron. The reason is that iron can break up their etheric bodies. Daemons, being purely ethereal, are even more strongly affected by an iron or steel blade. It is the magnetic property of iron that affects them by unbalancing the magnetic and electrical (yin and yang) forces within aether.

In *The Practice of Magical Evocation*, Mr. Bardon describes carved wooden wands as "simple wands," as distinguished from wands constructed out of metal and containing fluid condensers of various kinds. Mr. Bardon lays out the theory this way in his book *Initiation into Hermetics*:

> [T]here are two main kinds of fluids, originating in the four elements, namely the electric and the magnetic fluid. The electric fluid comes from the fire-principle, the magnetic one from the water-principle ... These fluids are the cause of every thing being (184).

By that last sentence above, I presume Magister Bardon means that these two polarized qualities or powers—the yin and yang, in Taoist terms—are the expressions of *akasha*, that "formless cloud" of the yogis from which all things are created and in which every idea ever thought remains a reality. Akasha can be identified with the aether of the Western alchemists. Aether is also called spirit, and it is thought to move from formless potentiality (in the divine dimension) into form by polarizing into these two "fluids." The light and dark, magnetic and electric occult forces exist within the etheric body of a metal or stone object as they do within our etheric and higher bodies—not as two separable fluids, but as two states of the quintessence, elemental aether.[24]

A fluid condenser, in Bardon's terminology, is a material which concentrates the two types of etheric fluids and allows them to accumulate. Bardon again: "Any object can be influenced by any fluid, regardless of being loaded electrically, magnetically, with elements or akasha, through the aid of the imagination and the will." However, not all materials are "suitable to retain an accumulated power for a long time or to accumulate it at all." Condensers may be physically liquid, solid, or "aeriform"—i.e., gaseous (*Initiation,* 195). So, we may observe that Magister Bardon treats magnetic fluid, electric fluid, the four elements, and akasha, or the quintessence, each as a class of essential power that may be stored and condensed.

In wandmaking, a solid condenser may be physically inserted into the pommel end of the wand. Liquid fluid condensers can be painted on before the coats of finishing oil. Any of these fluid condensers must, according to Bardon, contain at least a small amount of gold. He also mentions that sperm or blood "will grant an excellent accumulative power" (ibid.), but these are only appropriate when making a wand or other tool intended for your own use. Using bodily fluids will create a bond between the person supplying the fluids and the magical object

---

24 I refer the reader to Leadbeater, DuQuette, and Fortune for an understanding of the four worlds and the astral dimension of bodies; see also part five.

or potion into which they are placed. In the case of wandmaking, this kind of bond can also be afforded by including some hair from the wand's user secreted inside the wand—for example, under the reservoir stone in the pommel.

Magister Bardon describes the inclusion of liquid fluid condensers in hollowed-out wooden wands, particularly of woods such as elder, which have a pith at their center that can be removed. However, as he points out, any liquid fluid condenser is likely to be absorbed into the wood and ultimately evaporate. Solid condensers are easier to include inside a wand. Magister Bardon gives this formula for the "Electro-Magicum of the old alchemists" (ibid., 201), a mixture of metals:

> 30 parts of gold
> 30 parts of silver
> 15 parts of quicksilver (mercury)
> 15 parts of copper
> 6 parts of tin
> 5 parts of lead
> 3 parts of iron

This alloy would be powerful (magically speaking) because it contains all the metals of the seven classical planets of astrology. Because they are so poisonous, it is advisable to substitute other metals for quicksilver (mercury) and lead. Lead and mercury poisoning have been the cause of more magi losing their minds, powers, hair, or lives than any number of magical curses. Zinc or ruthenium may be substituted for mercury,[25] while nickel or palladium may be substituted for lead.[26]

I have not experimented with this process, so I cannot offer any firsthand practical advice on how to combine these metals. Apart from the costs involved, however, one must learn

---

25 Ruthenium? Yes, and here's why: the atomic number of mercury is 80, which reduces to 8 via gemetria. Ruthenium's atomic number is 44, which also reduces to 8. Ruthenium is also amenable to blending with precious metals. For sourcing on all these metals, see the Metallium, Inc. website in works cited, under minerals.

26 Palladium is about $50 a gram; nickel is about $2 a gram. Palladium is even denser than lead and so brings in this property, but nickel is a common meteoric metal with magnetic properties, which brings these qualities into your alloy. Lead is Saturn's metal, so to my mind density is more important because Saturn's power is one of heaviness and limitation. However, you need five grams for this recipe, and in palladium that would cost you about $250—more costly than gold at the moment.

enough about melting and alloying the seven metals together, including building a suitable furnace for smelting. Once these hurdles have been overcome, the process would in part depend upon successfully casting the liquid alloy into a mold to produce a relatively slender rod. (See "Alloys" article in the Encyclopaedia Britannica for a good discussion; also rotometals.com and backyardmetalcasting.com.)

Another recipe given by Bardon adds aloe resin, animal charcoal, and mineral coal to the metals in powdered form. This produces a powdered fluid condenser, which is easier to handle than molten metal when trying to introduce it into the center of a wand. One should still wear a breathing mask and gloves when mixing even the powdered metals. I am not entirely sure all seven metals could be found in powdered form. Bardon himself suggests constructing wands using metal pipes instead of wood, which has two practical benefits. First, it is easier to fill a metal pipe with the powdered or liquid condenser. Second, it is suitable to Bardon's theory of magnetic and electrical fluids, and to a belief that certain material substances can conduct these fluids better than others, just as silver or copper will conduct material electricity and iron has magnetic properties.

Bardon suggests a wand for the manipulation of electric fluid be made of a copper tube filled with powdered amber. For operations with magnetic fluid, he suggests a steel pipe filled with pulverized rock crystal. Or, for the ultimate electromagnetic wand, the maker can combine the two into a single rod, joining the steel and copper tubes end to end.[27] Again, I must emphasize that I do not mean *material* electricity or magnetism but the essential etheric forces that underlie those material manifestations.

Bardon also suggests a particular design for a wand used in the conjuration of the intelligences of the planets. In this case, a wooden wand is fitted with seven bands made from the seven planetary metals arranged in Kabbalistic order—that is, lead, tin, iron, gold, copper, brass (or mercury), and silver. (But obviously you have to substitute for mercury at least because it is liquid at room temperature.)

This design suggests that one should not think of a fluid condenser as if it is operating literally as a conductor of electricity. That is, the ingredients or components do not need to be contiguous, nor does the etheric fluid flow through them like an electrical current of moving electrons, which can be interrupted by a break in the conducting material (such as a broken wire). The seven metals are included for their spiritual—which is to say *imaginal*—power and

27 How do you join steel and copper pipes? Bardon does not say. Duct tape, perhaps.

value. To give another example, it is not necessary for the fluid condenser used as a wand core to extend all the way from one end of the wand to the other. It should extend at least through the handle of the wand, but it does not need to go all the way from pommel to point.

That said, one way to include such a condenser core is to fashion the wand in parts. If the point and pommel are crystal and stone, set in the wood with epoxy on the handle and shaft, this makes it possible to bore out a soft, pithy core all the way through and insert the metal rod you've created. In this way, the two stones are in physical contact with the material condenser, and you have a physical structure to support the flow of etheric energy. Just bear in mind that what is going on is not the flowing of a material substance or atomic force, it is the movement of prana. It is possible to project prana simply as a physical force against the strength of an adversary, but in most magic what you are doing is impressing a pattern upon prana. You are shaping it into a specific causal force shaped by your intentions. The wand can hold a reservoir of your prana, but it is your astral and mental ability that weaves it in a pattern to *do* something.

It will be obvious from the preceding discussion that the significance of metals is partly due to their association with the seven planets and their corresponding Roman divinities. As a druid, I believe that each metal and every kind of stone or crystal has intrinsic magical virtues, but in the case of the seven planetary metals, this magical virtue flows from the powers of the respective planets. For druids, the sun and the moon are symbolic of the two most powerful cosmic forces—the king and the queen—so gold and silver are most highly prized and powerful.

PART FIVE
Water

*For true love is inexhaustible; the more you
give, the more you have. And if you go to draw
at the true fountainhead, the more water
you draw, the more abundant is its flow.*

———————————

ᕲ Antoine de Saint-Exupéry

The Spiritual Dimension of Wandcraft

*W*HEN YOU PICKED up this book, it may be that this was the section you were looking for. What sort of tools do I use to carve wood, what sort of stain or finishing products, etc. — that is, instructions in how to physically make a wand. But the technique of any art is not just about physical technique. Carving and finishing a wooden wand employs the mind, the senses, the hands, and the soul.

Why do I give this chapter on the techniques of woodworking to elemental water? Because water, in the alchemical sense, is not just H_2O; it is also the essence of feeling, emotion, love, and connection. Elemental water is, on an astral level, the magnetic fluid, the yin that completes the yang of the artist's will. Technique must be learned consciously at first, but in order to master any technique, it must become unconscious. It must recede from the ego and into the dark depths of the psyche, into the ocean of the soul.[28]

The craft of woodcarving is itself a broad field, and there are many excellent books and DVDs of general instruction. I will not attempt to reproduce their contents here but will describe some of the tools and techniques that I use. It is not easy to teach carving without hands-on demonstration. My recommendations of books may be found in the bibliography, but there are many others.

---

28 If at this point you are saying, "Enough poetry already; I want to know how to carve!" then go find a copy of the book *Water and Dreams* by Gaston Bachelard and read it before continuing.

The basis of woodcarving is to remove some of the wood from your stock piece. Start with a stick or a dowel, and then use your power of imagination to see the shape you envision in the end. In woodcarving, one must examine the wood itself—its grain, knots, and other features that often indicate the natural lines on which a design is based.

In addition to the manual technique involved, there is a spiritual dimension to every craft. Even carvers who are not overtly magical feel the personality of the wood when they are working with it. Each type of wood has a history of relationship with human beings. Men and women have used wood to make tools, household implements, baskets and other containers, and indeed whole houses, ships, and other structures, for thousands of years. Behind your relationship to that particular piece of birch or oak lie countless generations of crafters who have come into intimate contact with the ancestors of that tree. It is in the element of alchemical water that relationships exist—the flow of fluids that connects one to another. The mixing of fluids creates each of us physically and emotionally. The water we drink connects us to other humans, to animals, to plants and trees. The water that flows in plants conveys nutrients from the soil and the light of the sun to feed all living things.

The relationship of mage and dryad is not exactly like having a relationship with another human being or an animal. When you approach the wood to make it into something useful, you intend to change it, to transform it with your tools. You may admire and love the living tree in one way, and when you come to carve and work its wood, you will carry some of that love with you. You also bring your love and excitement for the wand you wish to create—an entity that, as yet, only exists in the astral world of vision. The carver standing over the rough branch of a tree with his or her tools approaches it as a lover intending to join with it to create something new. The spirit of the wood and its divine creator made the branch's physical form. Your spirit and the spirit of the wand itself will now alter that form to make it something else, to form a wholly new relationship.

These aspects of woodcraft are true whether you are making a table or a magic wand. One can see in the work of the great woodworkers that they were aware of this soul-bonding of human and wood. In the act of working with wood and shaping it, one enters a state of light trance, a focused attention in which the center of consciousness has risen into the astral and mental planes. I believe that great woodworking is always a product of this intimate and transcendental relationship between the crafter and the wood. The relationship, in short, is love. The crafter's caresses and touch are as important in shaping wood as they are in human love. This is perhaps another reason why I feel that using power tools detracts from the intimacy of skin and wood. And the noise and inherent danger of power tools makes a state of trance more difficult to sustain.

For me, the act of woodcarving is itself a form of meditation. Through the imagination, I enter into contact with the spirit of the wood and let it tell me what it wants. I am not sure why dryads have particular ideas about wand design, but they do. It is not uncommon for me to receive very firm messages from wands in process telling me how they want to be carved or which stones or crystals they want to have—or which stones they do not want. So, listen to the dryad carefully.

Carving Tools

TRADITIONAL WOODCARVERS CAN carve beautiful pieces with nothing more than a straight carving knife. However, there are other more specialized tools also. For me, the most important tools are the saw, drawknife, the V-tool, the shallow gouge, and the rasp. In this chapter, I will introduce and discuss these tools in turn as I use them in the example carving pictured.

Carving tools may be purchased in many shapes and sizes, with differently shaped handles. Professional carvers often have a whole array of gouges and blades, each with a particular purpose. Many specialized tools are designed for flat-relief carving, which is the sort of carving you might do on a box or panel. Carving in the round and in a very small scale, as in wandmaking, requires fairly small, delicate tools. In the end, it is best to experiment a little until you figure out which tools are right for you.

I like Flexcut tools because of the particular rounded shape of their handles and because their blades are very sharp right from the store. The drawback to very small blades is that if they get nicks and lose their edge (often because of cutting into end grain or knots), they must be discarded and replaced. A truly adept carver will keep his or her blades perfectly sharp at all times and avoid overworking them to the breaking point, but sometimes it happens.

Basic Tools for Wandmaking

SAW: A wood saw has teeth that are very sharp and usually cut as you pull the saw toward you. A handsaw has a round handle and is small enough to cut branches or small wood stock. It should have fine-enough teeth that it can leave a smooth cut.

V-TOOL: A carving blade shaped like the letter V. It cuts a fine line, like a miniature river valley. These tools come in different sizes usually measured in millimeters. For wand carving, 1, 2, and 4 mm are most useful.

GOUGE: A carving blade shaped like the letter U. The shape of the U may be steep-sided or very shallow, like a glacial valley. The gouge can be used with the open side up to remove large amounts of wood at a time. It may also be used with the rounded side up so that the curve follows the curve of the branch. In this position, the carver uses it more lightly to remove smaller amounts of wood, often to carve beads and coves across the grain.

RASP: A coarse steel file, the surface of which consists of many small teeth. Rasps come in many degrees of coarseness, like sandpaper, and these are used to remove large amounts of wood to perform general shaping. A rasp leaves a somewhat rough surface lined with grooves. It tears away the wood fibers rather than cutting them as a blade does.

MICROPLANE: A plane is a tool used by cabinetmakers to smooth the surface of boards. It is essentially a sharp, straight blade held at a shallow angel to the wood so that it shaves off thin layers of wood. A microplane combines the qualities of a plane and a rasp, consisting of a steel surface punctured by many small shaped blades raised only slightly from the surface. Unlike a rasp which removes wood by tearing it, a microplane cuts the wood and produces very small shavings. It will leave a relatively smooth surface to the wood.

SANDPAPER: As a rasp removes large amounts of wood—more or less, depending on its coarseness—so sandpaper removes wood by tearing it. The sand particles on the paper tear at the wood as do the blades of a rasp or file but much more finely. The fineness of sandpaper is rated with a number and the term *grit*; 150-grit sandpaper is coarse and will leave a rough surface, but it is good to remove the grooves left by a rasp or other unevenness. The 240 grit has smaller particles of sand and smoothes the wood more finely. At this level of tearing, the cells of the wood are actually being filled with the fine dust that comes off the wood. This is what produces what we feel as smoothness. The 400-grit paper has such fine grains of sand on it that the paper itself will feel almost smooth to our fingertips and leaves the wood feeling absolutely smooth. Some brands of sandpaper today use artificial grit rather than actual sand and last longer as a result.

These are but a few of the V-tools and gouges used for carving and some rasps used in shaping and smoothing. Left to right, front row: large shallow gouge, four different sizes of V-tool from 1 mm to 10 mm, and a small shallow gouge. Top row: rasps from coarse to fine.

Sharpening

ℒET'S START WITH sharpening—not because you will need to sharpen your new tools right out of the box, but because the sharpness of your tools is of the first importance. Sharpening tools is a whole craft in itself. It is a crucial aspect of woodcarving. I cannot overemphasize the need for tools to be kept sharp. As long as you don't let them get chipped, you can sharpen your hand tools with small sharpening stones and a strop with sharpening compound on it. Practically every book on beginning carving, as well as many websites, will give you advice on this matter. The rule is that the cutting edge of a blade must be razor sharp. If you look at it through a magnifying lens under a light, you should see no reflection at all from the edge. This is because the perfectly sharp steel blade is only a few molecules thick, not enough to visibly reflect light to our eye.

Working on a blade has some similarity to smoothing wood with sandpaper. You progress from a coarse sharpening stone to a finer one and then to the leather strop with two degrees of sharpening compound (usually colored yellow and white, respectively) to get it down to that sublime quality of sharpness in which the edge is invisible to the eye. Sharpening or polishing compounds, sometimes called Tripoli or jeweler's rouge, come as a block or stick of chalklike consistency. Yellow is more coarse than white.

An Arkansas stone is a white sharpening stone that is very hard. Running a blade over an oiled Arkansas stone will give it a keen edge. The tricky bit is keeping a straight blade (such as the two sides of a V-tool) at a consistent and correct angle to sharpen the edge rather than flattening it. Jigs are sold that keep the blade at the proper 30-degree angle. You sharpen the outside angle of the blade until it shines and then lightly run a leather strop over the inside

Here's what a V-tool looks like close up. There are two
razor-sharp cutting edges that meet in a point.

of the blade. The leather strop is rubbed with sharpening compound. The last step is necessary because if you have sharpened the cutting edge perfectly, an invisible burr will form on
the opposite side of the edge. You can feel the burr with your fingertips. Once this burr is
removed, the blade is as sharp as it can be.

The basic movement for sharpening is to draw the blade smoothly across the Arkansas
stone or leather strop. The Arkansas stone must be oiled with sharpening oil. The stone cuts
away the steel at a molecular level, and the particles removed are carried away with the oil.
The oil also prevents the steel from heating up too much, which will deform it. Another kind
of sharpening stone is called a Japanese water stone and uses water rather than oil as the cool-
ing medium. This use of oil and water is your introduction to elemental water, the fluid that
produces the necessary sharpness in your cutting tools. Keeping a steady hand and the correct
angle takes practice.

For gouges, which have curved blades, the sharpening technique is more difficult to explain.
The gouge blade must be drawn back against the oiled stone and then moved in a figure-eight
motion to work the whole curve of it, always maintaining the same correct 30-degree angle.
You will want to sharpen your blades every so often as you are working, and if you carve much,

you will begin to be able to feel when the edge is dull. It starts to tear the wood rather than cleanly cut it. Different types of wood are harder on blades than others. For example, oak is very coarse grained and hard, so it can wear down a blade more quickly than fine-grained wood like linden, rowan, or apple. Cherry wood is a good example of a fine-grained wood that is very hard and dense, so is harder on the blade. Plum and blackthorn are extremely hard and difficult to carve. Ebony and lignum vitae are the hardest and most dense, and consequently will dull a cutting edge most quickly.

The only way to get nice, clean lines in carving is to use a sharp tool that slices through the fibers of the wood. Tearing will never produce a smooth, clean edge, and no amount of sanding can correct torn fibers. It is good to remember that when you are carving with a sharp tool and working with the grain, not against it, your surfaces will ideally not even need sanding to be smooth. Working "with the grain" means cutting in the same direction the lines in the wood are going; those lines you see are the grain. In some types of wood, you will hardly see the grain at all. This is called fine-grained wood.

Even if you are careful to go with the grain, you will still need to sand to get out blade marks and irregularities, but these marks can also be left alone. They give the piece a more handmade look. Getting the surface smooth with the blade will save work in the sanding stage. However, if you are going to carve designs into your wand, you will alternate stages of sanding with carving for reasons that I shall explain as we go.

This is the hazel branch I will use as my example in the following photographs. Note that hazel's bark is fairly smooth and thin, but there are several knots that we need to deal with.

The Vise

*Y*OU WILL PROBABLY want to have a small, adjustable vise in addition to the carving and sharpening tools. A wand carver must be free from vice and pure of heart, but one without a vise will bear the scars of his or her errors. In other words, you need a vise to avoid cutting up your hand and to have better control over the piece and the cutting blade. Vises for carving can be purchased from woodworking shops or online. What you will need is a vise with nylon or padded jaws to hold the wood in place without denting it. If it is a vise with a ball joint that allows it to be tipped and turned in any direction, you will find this useful; PanaVise is a well-known manufacturer of this type of small vise. Once I have stripped off the bark, I use a piece of leather in the vise jaws to pad them further.

Now you are ready to begin carving. But let's take a moment to consider the anatomy of the branch.

A vise that can be positioned at different angles is very useful
to secure the piece and move it during carving.

Confronting the Branch

ϒOU HAVE BEFORE you, in your vise, a branch from a tree. You have harvested it according to the rigors of your particular magical tradition, speaking to the tree and giving it a gift in return, perhaps, or maybe the branch was gifted to you by a tree dropping it in your path. The first decision to make is whether you wish to remove the bark. In some woods, such as birch, oak, or beech, the bark is itself so lovely and so characteristic of the tree that you might want to preserve at least some of it. To make this decision, it helps to understand the structure of a tree.

A tree grows in layers, called growth rings. Essentially, each year, the tree grows a new layer of its outer bark, increasing slightly in diameter. The branches do this as well as the trunk. Just behind the outer bark is a layer called the phloem. This is like the tree's circulatory system. It draws up water from the roots and sends it up into the branches and leaves. When you set a branch to dry, it is the moisture in the phloem layer that needs to evaporate. Further inside the tree are several growth rings that continue to be alive, with water and nutrients flowing through their pores. These layers are called the sapwood. Between the phloem and the sap-wood is a layer called the cambium, and this is where the new growth ring is created each year. The cambium is like an inner skin. The bark protects the life process going on inside. As a tree ages, the bark sometimes becomes much thicker and develops deep fissures; oak and ash trees are the classic example of this kind of bark. In other trees, the bark remains relatively thin; cherry, beech, and birch are good examples. Of course, the bark is much thicker on the trunk and larger branches of the tree than it is in the smaller branches you want for wandmaking.

It is the heartwood that most interests the wandmaker. Heartwood is considered dead by biologists, but it serves an important function, for the heartwood is like the bones in a skeleton, supporting the whole structure, bearing the weight of the whole tree at its widest point. I think of a tree's heartwood as its whole history or its memory—a memory that may extend back many human generations. In wand branches, the heartwood is the wood that may be stained to show the grain of the wood. The grain is the pattern of vascular rays that run perpendicular to the rings, transporting water and nutrients laterally through the layers. The cells in the rays are often darker than the surrounding cells. The heartwood is harder and more durable than sapwood, partly because its pores have been filled up with waste products from the tree's metabolism. These include resins, tannins, oils, and gums. These lines in the wood form the grain that is so beautiful when the wood is finished but which is tricky in the carving and sanding process.

The wandmaker who wishes to leave some or all of the bark on the wand must choose the wood carefully and make sure it is thoroughly dried; this can take up to six months. In some trees, this drying time is important because as it dries, the bark becomes loose. As the moisture leaves it, the phloem layer will shrivel up and the bark will separate from the sapwood and heartwood underneath. Trees such as oak, beech, and hazel hang on to their outer bark. Cherry and rowan are examples of trees that do not hang on to their bark so well. Milled pieces of wood will be already dry and ready to carve. It is possible to peel off the bark of some green branches (willow, for example), but one runs the risk of the wood cracking later as it dries.

In addition, the bark of a branch may conceal bugs or larvae who have taken up residence in the branch and are using it as a both a hotel and a smorgasbord. A close examination of the branch is necessary. If there are small holes in the bark (the size of a pinprick, in some cases), you will be wise to strip off some of the bark to find out what is going on. In some cases, you will find that an otherwise sound branch has tunnels all through it, and these tunnels are filled with soft—um, well, let us just say *digested* wood. The larvae might still be in the holes too. If you want to use a branch that has been tunneled through, it is not a bad idea to treat it thoroughly with alcohol to kill off any still-living residents. Sometimes, as larvae tunnel through the phloem and sapwood, they leave patterns carved into the heartwood below. They are very shallow patterns and are sometimes beautiful. As long as the wood is not decayed and there are not deeper tunnels that might compromise the structural integrity of the wand, these designs made by the parasites may be left intact.

Pictured here from top to bottom are a fine-toothed handsaw,
a microplane, and a curved drawknife.

In any case, it is the heartwood and its finishing that will produce the most beautiful object, a wand that is fully a wand, a creation of the artist, transformed out of nature's work. There is symbolic value in creating a wand that is no longer a branch, but there is also symbolic value in letting the wand be connected to nature with some bark on it, especially on the grip, where it serves a practical purpose as well. If you remove the bark, you can taper the wand and carve it. If you leave the bark on, your wand will have only what little natural taper might exist in the branch. This is quite adequate if you plan to give it a crystal point, but to alter the shape of the branch, you will have to remove the bark. To do that, the best tool is a two-handled drawknife.

On the facing page is an illustration of some of the cutting tools that you will apply to take off bark and shape the branch.

The drawknife is a large blade that may be straight or curved. Grip the tool with both hands and draw it over the bark at a shallow angle, just steep enough to cut into the surface. Don't try to dig too deep. Take off thin layers, and pay attention to the feel of the blade. If it catches or gets stuck and you continue jerking at it, the blade will dive down into the wood, following the grain, and take a big chunk out of the piece. This can also happen if you are carving against the grain. One side of your stick will have the grain running one way, and when you turn it over, the grain will run the other way. You have to cut with the grain to cut the wood smoothly.

Another hazard are knots in the wood, because around a knot, the grain goes in every direction and has to be treated gingerly. It is best to smooth knots with a coarse rasp or a microplane before using the drawknife.

To get at the beauty of the heartwood, you will need to also remove the sapwood layer beneath the bark. This can be done with the drawknife also, but often it is easier to use a coarse and medium rasp.

Use a coarse rasp to smooth knots before using the drawknife. A rasp is a steel instrument with many small parallel lines of teeth. Rasps tear away wood, while microplanes slice it away.

Here is the finer side of the rasp; note the smaller rows of teeth. This will smooth out the marks left by the coarse rasp. Here is a knot in the hazel branch that has been smoothed flush with the rest of the wood.

Rough Shaping

*T*HIS STAGE OF the work is different depending on whether you are using a natural branch or milled lumber. If you are using a piece of cherry or beech lumber, for example, this will come in boards. For wands, it is generally desired to have a board one inch thick and as long as you want the wand to be. Since boards are usually sold in widths of at least four inches, an electric table saw will be required to cut the board into 1 × 1 stock. Some lumber and woodworking stores will be happy to cut the wood for you in their shop.

If you use a dowel, you can skip the next step. Doweled wood is machined into cylindrical form and sold that way in various lengths and diameters. Oak, walnut, maple, cherry, and birch are available in many woodworking stores. The only observation I would make about dowels is that their grain is very broad—more broad than in a branch of the same size—because they have been cut from the trunks of the tree. So, a dowel will have grain similar to what you see in boards (for example, in a wooden tabletop).

Less-common wood you may have to buy as boards, and then get the wand into the shape you want, which is usually circular in cross-section. That means taking off the corners of the wood stock (unless you work from a dowel). Taking off the corners with a drawknife is sometimes tricky, and you will have to reverse directions as you go to keep your cut with the grain. Going against the grain with a drawknife on a piece of milled lumber often causes a deep split that is very hard to work out.

The drawknife should be kept at a very shallow angle. Cut with the grain,
and shave off one layer at a time. Take short cuts. Don't try to take off a strip
that is the whole length of the branch unless the bark is very loose.

For removing the bark and sapwood from a branch, I like to use a drawknife. For rounding the corners of a square-milled piece of stock, I find that a coarse rasp is the best tool. It will take off the wood quickly, leaving a rough surface, but this can be worked smooth once the general shape has been achieved. Use a coarse rasp with big teeth and then a finer one until the grooves left by the big teeth are smoothed out.

Taper the point as the next step after removing the bark and sapwood and smoothing all the knots. A microplane is sometimes useful too, made up of tiny blades that slice away thin layers of wood rather than tearing them off, as rasps and sandpaper do. If you are tapering the wood to a point, let the wand and your own creativity guide you toward the exact shape. Of course, you may wish to make some sketches beforehand. Rounding the end of the wand to a point takes a good deal of patience and careful work with the rasp. Take care to keep the sides even so that your point does not end up off-center.

If the wand is to have a crystal set in the point, then things are more involved. You will still want some taper from the pommel to the point, but in this case, you must measure the base of your crystal against the wood's end grain. Then taper the piece until it is just a little larger than the base of the crystal—approximately 2 mm larger. You may wish to carve the wood that will surround the base of the crystal into a design of more or less complexity, and the key is to leave enough depth to the wood to carve your design in relief. In the case of an animal head holding the crystal in its mouth, you may leave half a centimeter or more beyond the crystal's diameter in order to carve the head of your beast.

The fine side of the big two-sided rasp I'm using here will
smooth the piece down quite well at this stage.

First Sanding

*T*HE NEXT STAGE is called the first sanding. Once the general shape has been achieved, apply increasingly finer grits of sandpaper. Sanding is dusty; there is no getting around that. When sanding, wear a face mask to avoid breathing the fine particles of wood into your lungs. Some woods, such as ebony and purpleheart, have dust that is quite bad for the lungs. Other woods might be dangerous because of microscopic molds or funguses in the wood. In any case, you do not want to breathe in all that dust. You may want to do your sanding out of doors to reduce the chance of inhaling dust and to avoid getting it all over your house or apartment. Professional woodworkers often have elaborate systems of ventilation and dust removal hooked up to vacuum motors to deal with this health hazard.

You will require several degrees of sandpaper; try 80, 150, 220, and 400 grit. These are mystical numbers. With sandpaper, the higher the number, the finer the grit. When you sand the piece, you will work from the coarse paper (80 grit) to the fine (220), and after applying stain, use the 400 grit, followed by medium and fine nylon sanding pads. These pads have replaced steel wool for this fine smoothing because they do not leave tiny metal particles of steel in the wood, particles which also are hazardous to your eyes and lungs. This process gradually gives most types of wood a surface that is smooth as a baby's bottom.

Another item in your carving toolbox is tack cloth. These are pieces of cheesecloth impregnated with resin to make them sticky. You run a tack cloth over your piece before applying oil or other finishes in order to remove as much of the sanding dust as possible. Fine sanding actually fills the microscopic pores of the wood. The resin unblocks the pores to make them receptive to stain or oil.

Generally, when sanding, you want to work *with* the grain—that is, the same direction that the lines run. Sanding across the grain scratches and tears the wood, which is not what you want. In this first stage of sanding, the goal is to create a fairly smooth surface on which you can draw your carving design in pencil. You do not need to work it down to 400 grit at this point, but you may. This first sanding helps the wandmaker to get a sense of the wand's overall shape and the characteristics of the grain and knots in the wood. Start with 80 grit and work out the marks left from the rasps, then proceed to 150 and 220 grit (and 400 if you like). Remember, as you carve your design, you will be removing some of this smooth surface from the first sanding, because when you rough out the carving, you lower all the wood around your design to set it in relief. The purpose of the first sanding is to check the overall smoothness, catch any rasp toothmarks you missed, and give yourself a nice, smooth surface on which to draw your design in pencil.

Drawing the Design

Once you have a nice, smooth surface and have the point of your wand tapered how you want it, take up your pencil and then draw on your design. If you like, you can work out some ideas on paper first. I like to look at the branch and let the wood dictate to me how to carve it. Often I have some ideas—an owl reservoir, for example, or a particular design in Celtic interlace. Working with clients, I usually have some ideas given to me and then have to see how those ideas work with the branch I've chosen. Knots particularly will dictate where you carve, because the wood around a knot is extra hard, and, since that grain runs in every direction around it, it is best not to even try to carve through a knot. Go around it instead.

First, draw on the four main parts of the wand—pommel, handle, shaft, and point—taking care that any lines that run round the circumference of the wand are straight and connected. You can always erase and fiddle with the design as you put it on the wood. The mark of the point section indicates where you want it to begin to taper. In some cases, the shape and curve may be more complex, tapering toward the handle as well as toward the point.

After working out the main divisions, if you are going to include a stone or crystal in either end of the wand, you will want to trace its rough outline for the hole you will make later. Knowing approximately where the stone will be set helps in knowing how much wood you can take away in carving pommel and point.

Next, I draw the lines that go around the circumference of the piece. This indicates where I will cut with the saw to create beads and coves (the valleys between the beads), and the steps in the pommel. If you remember the earlier discussion in part three on design, beads are the term for carved sections that curve or jut outward, while coves is the term for carved indentations

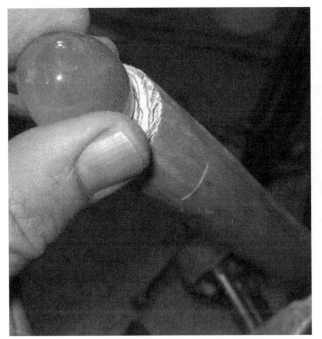
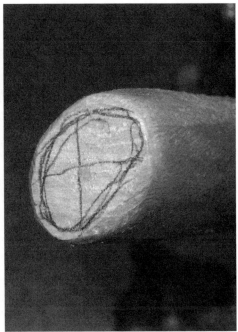

(Left) Here I am tracing around the stone that will be the reservoir of the hazel wand. This outline will serve as a reference as I carve the pommel to fit it. (Right) Here's the outline of the stone.

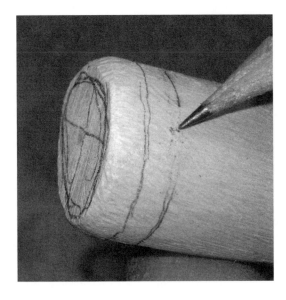

Make sure your lines meet and are straight as they circle the wand, or you will get slanted or wobbly beads, and nobody really wants that, do they?

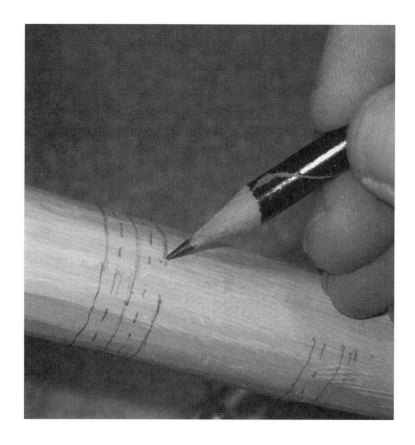

For the beads at the middle of the wand, I use solid lines to show where to saw and dashed lines to show where the high edge of the bead will be. These will be sharp beads, as you shall see ...

that set off the beads (see illustrations on page 73). In the hazel wand I carved for this demonstration, the setting for the pommel stone is a raised ring and a step down toward the stone (see the bottom photo on page 158).

Now, we saw on the lines, again being very careful to follow the line. If you place a piece of masking tape on the side of the saw parallel to the teeth, you can better keep track of how deep you are going. You may want to make a cut anywhere from $\frac{1}{32}$ of an inch to $\frac{1}{8}$; it's better to cut too shallow than too deep. You can always make it deeper and even it up later with the large shallow gouge.

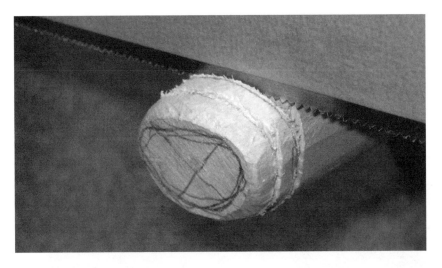

Here I am cutting the places where I want to make steps. This is tricky.

These are the lines of the beads and coves at the middle of the wand. There will be one large bead flanked by short, sharp coves and beads. Remember, only cut on the solid lines!

Once you have the grooves cut with the saw, the next step is to shape the beads and coves with a large shallow gouge or a knife. I like to use the gouge with the curve up to follow the curve of the branch. Taking small cuts, work around the piece, starting at your dotted lines for the short, sharp beads. For the large bead in this example, I am just eyeballing the curve I want.

Shape the large bead first, because the smaller ones are delicate and one slip can break them. The motion here is partly slicing and partly shaving. Push the gouge into the wood and give it a bit of a twist to slice off small bits. The smaller the bits you carve in each motion, the easier it will be to fix your mistakes.

Shaping the small beads and coves. The coves are the valleys between the beads. I start
at the dotted line that marks the midway point where I want it to be pretty sharp.

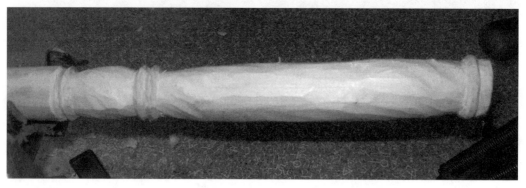

Here is the whole set of beads and coves roughed out with the gouge, top.
Underneath, here is the handle and pommel roughed out too. Ready for rasping!

Once you have the parts of the wand roughed out, return to the places you have cut with smaller rasps and coarse sandpaper to smooth them again. The places you have not carved will still be smooth.

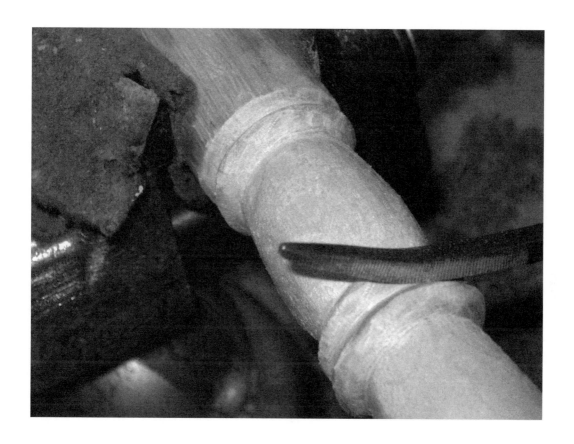

A small, flat rasp is good for the larger areas like the handle, but in the narrow parts you will want a V-shaped rasp, as shown here.

Drawing the Surface Designs

ONCE YOU HAVE the wand shaped and smoothed the way you want it, you can take up your pencil again and draw on any surface design or inscription that you want to include. These designs will be carved in low relief, which means that you will be cutting away the negative space in your design. If it is a vine climbing up the wand's shaft, then you will cut away everything that isn't the vine to a depth of about 1/16 of an inch (a millimeter or two). You can carve whatever you like, from lifelike representations of leaves to abstract knotwork animals or iconic symbols and sigils. For inscriptions, it is usually best to carve these into the wood directly rather than in relief, but it's up to you.

We discussed inscriptions and symbols in part three. Now you will need to actually lay out those letters or symbols onto the wood itself and plan how to carve them, depending on what alphabet you are using. If you carve a ribbon that winds around the shaft of the wand to bear the inscription, then take care to space your letters out so they will all fit evenly and you do not end up with too little space at the end of your ribbon.

At this point, you are not going to actually carve the letters of the inscription, you are only drawing on your design. Writing them on the wood will help you plan how they will be spaced later, when you have finished carving everything else that may go around them. The ogham letters are a handsome form for inscriptions on wands because you can essentially lay out your center line onto the wood, draw two equidistant parallels, and then draw the letters in between those two parallels. Take care with spacing ogham letters, however, because they vary a great deal in terms of length.

On this wand, I am going to decorate the handle with oak leaves and acorns.

Carving

*A*FTER THE DESIGN is worked out to your satisfaction (and to the satisfaction of the dryad spirit), take up a medium V-tool (4-10 mm, as seems right) and begin cutting away the outline of your design. Every line you have drawn should indicate a place where the V-tool goes to remove wood. For tricky, delicate designs, you may wish to start with a 1 mm V-tool just to get the outline.

With the wand secured in your vise, take your V-tool in your right hand (if you are right-handed) and hold it comfortably. With your other hand, guide the tip of the tool so that it follows your lines precisely. Hold your tool at about a 20- to 30-degree angle and just nick the bottom of the V into the wood. Push gently, maintaining your angle, and then lift slightly to end the cut. You should produce a thin shaving of wood and a smooth parting of the wood fibers where your pencil line was.

After outlining the entire design, you can take a larger V-tool and begin slicing away the part of the wand that you want to lie lower than the relief design. For example, if you are carving oak leaves in relief, you will carve away all the surrounding wood to about 1 to 2 mm lower than the original surface to set off the leaves in relief. You can smooth this lowered surface or texture it using a 1 mm V-tool or gouge. Carving away all the wood that is *not* your design takes considerable patience and repeated examination by eye and with your fingers until the surface is to your satisfaction and your relief design is raised as much as you want it to be. (See the color pages for a photo of a finished oak leaf handle.)

You do not have to cut a design in deep relief. You may prefer to establish the outline and leave it at that. This is especially true for inscriptions. Staining the wood will bring out the lines and make them appear darker than the smooth surfaces around them, which gives a very handsome effect to the wand. The reason the carved parts of the wood will stain more darkly than the smooth surfaces is that each cut exposes the sides of the wood cells so they have a rougher and more porous surface.

As you carve, pay attention to which way the grain is going. If you carve across the grain, you risk tearing the fibers of the wood and not getting a smooth surface. Some woods are more difficult in this respect than others. The solution is to stop and turn yourself (or the piece) around and carve the other direction along your line. If it still seems to be giving you trouble, stop and check that your blade is sharp and not nicked. If you think about a curved design like vinery winding around the shaft of the wand, you can readily see that you will have to adjust the direction of your cut as you go along and the line changes direction. If one side of your vine cuts nicely, then you know you are going with the grain. That also means that the other side of the vine stem will need to be cut in the opposite direction.

The only way to make parts of the wand larger in diameter than the rest of the wand is to reduce the diameter of everything but what you want to be the largest diameter. You have to think out those aspects of the design before you even pick out your branch. The essence of carving is that you are removing wood, so the highest points in the design have to have the least amount of carving done to them.

To round the pommel if it is going to be wood, the best tool is a coarse rasp, followed by the finer side of the rasp, and then finer rasps and the shallow gouge as described above, with the curve of the blade going with the curve of the wood. Shape the pommel as you wish by eye to its general shape. There are many options for the shape of the pommel or reservoir. It can be spherical or ovate (egg shaped), onion shaped (like the onion domes on Russian cathedrals), or shaped like a beehive. The beehive shape (one of my favorites) is achieved by making the end of the pommel somewhat conical, rounding toward its bottom like an old-fashioned woven beehive. Then, with a small V-tool, carve a spiral from the top point to the base of the hive. You can draw the spiral line first, of course.

Another favorite of mine is the pommel reservoir carved as an acorn. The acorn can look like a woman's breast if you take the time to give it its little nipple or, when placed on the point of a wand, it can take on a distinctly phallic character—so it works both ways. To carve an acorn, start with a generally ovoid shape, then divide it about one-third of the way from the top. The bottom two-thirds are carved inward slightly with the concave side of a shallow gouge so that the nut is inset from the top third, which will be the acorn's cap.

The cap may be carved in a pattern of cross-hatching. Cut the lines across the grain first to minimize tearing with a straight, sharp carving blade. Use a field guide to the many kinds of oak to get some ideas for your acorns.

Another iconic design for the pommel or carved reservoir is what I call the stupa form. A stupa is an ancient temple form from Asia that is essentially a stepped building—like a step-pyramid, only round. This design is very easy to produce on a lathe but takes a bit of finesse to do manually. The sections can be marked off with a saw but should be worked down carefully with a V-tool or shallow gouge. A rasp works even better, in my opinion, though the process is slower. The trick is to get the sections to be concentric circles.

The pommel can be carved into the likeness of an animal too. This can get as elaborate as you like and your skill as a carver permits. Owls are a particular favorite of mine, but you can carve gods and goddesses, druids, wizards, lions, wolves, etc., if you like. If you want an animal with a long beak—say, the head of Thoth (whose head is an ibis) or any design that extends far outward to the sides—it is probably going to be easier to do that carving as a separate piece and then affix it to the handle of the wand. Finding a branch that is large enough in diameter for that sort of animal carving is tricky and might involve removing a great deal of wood from the other parts of the wand.

If you want the wand to be one solid piece of wood, one way to approach it is to take a thick branch and turn the point-end down on a lathe to the desired diameter, leaving the pommel-end as a larger block for carving your figure. Bringing down the diameter of the stock with a drawknife can also be done, though more slowly and with the application of more elbow grease.

One other staple of my own carving is Celtic and Norse interlace. These intricate knotwork designs are an art in themselves, and masters of the techniques learn how to create the complex symmetries that were produced on medieval Irish manuscripts and other great works of the illuminator, jeweler, and carver. There are many good books on this sort of design, and I have listed some of my favorites in the bibliography. Some of the designs are purely geometrical. Others are zoomorphic—which is to say, they include stylized animals such as dragons, gryphons, dogs, lions, horses, and birds. After preparing the surface of the wand through the first sanding stage, lay out your interlace design along the shaft or handle (wherever you want it to go). It might be in a panel on the handle of the wand or it might straggle off down the length.

Another tricky sort of animal carving is on the wand's tip when it has a crystal point. It is not easy, but it is possible to carve an animal in the round at the tip of the wand and insert the crystal into the animal's mouth. The hole for the crystal point is very carefully drilled into the end grain, leaving enough wood around it to carve the animal's head. The open mouth must be carved in such a way that there is an opening on each side and the teeth wrap around the crystal. This is easier with a mammal—a lion or even a dragon—than with a bird. I've done ravens this way, but getting the beak the right shape is hard to do without making it look unnaturally wide. For a stone of substantial size, you need an animal with a fairly large mouth.

One of the difficulties of this sort of design is in working with the end grain, which is where you cut the branch when you first cut it to length. End-on, the grain goes in circles, and the spaces between the grain are often difficult to smooth. Ideally, one should leave as little of the end grain exposed as possible. This means curving the surfaces—such as nose, lips, and teeth—so that the front of the animal's face does not present any flat surfaces.

Human or animal images can be as realistic or as stylized as you wish. If you are trying for a very realistic, in-the-round bird, for example, you can make the feathers as detailed as you wish. Study photographs and drawings of the bird you wish to use as a model. Notice the different sizes and textures to the feathers of the wing, back, breast, and tail. The wing and tail feathers are the ones that will most need to be carved in detail because the back and breast feathers of birds are so fine and smooth that they don't really show as individual feathers. Study the structure of feathers. Each feather is made of a central stem, called a rachis, and tiny parallel barbs that go out at an angle from the rachis. Often it is enough to indicate some of the individual feathers and the rachis down the middle, but if you want a very detailed and realistic carving, you can take a very fine 1 mm V-tool and lightly carve in the barbs.

These are a few tips and suggestions for the carving of figures, leaves, and relief designs in your wand. In the final analysis, you will need further instruction one way or another, either by taking a class in carving or by studying books that teach step-by-step with lots of photographs. DVDs are even more valuable. I have made a few recommendations in the section of the bibliography on woodworking; see especially Congdon-Martin, Ellenwood, Jones and George, and Robertson.

Letter Carving

ᴀFTER EVERYTHING ELSE has been carved, if you have left a smooth ribbon, ring, or other surface on which to make an inscription, give it a final sanding and buffing and then do the lettering. You will want to draw the letters on the wood again, because all the sanding probably will have obliterated your original sketch of them. Pay attention to spacing again. If you get the letters too close, they will not only look cramped but you will have trouble keeping your tiny V-tool or pyrography point from slipping and joining letters together.

You will find that some alphabets are easier to carve than others. Our Roman letters are made for carving in stone, but bear in mind that when lettering, you have to pay attention to the grain of the wood here too. Carving very small letters is more difficult than carving larger ones, but the curved letters such as C and S require a steady hand. It is possible to turn the V-tool in a curve as you carve, but here again, the smaller the curve, the more tricky it is. Sometimes it is better to make the curve in a series of very short cuts rather than a single curving cut; it depends on the wood you are using. Apple, rowan, and hazel all take inscriptions beautifully because their grain is so fine. Oak, on the other hand, has such a dark and complex grain that you may find even if you succeed in carving your inscription, the whole thing vanishes when you oil the oak and the grain comes out.

Other lettering systems, such as the Norse runes, Dwarf runes, Elf runes, and the Bardic ogham signary, are better adapted to carving than are Roman or Hebrew letters, because they use straight lines. With Futhark runes, for example, the whole lettering system is built on six lines radiating from a center. This makes carving easier. The ogham fews are easiest of all to carve and make an elegant pattern that will not be immediately recognizable as lettering to most people.

Theban letters are popular among witches. Theban is called the witch's alphabet. There is no question that it is very beautiful and mysterious. However, it is also very curvy and so is tricky to carve. As with calligraphy on a piece of vellum or paper, it is best to make fine guidelines for both the baseline and the top of your letters in order to keep them all proportioned correctly. Whichever letters you use, I recommend making a test wand on which you can practice. Try out a few alphabets and get the feel of them. For further guidance, you may wish to procure a book on lettercarving in wood (see Pye). See appendix I for three examples of lettering systems.

Staining and Coloring the Wood

*A*FTER YOU HAVE done your carving and inscriptions, it is time to make another go with the finer grades of sandpaper. Pay special attention to removing any tiny flakes of wood or splinters that result from the tearing of the grain. Lightly sand the surfaces with 400-grit paper. The goal at this stage is not to get a finely burnished surface; that would actually work against you when applying oils and stains. You want them to penetrate into the pores of the wood, and sanding creates its smooth feeling by filling in those microscopic pores with dust. Get a reasonably smooth surface, and then apply your stain or oil.

Skip staining if you prefer to have a wand that is the natural shade of the wood, especially if you are working with wood such as ebony, purpleheart, yellowheart, cedar, or black walnut, all of which have a beautiful, rich color of their own. For these woods, you can simply apply an oil finish to bring out the inner glow of the color and seal the pores of the wood.

When it comes to wood stain, there are many brands made in different ways, and many colors, both natural shades of brown and also red, green, blue, yellow—you name it. The basic idea of wood stain is to penetrate the surface of the wood, to seal its pores, and also to color the wood. Paint will sit on the surface of the wood and can be scraped off. Stain penetrates into the wood and is more permanent.

As you can discover from walking through any forest, wood won't last if it isn't sealed. Moisture will penetrate the wood's pores. Worms and bugs move in and assist in the process of decay. Over time, a branch or even a whole tree trunk is reduced to a crumbly, damp pulp and finally to humus. That decaying wood is very lively in the biological sense and is undergoing a miraculous magical transformation—but you don't want your magic wand to be alive in the wormy, bacterial sense. You are creating it for a kind of immortality, a new existence that is spiritually alive in quite a different way than its biological state. So, seal those pores.

You can stain the whole wand one color or carefully work with small brushes to apply different colors to different parts of your design. In the case of inscriptions, I take an open steel calligraphy nib and use that to apply red ink. Red is traditional—what you will find in old runestones, for example—but you can obviously use any color you like. On inscriptions I use ink rather than stain because it flows well into small grooves. However, you could also use colored stains, which will penetrate the surface more than ink does. Have a look at the photos of the elm wand in the color section. It is stained in two colors and has gold paint applied to the leaves.

The major choice in stain is between water-based and oil-based formulae. There are also products that are based on polyurethane, which is an organic polymer produced in chemistry labs. It is widely used as a kind of plastic or a substitute for rubber, and it is quite popular in the wood-finishing business because it gives a hard, waterproof top coat. I do not think it is the best choice for wands, however. Using polyurethane is really just coating your wood in plastic. So, I recommend you stick to the old-fashioned ways of finishing wood. Water-based stains are perfectly suitable and more environmentally friendly than oil-based stains, mainly because the waste can be disposed of more easily. Some oil finishes are actually rather dangerous and can spontaneously combust if you throw a used rag into a wastebasket with paper or wood shavings. Dispose of your rags carefully.

Oil-based formulae usually employ tung oil, which is a natural product expressed from the seed kernels of the Chinese tung tree. One product that is based on tung oil is called Danish oil finish. It is one of my favorite oils and comes either without color or in various tints such as oak or cherry. An oil finish such as Danish oil will give a smooth and rich finish, bringing out the grain and color of the wood. It will yield a satiny patina, not a glossy finish. With an oil- or a water-based stain, you may still feel the grain of the wood, even after careful burnishing. Apply three coats of stain and be sure to follow the instructions on the particular product you use. A day of drying time between coats is normal. That is usually sufficient and will give a rich, deep patina to the wood.

It may be worth mentioning that turpentine, used as a solvent and often for cleaning brushes, is another tree product, made by the distillation of pine resins. So, you might think of turpentine as the whiskey of the arboreal world. Don't drink it, though, and don't give it to your trees as an offering. There is no avoiding the fact that many of the finishing products used in woodcrafting are toxic to humans. There are oil finishes that are designed for finishing bowls, wooden spoons, and other wooden implements intended to hold food and drink. These oil finishes are called "food grade" oils. Walnut oil or almond oil are suitable for this kind of finish if it suits you. Do not, however, use olive oil or other vegetable oils, as these will turn rancid over time.

Once you have achieved the color you desire, burnish the surface with steel wool or the nylon 3M sanding pads that come in various degrees from coarse to fine. I prefer the nylon pads because they will not accidentally leave tiny bits of steel in the wood, which may eventually discolor. Work the surface until it is quite smooth.

Varnish, Shellac, and French Polishing

$\mathcal{T}$WO OTHER OLD-WORLD products for finishing and getting a high gloss are varnish and shellac. What is varnish? One doesn't find varnish finishes on furniture much anymore because synthetic products are easier to apply and give a harder, more durable surface. It is still used in making the rich, glossy finish on classical string instruments such as violins. Varnishes are made from resins such as amber, copal, or rosin dissolved in a solvent (usually turpentine or alcohol) and combined with a drying oil such as linseed or walnut oil. Spar varnish is perhaps the most durable of all. It is the kind used on boats and the masts, or spars, of wooden ships. Spar varnish is both waterproof and sunlight resistant. The latter characteristic is an apt feature when working with woods such as purpleheart that lose their lovely color when exposed to ultraviolet light.

These finishes are applied with a brush in several coats just like paint, but because varnish has resins in it and not pigments, the light will pass through it, reflect off the wood surface, and shine back through the varnish, giving a particularly rich glow. It creates a hard protective coating. (See example of a varnish-finished wand in the color section.)

Shellac is similar to varnish but is made from a resinous substance called lac that is secreted by the lac beetle (*Coccus lacca*) as it feeds on trees in Thailand and Assam. The resinous flakes of lac are dissolved in denatured alcohol, so if you use shellac you will need to procure some of that to clean your brushes and thin the shellac. Varnish and shellac are both more finicky and more delicate finishes than a penetrating oil finish. They will give a much more glossy surface and rich amber colors, but they can be scratched or chipped more easily and can be damaged by heat or alcohol. However, because they are applied in layers on top of the wood surface, the varnishes and shellacs do protect the wood. You scratch the varnish, not the wood.

French polishing is a term that refers to a particular method of applying a shellac finish. It is an art in itself and mostly is used in the finishing of wooden musical instruments such as guitars and lutes. For more thorough information on this method, see Bob and Orville Milburn's tutorial on the Internet, cited in the bibliography. French polishing involves laying on many thin layers of shellac and using pumice to fill the pores and give a perfectly smooth surface to the wood. This type of finishing is typical of that on classical guitars, providing an almost glassy-smooth surface.

French polishing is a very involved process, and detailed instructions for it are beyond the scope of this book. However, it is useful to make a few remarks about using shellac as a finish in wandmaking. While the wandmaker is seldom after a perfectly glassy finish, shellac will give the most shiny and rich appearance. You can mix your own shellac from flakes and alcohol or purchase shellac already in liquid form. The main trick in applying it is to keep moving. Whether using a brush or a layered pad (for the traditional French polishing method), you do not want to pause while in contact with the wood or the finish will be marred.

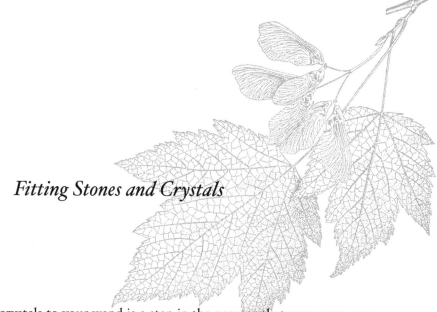

Fitting Stones and Crystals

*A*DDING STONES AND crystals to your wand is a step in the process that may come somewhere in the middle of applying the finish. Usually I create the holes or receptacles for the stones before applying stain, then set the stones after the wood has been stained. You can also add them after all the finish has been applied, but then you will need to take special care not to spoil the finish with adhesive.

Let us first consider the matter of carving the receptacle for the stones. Working with wood's end grain is always a challenge. The end grain is what you get when you cut off a branch to make a straight edge. You will see the growth rings head-on. It is very hard to carve end grain because the direction of the grain is changing at every point as you move a tool. Going at the end grain of some hardwoods with a small V-tool or gouge is a good way to ruin its edge. Instead, try using a small, rather deep gouge (preferably less than half the diameter of the wood). The gouge should be applied in a circular motion, which is the only way to carve with the grain in a situation like this. There are limits to how deep you can get the hole with this method. For setting rounded reservoir stones, it is adequate. In the case of rounded stones on the pommel end, your goal is to get the hole as nearly matched to the shape and contour of the stone as possible so that when the epoxy is applied, they will bond tightly.

In the case of crystal points, the hole must be much deeper. Typically, you will want from one-eighth to one-quarter inch of the crystal to be imbedded in the wood, and for this it is best to drill. This is one of the few instances when I make a concession to power tools and use an electric drill. However, it is possible to use a hand drill if you can crank it and keep your bit steady at the same time, while poised on the end grain of a branch.

In either case, you must get your piece firmly clamped in an adjustable vise so that the end grain is up and the piece is gripped well enough in the vise jaws so that it will not slip when you apply pressure to the drill. Use a bit that is just about exactly the diameter of the crystal. Through the careful use of a V-tool, it is possible to carve out a hole that will exactly accommodate the shape of an irregular stone or crystal. However, unless the crystal is cut (rather than natural), and so of an even and symmetrical shape, this is fairly tricky work that requires a good eye. An easier way to achieve the goal of a firm bond is to drill the hole or shape it to the approximate size, and then fill it with epoxy putty.

Epoxy is a heavy-duty adhesive that comes in two parts: the resin and the hardener. When separate, each of these will stay liquid or like putty, but when combined the two parts solidify and will bond stone to wood. One product that I can recommend is QuikWood, an epoxy with the consistency of putty. It is packaged in such a way that you need only slice a bit off the roll like dough, knead it between your fingers until the resin and hardener mix, then apply it to your work. It will fill the hole you have made for your stone or crystal and when you press the stone into the putty, it will shape itself perfectly to the irregular surfaces of the stone.

While the epoxy is curing, you may work it smooth around the edges of the hole with a small pallet knife. When it has completely hardened, which for QuikWood takes only forty-five minutes, you can use a small straight blade to shape or shave it further. QuikWood has the advantage over regular clear epoxy in that it is tinted and will take paint or stain. Note, however, that it won't take the stain quite as well as the wood itself and so may require some careful blending if you want the joinery to all look like the wood. Applying brown or black ink to the exposed epoxy is one way to disguise the joining of the two materials.

Another aspect of applying stones to wood is the shape of the actual joint. Do you want it to be a flat cut, with the stone simply set into it? Or do you want carving around the stone's setting, to make it look more organic?

One can also carve wooden "fingers" to hold the reservoir stone. (Look at the setting of the linden wand's white stone in the color section.) This method gives a more organic look and exposes more of the surface of the stone than a flat end does. It also draws the edges of the wood all the way up to the edge of the stone so that little of the end grain and only a thin line of the epoxy remains exposed.

Polishing

𝒲HEN YOU HAVE passed through all these stages and achieved the final burnished finish you desire, the final step is to polish the wand and buff it up nicely. A product containing beeswax is the most suitable. The wax made from bees is magical stuff in itself, possessing powers to purify and bless. The sacred bee is a subject unto itself (see Ransome).

Another lovely final polish can be carnauba wax, which is found in hard blocks and must be applied to a buffing wheel and then to the wand itself. Renaissance brand micro-crystalline wax polish is a product that I particularly like, even though it is a synthetic compound. It was formulated by the British Museum in the 1950s to protect and restore fine works of art, from stone and bronze statues to armor. It is synthesized from petroleum, so it is distanced from trees and vegetation by several millions of years. Its advantage is that it provides a very impermeable coating that is especially resistant to acids in the air and in human skin. This is most important when dealing with works of art that are hundreds of years old. It is very easy to use, requiring no drying time. Just wipe it on and buff it immediately.

In the end, the craft of wandmaking is inseparable from the magic of woodworking and vice versa. The many potions and secret formulae developed over centuries using the gums and resins of trees and the secretions of insects are all a part of the world of magic. In the world of wandmaking, one comes to see the spirit and the wonder even in turpentine and pumice. You are working together with water, that most marvelous of substances, the fluid of life. You work with pigments taken from nature, oils from seeds and nuts, resins from pine or the secretions of an exotic Asian beetle, or amber that is the sap of trees preserved and hardened for perhaps millions of years.

In your woodshop, you mix and stir together the vast expanses of time, the grandeur of living processes in the wild forests, as well as the work of many other human beings who painstakingly harvested the raw materials and used their alchemy to produce that marvel in a can. Finally, when all is done, you take beeswax from that most sacred of animals, the bee, giver of honey and wax for candles, pollinator of our farms and orchards. You rub the fluid wax until it shines, capturing the light of the sun, moon, and stars.

Approach the craft of carving with elemental water in mind, and work with a feeling of relationship to the wood. Then you will sense how this craft has its magical dimension and is as involved in the employment of thoughtforms and the moving of prana as much as other ritual work. Craft is ritual if you make it so. The flow of liquid oils and varnishes embodies the flow of one's intention and emotion. The sensual rubbing of the wood with successive grades of abrasives and liquids forms a dance in which the crafter's love is conveyed through the mysteries of friction and lubrication. The ultimate goal is to create a beloved object. If you are making your own wand, you enter into the wood through sight and touch. Your touch draws beauty and light from the wood in a way that mirrors how the tree, in life, drew light and life from the sun. Like the layers of fine wood finishing, there are higher planes of technique in the art of wandmaking. Understand the fluid flow on all planes and you will have gone far toward mastering the wandmaker's craft.

PART SIX

Quintessence

Man is a microcosm, or a little world, because
he is an extract from all the stars and planets
of the whole firmament, from the earth and
the elements; and so he is their quintessence.

~ Paracelsus

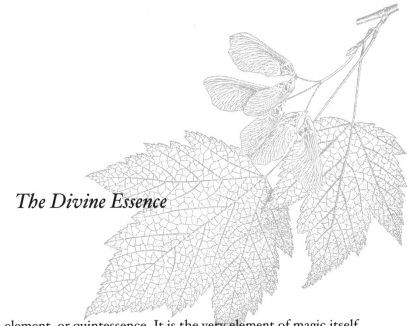

The Divine Essence

*A*ETHER IS CALLED the fifth element, or quintessence. It is the very element of magic itself because it is that substance beyond energy or matter, invisible pure potentiality. In this final part of *Wandlore*, I will give a very brief introduction to the quintessence itself, then touch on the most obvious magic of wandmaking: the enchantment of the wand, including its magical core and its consecration, dedication, and use. The scope of this book does not permit a complete exposition on the magical arts, but I offer some pointers necessary to understand the workings given here. A wizard must understand the four elements of manifestation to work magic, but that is not enough. It is necessary to understand the quintessence that underlies the four.

Although quintessence is called the fifth essence, it is, in fact, the *first* essence, the very essence of being. The alchemists named the quintessence aether (or ether) and hypothesized that it was an invisible substance (hence the term *ethereal*). Even into the nineteenth century, scientists posited that aether was the invisible medium through which light waves were propagated in outer space, and so were called luminiferous ether. It was considered to be a substance that was everywhere yet was too subtle to detect with ordinary senses and instruments.

Unable to prove aether existed, scientists abandoned the idea in favor of an empty vacuum and the idea that light was a particle (photons) that could fly through a vacuum. It just happened that light also behaved like a wave. The idea of an atom giving off photons in the transmission of energy to another atom has served us well in understanding the relationship between matter and electromagnetic energy. By means of this model, we explain the four states of matter. It has led us to discover a seemingly endless stream of new subatomic particles and forces. Scientists postulate and long to find a Unified Theory of Everything that underlies all of the various theories of nature.

Yet, aether remains that mysterious substance sought by alchemists and revered by wizards throughout the ages, which transcends the material world and unites the four elements. Four is the number of wholeness in the material plane. There are four cardinal directions, four seasons, four winds. The fifth essence is like the vertical dimension that intersects that four-fold plane of ordinary existence. When our consciousness is shifted into that spiritual dimension of the cosmos, we can see into and reach into every aspect of the mundane world. A hawk soaring above the ground may see a rabbit that is far away and out of sight to an observer on the ground. The hawk may plunge downward and seize its prey. From the point of view of the rabbit, the appearance of the hawk is inexplicable. The hawk has come out of another dimension.

Some among the wise have considered quintessence to be the life force itself—prana, as the yogis say; chi, as the Taoists call it; the élan vital, as we have it in French; mana in Melanesia; and awen in the Welsh bardic tradition. Some scientists outside the mainstream relate aether to Reich's orgone energy and describe it as mass-free and non-electromagnetic. The term has also been used by quantum physicists for "dark matter" or "dark energy," the undetectable *something* that is necessary to explain the universe's rate of expansion.[29]

In the classical era, the Greeks considered aether to be the highest heaven above the realm of the elements. Literally, it meant "clear air" and was considered to be the medium of the gods—the air they breathed, so to speak—all of which can be understood as true, if one keeps a poetical and metaphorical mind.

I started this book with the statement that the magic wand is an instrument of the will, and that the will proceeds from elemental fire. Aether lies behind and above all the four elements, and so it is the manipulation of that quintessence that is the heart of all enchantment. When you enchant a wand after all the work of physically constructing it, you apply your ethereal body to the etheric body of the wand. The etheric body is where the power of imagination lies, the ability to affect changes in the astral dimension of existence through one's mind. There are many ways to be trained to work magic, and within each path are differences in method.

29 See aetherometry.com for an interesting source of discussions about aether.

The process I employ is not the only way to enchant a wand; quite the contrary. Each wand-maker should devise his or her own method. I offer mine merely as an example to illustrate the principles involved. There are seven parts to my method of enchanting wands, as indicated below:

- Consecrating the wand with fire, air, and earth

- Anointing it with the oil of the sun and the water of the moon

- Awakening the dryad spirit with the breath of life

- Adding the imaginal inclusion of a hair, feather, or sliver of shed skin from a mythical creature

- Charging the wand with prana and intention

- Sealing the enchantment with primal sound and declaration

- Receiving the secret name of the wand

These steps are followed by a farewell blessing in cases where I have made the wand for a client. Before going through these steps in order, I first must take up the matter of wand cores and mythical beasts. If you plan to include a magical beast's essence in your wand, you will probably want to plan it in the design stage, though sometimes the wand itself will tell you what kind of core is most appropriate. It is at the time of enchantment that this last component of the wand is included in the wand's makeup.

Beastly Wand Cores

BECAUSE WAND CORES are ethereal, I include the subject of magical wand cores here, in the quintessence section of the book. A core is placed inside a wand in the astral plane, not physically. The mage employs the mind not in an intellectual sense, as we discovered in the Wind section; instead, he or she employs the mind as an organ of imagination. Imagination is the ability to visualize things that are not immediately present to the material senses; for example, a phoenix feather or a hair from the tail of a hippogriff. The ability to visualize and manifest an image in the astral dimension of reality is the very essence of enchantment. Enchantment is used to insert a phoenix feather or unicorn hair imaginally into a wand.

The astral plane is all about images and feelings, and this is what makes any magic effective. It is possible to perform a ritual on the material plane of being without consciously engaging on the higher levels by merely going through the motions. It is also possible to perform a carefully orchestrated piece of magic with only the material and mental parts of one's being—that is, without consciously engaging the astral part of one's being. In such a case, the magic would be ineffective for lack of feeling and visualization, and it would not be under conscious control either, even if you think it is.

To engage with phoenixes and unicorns requires that one be conscious on the astral plane of reality, because it is in that dream world that such beings exist. Without that shift of consciousness, if you are performing the magic only intellectually and physically, as a combination of abstract symbols, then you will leave yourself open to astral attack by the very creatures you seek. All of them are beasts and defend themselves. Some (dragons and gryphons especially) are predators, and the last thing you want while collecting a core material is to have your astral body eaten. So, make sure you are comfortable with visualization and using emotion astrally before you try this at home. Most magical traditions begin by teaching these astral skills (see Bardon, *Initiation*).

The invocation of a mythical and imaginal creature into a wand completes its many layers of being. The wood of the wand is of the vegetable kingdom, the crystal or stone is of the mineral kingdom, and the dryad spirit of the tree exists in the ethereal plane that animates the physical body of the wood. The phoenix, unicorn, or gryphon have their center of being in the astral dimension. It is by shifting consciousness into the ethereal reality underlying the material world that the wizard passes upward into the astral world of imagination and finds it to be as real as the familiar material world. Children understand better than adults how real the imaginal world is. Adults have imagination too, of course, but have been trained to apply it to precognition—imagining the outcomes of material plans and actions in the mundane plane. So, how do you find a dragon? Visualize it and it will come.

In the fictional world of the Harry Potter stories, author J. K. Rowling describes wand cores in plainly material terms. For example, a unicorn hair is a material hair taken from a material unicorn and (somehow) materially placed into the wand. This is characteristic of many literary fantasies: no distinction is made between the material and astral worlds. Instead, magic appears to be a violation of physical laws and only "muggles"—people with no imagination—fail to see it as a part of material reality. Close, but no cigar.

That there are different levels or dimensions of existence is fundamental to magic. The only reason nonmagicals can't see unicorns is because they have not developed their higher senses to see into the dimension where unicorns live.

How Do You Get There from Here?

In our nonmagical culture, if a thing does not exist in the material dimension, it is said to not exist at all. It is "only" a dream, a fantasy, a vision, etc. This ordinary way of classifying things as either existent or nonexistent has a great deal of survival value for animals, including human beings... until you run into an ethereal being.

In magical philosophy, by contrast, an entity lacking corporeal manifestation exists and is every bit as "real" as something that is manifest corporeally. In the magical cosmology, there are also entities that manifest in only partial or temporary corporeal form at will—gods, angels, daemons, giants, the Hidden Folk, Faeries, and the so-called magical beasts. A moment's reflection will reveal that all material forms are temporary. Temporality is an intrinsic quality of material forms. However, we must also admit that some things are more ephemeral than others. Some take physical form for a short period, others for longer. Some beings, such as unicorns, may take a physical form in one world and pass into another world at will (or by instinct). Such beings seem able to dissolve their material bodies at will to disappear into the astral plane.

Or it might be clearer to say not that the body "dissolves" or even that it "disappears," but that it *relocates* in time and space. We do this all the time. A body in motion is constantly relocating itself (or being relocated by some other action upon it). The relocation of a material body by moving its ethereal body can be compared to what we see as the ordinary feat of locomotion. The only reason ethereal locomotion seems magical and inexplicable to us is that we have not been trained to perceive it and cannot do so with our material five senses. Even in material space-time an object moving fast enough will elude the eye, and we often say that something or other happened "in the blink of an eye." Ethereal locomotion is not instantaneous either, but it can be very fast, and only adepts are trained to expect it.

Astral locomotion is also possible—as distinct from ethereal locomotion—and this is the sort of traveling wizards do to find phoenix feathers and such. If you relocate your astral body while leaving the material and etheric bodies in place, your material body does not disappear, but the astral part of you leaves its lower dimensions of self to move within the astral world. Consciousness is shifted away from the material body and into the astral body. When wizards do this, it is called astral travel or astral projection.[30]

Whole books have been written on this subject, so I will not attempt to offer detailed instruction here. Suffice it to say that entering magical states of consciousness is the way to find dragons and phoenixes. Don't imagine it to be all fairyland sweetness and wonder; in fact, the astral world is not for the faint of heart. When you move your consciousness into the astral world, remember that it is distinct from the mental plane, and so the astral world and its denizens are not always subject to reason. That is why in the astral plane almost anything can happen. That is also why you can get distracted very easily, as you do in a dream.

So, the magical creatures that we like to use in wand cores exist primarily on the astral plane. I emphasize again that this fact does not make them less "real" than a rhinoceros or a baboon. They are just as real as, for example, angels. Mythical beasts can appear and disappear

---

30 See Leadbeater or Denning and Phillips.

materially but very seldom actually do this because they are fundamentally not creatures of the material plane. This is why they are so often encountered in fantasies, dreams, and artistic visions, which all emanate from the astral dimensions of the seer's own being. Unicorns, phoenixes, dragons, and gryphons all are born with the center of their consciousness in the astral dimension, and that is where their lives intersect with ours.

Are Magical Cores Necessary for Magic?

In short, no. J. K. Rowling's books suggest that a unicorn hair or phoenix feather is the critical thing that makes a magic wand magical. The phenomenon of etheric sensations of emotion generated by astral entities can certainly make the presence of an astral creature *feel* more magical, but to suppose it is actually the *source* of the magic would be less than correct.

This said, I do feel that the inclusion of the hair, feather, or skin[31] of an astral being in a wand certainly imparts to it an especially powerful quality. It is neither more nor less important than the inclusion of a stone or crystal or the evocation of the dryad spirit of the tree into the wood. Still, while I do make wands without stones, I have never felt comfortable enchanting a wand and leaving out the core.

If a core of the magical hair or feather is not absolutely required, then why do I include them? By including a core, one draws together the vegetable and the animal kingdoms. Adding stones and crystals, one also includes the mineral kingdom. A further consideration is that the inclusion of a purely astral hair, feather, scale, etc., helps the dryad spirit of the wand to keep its own consciousness (such as it is) always shifting toward the astral plane. That is where magic is done, and so a wand that has a pull to the astral built in (so to speak) will pull along its user more easily into his or her own higher dimensions of being.

Think of the totem animals of the Native American medicine man or woman. Think of the animal spirits that guide the shamans of the Tungus or the seers of African tribes. The animals represent the nonhuman world, a world of qualities that are different from our own. Animals also have their godforms. The ancient Egyptian religion is particularly notable in emphasizing

---

31   Any ethical wizard will only use the cast-off skin of animals such as snakes and dragons who naturally shed. Indeed, hair and feathers are almost always gathered after having been shed. Pulling the hair off a unicorn is likely to result in one's premature removal to the higher planes.

the importance of creating the link between the animal and the human, as nearly all their gods and goddesses have animal qualities and often animal heads on human bodies.

Helpful animal spirits and guides are an important aspect of the universe. Many animals who regularly take material form are also magical creatures—owls, wolves, cats, dogs, eagles, ravens, hawks, snakes, seals. These are magical animals because they have been endowed with spiritual meanings by us.

The Astral Power of Mythical Beasts

*W*HAT IS THE meaning of a unicorn? As with all things and beings that contain the symbolic meanings of the etheric and astral worlds, each one of us must articulate those meanings for ourselves. Some meanings are quite individual. At the same time, there are some traditions to draw upon that give us a glimpse of what these beings symbolize for the collective unconscious. Reading stories about such animals is the best way to gain an intuitive grasp of their symbolic power. Meditating and astrally journeying to encounter them will add personal knowledge that will help you establish relationships to each species of creature. You must grasp that these astral beings were brought into existence when someone thought of them—*imagined* them. They are the products of artistic inspiration; however, that does not mean they aren't real. In the astral plane, all of our imaginings take a form that is just as substantial and independent of the human ego as wild animals are in the material world. It is just that in the astral world, if you think of an animal that is half eagle and half lion, it will actually appear. This is why your mother always told you to be careful what you wished for. Even species that are real on the mundane plane can have magical characteristics and quite different characters in the astral plane.

Take owls. In myth, owls are endowed with wisdom, knowledge, and a penetrating, knowing eye. Ornithologists may tell you that owls are not particularly bright birds, compared to, say, ravens. That may be true on the material plane, but on the higher planes, owls are wise, and ravens are even smarter there than on the mundane plane. Owls are linked to the archetypal goddess of wisdom, Roman Minerva and Hellenic Athena.

Similarly, we find ravens linked to the Morrigan, an Irish goddess who expresses the Great Queen archetype, the sovereign power of the Great Mother and Mother Earth herself, a power to devour her children, returning them to her body for rebirth and renewal. The Morrigan is sometimes called a war goddess, but I do not think this does her justice. In myths, war symbolizes death and sacrifice. The involvement of the Great Queen in the warrior's death on a battlefield is symbolic of the Great Mother's involvement in all deaths. She who gives birth to us also takes us back; all that is born of her returns to her as carrion, blood, and dust.

We might also say that the higher dimensions that gave birth to our material form will take back and hold together our being, fashioning a new material form that has always already been a part of our greater being. Raven brings down this archetypal current into the astral, ethereal, and material planes as a harbinger of war, death, and inhumation. Raven, however, is also depicted in other myths as a Trickster, a wise guy who steals the sun or the moon or outwits the less witty. Thus, mastery over death is a quality that points toward wisdom. If we look closely at owls, we see that they are often associated with death too.

Similarly, the serpent, snake, and dragon are all linked to death and to wisdom. They embody the mysteries of eternal life, which is the prerequisite to accumulating experience that leads to wisdom. The serpent in the Garden of Eden is the bringer of awakening, of knowledge of our inner divine nature. But the serpent is also the bringer of mortality to Adam and Eve, the archetypal human parents. This myth holds a great lesson about the intertwined reality of matter and the higher dimensions, and the road that beings with their consciousness centered upon the material plane must walk to find wisdom. Every religion and magical tradition in the world has pointed to death and rebirth as the center of the mystery of achieving enlightenment. Animals are our assistants in this human struggle for enlightenment.

What about the other mythical beasts such as unicorns and gryphons, animals that seem to be combinations of ordinary material animals? Here are some ideas, based partly on research into traditional stories and partly on my own experience. When choosing an animal to provide the spiritual core of a wand, consider all of its qualities.

The alchemical union of opposites is key to understanding all of the composite animals.

Gryphon

The gryphon has the forequarters of an eagle and the hindquarters and tail of a lion. It combines the predatory ferocity of both of these animals—the king of the jungle, on the one hand, and the king of the skies on the other. Gryphons have been depicted as gigantic creatures in myth and legend, which I suspect is partly just the storyteller's tendency to exaggeration and partly due to regional differences. In his *Book of Gryphons*, Joe Nigg notes the many differences in the way these beasts have been described across time and cultures—sometimes as a lion-headed bird, or with a snake's tail, and so on. Indeed, there are about as many different historical versions of the gryphon as there are ways to spell its name. Moreover, it has cousins. The Renaissance Italian Ariosto, author of *Orlando Furioso*, invented the hippogriff, mating gryphon and horse for a tamable mount like a knight's charger, only airborne (see page 195). There is also the opinicus, preserved in heraldry, which differs from the gryphon in having a lion's forelegs instead of an eagle's. The falcon-headed sphinx of Egypt differs only essentially from the opinicus in lacking wings.

One tends nowadays to think of the great lions of Africa when one hears *lion*, and the tail of the heraldic gryphon usually has that bushy end like the African male lion. Indeed, the luxuriance of the gryphon tale goes far beyond the lion. However, one should take as a clue the forequarters of the animal and realize that the size of even the largest eagle is not compatible with a lion of that magnitude. Of course, when it comes to fabulous beasts, there are no rules about plausibility.

My experience with gryphons is that they are about the size of golden eagles and the North American mountain lion—that is, about the size of a large dog, not a horse. Many stories tell of gryphons acting as draft animals, in particular pulling the chariot of Nemesis, Hellenic goddess of vengeance. This association alludes to the belief that these animals are particularly rapacious and big enough to easily bear off a human baby. It does not suggest that they can be put into harness by just anyone. Their presence always attests to the high nobility and power of the person the gryphon befriends.

The gryphon is a remarkable creature because besides being half eagle and half lion, it has distinctly pronounced ears that sit erect on its head. When sitting high in a tree, gryphons may be mistaken for eagles, but the ears are a definite giveaway. The significance of these ears is that gryphons have the hearing of dogs and the eyesight of eagles. Yet their temperament is that of a feline, and I can tell you that they do not make good pets. Like dragons, gryphons are carnivores and hunters, and they are not any more friendly to humans than your average eagle and mountain lion combined. They are elusive and sudden in their attacks, capable of jumping out of a tree or low brush as easily as out of the sky. Almost no creature can elude their talons or the deadly raking of their hind claws.

Yet the combination of two animals in the astral world is always metaphysical as well as physical. The eagle and the lion are the monarch of the skies and the king of the beasts, respectively, which gives them the symbolic qualities of royalty, nobility, command, initiative, and the obedience of two worlds—that of earth and that of air. Consider this in an elemental sense and you will see that the gryphon's regal mastery reaches from earth to heaven, from the depths of our unconscious instincts and urges, up to the heights of abstract reasoning and language, that crowing achievement.

So, while the predatory character of gryphons is most notable on the surface of their myths, other positive traits emerge beneath the symbolism of air, earth, and sun. They reputedly were loyal guards of treasures and indeed liked to line their nests in gold and just gaze at piles of gems, entranced. These traits allude symbolically to the sun (gold) and to the many spiritual powers of precious stones, and also to the hidden treasures to be found in the astral realms—not material gold and gems but spiritual riches. In a wand, the inclusion of a gryphon feather carries with it the power of vigilance, ferocity, perception, strength, loyalty, dependability, and, on the negative side, just a touch of avarice, which while not good for one's character is at least good for finding treasure. The powerful eyesight of the gryphon also enhances clairvoyance. The large ears are translated spiritually to the wand as the enhancement of clairaudience (far-hearing). One collects gryphon feathers after they have been molted. If you're smart, that is.

Unicorn

Unicorns are hardly less frightening in person than gryphons. Encountering one on the astral plane is more often terrifying than an occasion to ooh and ahh. Unicorns are not carnivorous, but they are extremely aggressive and will attack if threatened. Being attacked by a creature almost as large as an Arabian horse with a two-foot bone lance on its forehead is about as cute as a charging bull. The unicorn, male or female, will defend itself very adroitly, charging and wheeling with the dexterity of a fencer and the momentum of a knight tilting at a joust. Their eyes have something of the gentle quality of a deer or llama but will turn fiery if a threat is perceived. Also, male unicorns are extremely territorial and, quite frankly, like to charge at anything that appears either afraid or belligerent. Older ones are like rhinoceroses in this respect: they lose their eyesight and charge at anything that moves. Females will attack only when defending their young.

Under no circumstances should you attempt to ask a unicorn for its hair. As with gryphons, one must seek out their habitat and find hair that has been shed from the mane or tail. I prefer tail hairs as they are somewhat stiffer and thicker. The only people unicorns will trust are virgins—that is, prepubescent girls. I have no idea why. However, it is a symbolic characteristic that hints at the unicorn's purity. Purity does not mean unsexual, as some people seem to think. It means an integrity of spirit and unspoiled essence—being totally one's self.

This idea of purity was developed in the Renaissance tales and the many paintings and other works of art depicting unicorns. One of the wonders of the animal was that it would kneel down beside a brook and dip its horn in the water to cleanse it of all poisons.

Unicorns also symbolize nobility of a high spiritual order. In his book *Unicorn: Myth and Reality,* Rüdiger Robert Beer describes a series of tapestries about the hunt and capture of a unicorn. He says that the figure of the lone unicorn corralled and chained is "a symbol of wounded and shackled nobility in an unappreciative world" (160). Always the unicorn alludes to the human relationship to the horse as a mount and service animal. However, the allusion is a negative one, for unicorns symbolize the untamable spirit of the horse, not the horse that has been domesticated. Unicorns symbolize a militant spirit, but not one that serves humans. Instead, it is their spiritual power, often connected to love, the unicorn serves, and most often to woman, because it is in her that true virtue can be found, or so the theory went in the Middle Ages. If you look at the men of that time, they were pretty lacking in virtue.

This virtue of the unicorn was expressed in another way: as a medicine. Unicorn horns were said to possess antidotal powers over poisons, which included many ailments. The powdered horn was prescribed in potions for epilepsy, fevers, plague, colic, vermin, worms in children, and rabies (Beer, 116). For the rich, who had to watch out for poisons in their food and drink, cutlery with unicorn-horn handles were used as poison detectors. The handles would sweat on contact with the poisonous food, and if there was poison in drink, it would effervesce when placed in contact with unicorn horn. Drinking vessels were made of the horn when it was in plentiful supply (Beer, 117). Some claimed the same power from unicorn hooves. For St. Hildegard von Bingen (twelfth century), it was the liver and pelt. She seems tacitly skeptical about the horn in the following passage from her notebooks, quoted by Beer:

Take some unicorn liver, grind it up and mash with egg yolk to make an ointment. Every type of leprosy is healed if treated frequently with this ointment, unless the patient is destined to die or God intends not to aid him...Take some unicorn pelt, from it cut a belt and gird it round the body, thus averting attack by plague or fever. Make also some shoes from unicorn leather and wear them, thus assuring everhealthy feet, thighs and joints, nor will the plague ever attack those limbs. Apart from that, nothing else of the unicorn is to be used medically (Beer, 114).

One wonders if St. Hildegard was just copying these notes from older classical or Arab authors or whether she had occasion to try them. In any case, the unicorn's hair, if not useful medically, is very useful as a wand core. It carries extremely potent powers for protection, finding treasure, purifying, healing, and spells to detect poison or disease. The latter is so finely attuned that a wand using unicorn hair for its core may locate the place in the body from whence the disease originates and also clear the body's meridians. Unicorn-hair cores also dispose a wand to working toward instilling or reawakening virtue in persons and places, and therefore are excellent for creating sacred objects and spaces, for activating the power of the Divine Feminine, and for spells of love, faith, hope, justice, wisdom, truth, and fortitude.

Now, again, to avoid confusion, let me remind you that the hair in a wand core is not placed *physically* into the wood. It is included by astral means, by the power of mind and will in the process of enchantment. Inserting a hair physically, without enchantment, would accomplish very little, magically speaking.

One final note to address something that may be going through your mind. Yes, a wand fashioned from a unicorn horn is possible, and it has been done. I was shown a marvelous example of superb workmanship in one of the kingdoms of the alfar (elves). This instrument was fourteen inches long, with a handle of hazel wrapped in unicorn leather and fittings of gold, including a large spherical reservoir of gold. It was made from a unicorn who had died after long service as a mount for one of the elfin kings. Extraordinary![32]

---

32 My own adventures in the Faerie realms must wait for another book to be given in full.

Phoenix

The phoenix is not a composite animal; it is all bird, but its ability to renew itself through self-immolation makes it a powerful symbol of rebirth, endurance, and even healing. Phoenix feathers also symbolize hope for immortality and beauty, for the firebird has beautiful plumage and exercises powerful charm over one who sees it or hears its call. The fire of the phoenix is elemental astral fire, and so the consumption of the bird by fire symbolizes overpowering passion and self-assertion to the point of remaking oneself. Its blood is ichor, a divine substance that can burn without being consumed and that possesses the power of immortality. Phoenix feathers enchanted into a wand convey this astral fire of transformation as a purplish-scarlet light that coils tightly in a helix through the center of the wood.

Phoenixes (phoenices, properly) are gentle herbivores but, like most birds, may be afraid of human contact. As with all of these creatures, if you have a wand with you on the astral plane, you can keep them from flight or attack. They instinctively understand what magic wands are. Approaching and even conversing with a phoenix to ask permission to use its feathers is a deep and sublime experience. Phoenices and dragons especially are very intelligent, and, as every child knows, in the astral world one can talk to the animals.

Because of their unique auto-regenerative ability, phoenices are bisexual. They lay eggs very rarely, which is why the population of phoenices increases only very slowly. In the astral realms, they are kept as pets, hunted for their plumage and their ichor, and are even eaten as a delicacy. (I know what you are thinking. No, they are not self-cooking.) Feathers taken from a dead phoenix are not suitable for use as a wand core. It is best to catch one when it is molting but not too close to its combustion. This requires the collector to observe a particular phoenix carefully for a long time to get a sense of its condition.

The virtue of a phoenix-feather wand core is that it greatly enhances the element of fire, which is the source of willpower, desire, passion, and intensity. Its healing powers are very strong, making it most useful for healing magic that employs elemental fire to destroy disease agents. Its fiery nature makes it also well-suited for treating fevers, including emotional fevers resulting from passionate attraction, jealousy, rejection, etc.

On Dragon's Scale

Green, red, gold, and black dragons are the most common types, and it is possible to harvest their shed scales without ever getting close to the creature itself, astrally speaking.[33] Dragon scales are large as compared to snakeskin, for example. One scale is sufficient for the creation of a core. This is not, however, as easy as making a core from hair or feather. The way I prepare a sliver to use as a core is to first procure a scale measuring from ten to fifteen centimeters in its longest dimension, then to secure it in a steel vise without the nylon jaws you want when working on wood. With a special ethereal spokeshave, I shave the scale into thin slivers or shards, barely 1 mm in width. After being shaved, the shard curls into a beautiful helix, which is quite pliable. The astral light of dragon scale is characterized by a very strong ultraviolet component so that the best way to describe its appearance is as being similar to black light. However, in red, green, or gold dragons there is an overtone of the dominant pigment of the scale itself.

I must digress a moment to say a word about the fictional wandmakers of the Harry Potter novels, who are said to use "dragon heartstrings" in their wands. Such a thing is a very bad idea. First of all, the only way to acquire "heartstrings" (by which presumably is meant sinew from that organ) is to kill a dragon. Killing animals and using their internal organs as ingredients in magic formulae is not something I recommend. The virtue of a dragon's power does not reside in its interior viscera; it lies in its skin. The magical properties of the soft-tissue parts of a dead dragon are quite unpleasant.

The special virtues of dragon-scale cores is that they lend intelligence and strong protective vibrations to a wand. This makes the wand very well-suited to spells of discovery and protection. Remember all those stories about dragons guarding treasure? Well, it's the same as the gryphon: dragons will loyally guard a treasure with great ferocity. Contrary to popular belief, dragons do not like to eat humans. Their prey are herbivores such as deer, cattle, sheep, and goats. A dragon will only take on a human if attacked near its lair. The gold dragon, well known in the Far East as a benevolent bringer of rain, is actually curious about other sentient creatures and will permit humans in need to ride on its back. They have strong telepathic abilities and can converse on some subjects with great wisdom.

---

33 Some wizards believe the use of an animal's bodily ephemera is as unethical as taking a hair from a human to include in spellworking. I leave that to your own sense of ethics. Yes, the hair or feather is a holographic part of the animal's soul. I myself do ask permission directly when I encounter the beast face to face, but some of them will just roar at you or lick their chops.

It must be said, however, that some dragons are quite misanthropic and live up well to their legendary bad temper. They won't eat you, but they will roast you with their fire breath. It is this ability to breathe fire that attests to the concentration of elemental fire in a dragon's body.

This means that a wand of dragon-scale core is well suited to magic of willpower, protection, questing, loyalty, wisdom, weatherworking, earthworking[34] (depending on the color), and summoning helpful spirits—oh, yes, and the ever-popular finding treasure. By color, the propensities are as follows: red for passion, protection, and vengeance; green for prosperity, earthworking, treasure finding, and "finding" spells generally; black to intensify intelligence, cunning, and vision into otherworlds; and gold for weatherworking, prosperity, wisdom, guidance, friendship, and fertility.

Hippogriff

Hippogriffs combine a horse with a giant eagle to get a more docile animal who can be trained to be ridden in battle. As mentioned in the gryphon section, the first hippogriff was bred by the Italian poet Ariosto for the hero Orlando, one of the Paladins of Charlemagne, king of the Franks. Since then they have proliferated, apparently by swooping down on unsuspecting mares. Like gryphons, these animals unite two different elemental realms. The hippogriff, with the forequarters of an eagle and the hindquarters of a horse, unites not only the realms of air and earth but also predator and prey. The horse is a prey animal and herbivore. The eagle a carnivorous predator. The result is an omnivore who is both fierce and skittish, a combination that makes it much like the human psyche. Aggressiveness and dominance are combined with calm grazing that can be easily spooked into wild running. Both sides also symbolize the wild energy of running or flying free—taking a determined path or soaring into the realms of imagination.

It is worthwhile to compare the character of the eagle+horse with the gryphon's eagle+lion. The gryphon doubles and intensifies the aggressive, predatory energy. The hippogriff moderates the symbolic meaning of the predatory eagle by combining it with the grass-grazing horse, which has so long served humans as a mount and beast of burden. It is a union of opposites. One is essentially untamed, the other tamable and an extremely useful partner in many

---

34 Earthworking is an elemental operation aimed at strengthening the earth element in the wizard and in turn protecting and preserving the mineral, plant, and animal kingdoms.

ways—transport, combat, moving heavy objects. Usually it is the feather that is used from the hippogriff, although it is possible to use the hair from the tail or fetlocks. The choice slightly emphasizes the corresponding side of the dual character of the animal. The hair emphasizes the earth element—solidity, manifestation, physicality, and intuition. The feather emphasizes the air element—thought, inspiration, higher worlds, and knowledge.

In a wand, the hippogriff's feather lends aggressiveness to the will and at the same time eagerness to help. It is well suited to any magical work involving elemental air or earth, or the combination of the two elements—i.e., unifying the mental and material aspects of a being or situation. This makes it useful for mind-body healing.

Hippocampus[35]

The hippocampus combines the forequarters of a horse and the hindquarters of a fish. There is a key difference here from the hippogriff, for having a horse's head makes these animals as proud of bearing and as fierce as a wild horse. But they are not predators. Moreover, the water horse, as they are known in Scotland, has its life only in the water. On land it has no locomotion, so it does not so strongly symbolize the union of earth and water. Rather, it introduces the idea of a mount, intelligence, and affectionate relationship with humans into the watery element, an element into which we cannot naturally penetrate and in which we may easily drown.

Hippocampi are usually shown with a long serpentine tail that ends in flowing fins, like those of an elongated and very large koi or mermaid. The hippocampus is not a deep swimmer and actually lives a life similar to that of a manatee or hippopotamus. They have fur on their forequarters and scales on the hindquarters, so that part of their meaning is the union of fish and mammal, cold-blooded and warm-blooded creatures, and the union of land creatures and sea creatures. Meditate upon the meaning these unions suggest. Magically, hippocampi are especially helpful in the creation of a wand intended for watery magic or magic that brings together elemental water and earth—for example, a wand intended for use in emotional and physical healing or developing clairvoyance or prophecy. It also enhances strength, service, and calm.

---

35 Not the ordinary animal called a seahorse nor the part of the brain given this name because of its resemblance to the animal.

The Astral Power of Spirit Animals

Spirit Owl

The feather is used in wand cores. These are not material owl feathers. The owl is sacred to Minerva/Athena and so will channel the goddess's energy and her character: wisdom, assertion, aggression, protection, disguise, secret aid. Because of the owl's interesting digestive system, digestion and cleansing are also special powers of this wand core. Owls eat their prey whole and digest all but the bones and fur, then cough up these indigestibles in a tightly packed ball, or owl pellet.

Digestion may be taken literally (magic to heal digestive problems) but also metaphorically: the ability to digest and assimilate knowledge, the ability to separate what is useful from what is not, the ability to distinguish truth and falsehood, friend and foe.

As with all predators, there is also the quality of drawing energy from other beings. Astral travel, flights of imagination, secrecy, and stealth are other qualities that arise from the owl's nighttime habits and ability to fly silently.

Spirit Raven

As with the owl, we are talking about the astral dimension of the creature and not the inclusion of material raven feathers in the wand (although this is obviously possible). A raven-feather core draws the energy of the Norse god Odin, known for his far vision, wisdom, cunning, and trickery. He is sometimes equated with Roman Mercury, though the analogy is a little loose. However, one can see how the raven takes advantage of another's loss to add to its own success. This is often the essence of success in business, so the raven energy is good for spells regarding business success and opportunities to prosper at someone else's expense.

Ravens are also joined to the Celtic war goddess Babh, who some consider an aspect of the Morrigan, or Great Queen. She flies over battlefields (as crows and ravens do). The idea of feasting on war is present in the myths of this goddess, but this image can be taken metaphorically to mean feasting on the hero-energy, internalizing it, and turning death and defeat into life and a new start. The carrion eater, after all, eats dead bodies as its food and sustenance. It also takes advantage of someone else's killing, rather than itself killing prey. This quality makes the raven different from the owl and other predators. It is neither predator nor prey but stands in the middle and takes the spoils of the predator's kill (on a human battlefield or not). The raven combines wisdom, cunning, intelligence, spying, and taking advantage of opportunities, including theft. It also gives vision flight through the spheres. Working particularly in the sphere of Mars and Mercury, raven magic is the power of death and rebirth, swiftness in thought and action, self-protection, business dealings, and conflict resolution.

Spirit Snake

The skin of the spirit snake is employed as a wand core. Its light is white and wavy like the movement of a snake. Sacred to Athena and a number of other goddesses (the ancient snake goddesses of the Middle East), the serpent energy is the energy of healing and rebirth (because the snake sheds its skin and renews itself). It is the power of knowledge, wisdom, and judgment. In the myth of the Garden of Eden, the first woman, Eve, must judge whether it is better to obey authority blindly (that of her father/creator) or to seek knowledge and make decisions of her own. The serpent is her teacher, opening her eyes to a different way of thinking. Represented in a circle, spiral, or helix, snakes can symbolize the whole cosmos.

A Complex of Meanings

$\mathcal{H}$OW THE DRYAD of a tree and the spirit of a magical beast join to form a new entity in a wand is a mystery of astral weaving. Each component of a wand carries its spirit into a new whole, and this complex of meanings forms the wand's personality, if we may apply that word. Some word lists may illustrate how it works. Let us take, for example, an oak wand with a gryphon-feather core and a reservoir stone of carnelian.

First, the complex of qualities exhibited by oak wood might include the following:

- Durability

- Strength

- Royalty

- Fruitfulness

- Lightning

Add to this the qualities exhibited by the gryphon, and the web grows larger:

- Double predator

- Fierceness

- Guardian

- Air and earth combined

- Heaven and earth united

- Self-assertion

- Loyalty

- Clairaudience

- Clairvoyance

And if we next add a carnelian to the wand's pommel, we create this complex of animal, vegetable, and mineral:

- Protection from evil

- Speeds manifestation

- Revitalizes

- Fulfills all desires

- Aligns body and spirit

- Balances creative and organizational abilities

- Strengthens concentration

- Increases self-worth

One can quickly appreciate from these lists the intricacy and breadth of character in a wand made this way.

But wait, there's more!

There is another complex of qualities that are introduced into the wand by the timing of its enchantment. These qualities come from the influence of the planets and stars at the moment of its "birth" as a new and distinctive entity. A wand has a natal horoscope just like anyone, but the key components are the elemental placement of Sun, Moon, Mercury, Mars, Midheaven sign, and rising sign. To a lesser extent, Venus can indicate the wand's disposition toward its owner and the seventh house, its approach to partnership.

It is in the act of enchantment that all of these forces are brought together with the unique moment of awakening, so that the wand's being is not merely a mixture of, in this example, oak dryad, carnelian spirit, and gryphon spirit. The final list, including the primary planetary and sidereal influences that I find to be most important in a wand's character, follows (more on astrology and the wand's nativity in a moment):

- ☽ Pisces Midheaven

- ☽ Mercury in Virgo

- ☽ Moon in Leo

- ☽ Mars in Aries

- ☽ Sun in Leo

- ☽ Venus in Cancer

- ☽ Gemini Rising

The wizard learned in astrology will appreciate that even this relatively complicated diagram is only partial, since each of the parts of the astrological nativity is itself a cluster of meanings and qualities. At the same time, the personality of the spirit in a wand is not the same as that of a human spirit. It should be treated with greater intimacy than one does some spirits, but do not mistake it for another human being. A study of wand personality would be an interesting book. However, the timing of the nativity of a wand—its enchantment—is an important part of the art of wandmaking.

Timing and Astrology

*T*HERE ARE DIFFERENT ideas about how astrology and timing may be used in works of magic. In wandmaking, the goal is to find a time for the wand's birth that is auspicious. Don't try to second-guess the cosmos and manufacture the perfect birth time for your wand. I have found that, like most births, a wand's enchantment will find its own ripe time, no matter how well you plan. To the extent that you do plan it, there are only a few major considerations. One wishes to find a suitable placing of the planets in the signs of the zodiac and their elements, with particular attention to fire because it indicates the power of the will. Doing this by hand can be laborious, but today computers make it very easy to look at the positions of the planets for dates and times in the future.

Skye Alexander, in her book *Magical Astrology*, suggests that a fire wand should be made "when the sun and moon are in fire signs (Aries, Leo, Sagittarius) and during the days and hours that correspond to the Sun, Mars, or Jupiter ... The Spring Equinox and Summer Solstice are ideal times to fashion this magical device" (140). If one adhered to this method closely, it would mean working on the wand only during those auspicious times. If one adheres a bit less strictly to the method, one could say that *starting* the work in the fiery hour and day is sufficient. In my case, I give most attention not to the influences during the time when I am carving a branch but to the influences when I perform its enchantment, which is its birth (or rebirth) as a wand.

If you are making your own wand, from the tree to the final product, you would also want to pay attention to the moment when you harvest the branch. If you do so and the branch is green wood, you will need to let it season for six months or so before carving.

Medieval magical theory suggests that one must pay close attention to the planetary days and hours for magic to be most effective. For example, say you consider that wand enchantment is something particularly under the auspices of Mercury as the planet and Roman god associated with magic. Then you would want to do your enchantment on a Wednesday, which is named for the Germanic god Woden and was dedicated by the Romans to Mercury. All of Mercury's particular specialties are considered to be more auspicious and harmonious if performed or begun on that day—for example, a divination ritual to determine if the time is right for safe travel. I consider any day of the week appropriate for wand enchantment, but you should consider the day and its planet as another factor in the harmonious construction of energies in the wand. A wand you intend to use for love spells or divination will struggle if it is enchanted on a Saturday or a Tuesday, for example, because these days are vessels for the energy of Saturn and Mars (Tuesday is named after the Germanic god Tiw or possibly the Celtic Teutates, both gods of tribal protection and battle).

The system of planetary times goes further to not only planetary days but planetary hours. So, you can also find the hour of Mercury on the day of Mercury, which will be even more conducive to magic of all kinds. Calculation of the planetary hours is done by taking all the hours of daylight in the day (calculated according to the time of year and where you are on the planet), dividing by twelve, and then with these "hours" (which may be more or less than sixty minutes), you assign the planets in the traditional Chaldean order,[36] beginning with the planet that rules the day. You do the same thing with the hours of night. In winter, the night hours will be longer than sixty minutes and the daylight hours shorter than sixty minutes. The reverse is true in summer, when there is more daylight—depending, again, on your latitude. Only at the equinoxes will the hours of daylight and darkness correspond to the conventional clock hours of sixty minutes (for further explanation, see Warnock). The following tables show how the planets are set into Chaldean order within the hours of day and night.

---

36 Sun, Venus, Mercury, Moon, Saturn, Jupiter, Mars—in that order. Not the order counting them outward from the Sun nor the order in the days of the week. Why? Ask the Chaldeans.

Planetary Hours of the Day

HOUR	SUNDAY	MONDAY	TUESDAY	WEDNESDAY	THURSDAY	FRIDAY	SATURDAY
1	Sun	Moon	Mars	Mercury	Jupiter	Venus	Saturn
2	Venus	Saturn	Sun	Moon	Mars	Mercury	Jupiter
3	Mercury	Jupiter	Venus	Saturn	Sun	Moon	Mars
4	Moon	Mars	Mercury	Jupiter	Venus	Saturn	Sun
5	Saturn	Sun	Moon	Mars	Mercury	Jupiter	Venus
6	Jupiter	Venus	Saturn	Sun	Moon	Mars	Mercury
7	Mars	Mercury	Jupiter	Venus	Saturn	Sun	Moon
8	Sun	Moon	Mars	Mercury	Jupiter	Venus	Saturn
9	Venus	Saturn	Sun	Moon	Mars	Mercury	Jupiter
10	Mercury	Jupiter	Venus	Saturn	Sun	Moon	Mars
11	Moon	Mars	Mercury	Jupiter	Venus	Saturn	Sun
12	Saturn	Sun	Moon	Mars	Mercury	Jupiter	Venus

Planetary Hours of the Night

HOUR	SUNDAY	MONDAY	TUESDAY	WEDNESDAY	THURSDAY	FRIDAY	SATURDAY
1	Jupiter	Venus	Saturn	Sun	Moon	Mars	Mercury
2	Mars	Mercury	Jupiter	Venus	Saturn	Sun	Moon
3	Sun	Moon	Mars	Mercury	Jupiter	Venus	Saturn
4	Venus	Saturn	Sun	Moon	Mars	Mercury	Jupiter
5	Mercury	Jupiter	Venus	Saturn	Sun	Moon	Mars
6	Moon	Mars	Mercury	Jupiter	Venus	Saturn	Sun
7	Saturn	Sun	Moon	Mars	Mercury	Jupiter	Venus
8	Jupiter	Venus	Saturn	Sun	Moon	Mars	Mercury
9	Mars	Mercury	Jupiter	Venus	Saturn	Sun	Moon
10	Sun	Moon	Mars	Mercury	Jupiter	Venus	Saturn
11	Venus	Saturn	Sun	Moon	Mars	Mercury	Jupiter
12	Mercury	Jupiter	Venus	Saturn	Sun	Moon	Mars

Tables adapted from Warnock, "The Planetary Hours."

After you've done the hours of daylight, you just continue on with the next planet in the Chaldean order in the first hour of night, as indicated in the table for planetary hours of the night.

After going through these calculations, one must consider which planet one wishes to be the governing force for the work. Planetary influences may be combined also; for example, enchanting on a Monday for the moon during the sign of Leo (ruled by the sun) and in the hour of Mercury. However, when it comes to wand enchantment, it all depends on what sort of magic you intend to do with the wand.

Arguably, Mars might seem the best planet to overlight a wand,[37] as the god Mars may be associated with willpower and self-assertion, i.e., elemental fire. Or one could make arguments for the sun and the moon because they are the two major luminaries. In the case of the moon, she is preeminently watery, not fiery, but elemental water is, as noted in part five, the source of the magnetic (or feminine) etheric fluid. A moon wand is well attuned to blue or white magic, and also black, as the waxing and waning phases of the moon send different energies. Alternatively, Venus would be appropriate if one were creating a wand to work primarily under the influence of that goddess in the pink, green, or red rays of magic. Astrology tells us the sort of magic associated with each of the planets, as shown in the following table:[38]

THE 7 PLANETS IN TRADITIONAL ASTROLOGY	
Sun	The higher self, one's deepest identity and source of power, the light on all planes, divine love and beauty, magnanimity, potency, rulership, kingship, orange and gold magic
Venus	Love, attraction, sex, relationships, beauty, art, music, joyful emotions, partnership, young feminine energy
Mercury	Intelligence, cunning, travel, trickery, youth, messages, information, heraldry, writing, poetry, memory, books
Moon	Home, emotions, feelings, domestic roles, intuition, seership, sensitivity, motherhood, mature feminine energy

37 *Overlight* means to extend its governance, influence, and protection—to channel the light of creation through its character.

38 The old Chaldean system does not take into account the modern outer planets, Uranus and Neptune, so you can't make a traditional table of planetary hours for them.

Saturn	Restriction, binding, restraint, reserve, limitation, prudence, boundaries, self-control, control of others, conservation and preservation, finance, time, death
Jupiter	Kingship, expansion, religion, philosophy, wisdom, riches, mature masculine energy, indigo magic, deep wisdom
Mars	Action, assertiveness, daring, lust, power, strength, guardianship, adventure, young masculine energy

So, which planet, then? In my own method of enchantment, I focus especially on the signs of the zodiac occupied by the sun, the moon, the Ascendant, and the Midheaven. The day of the week and the planetary hour are secondary considerations.

The enchantment of a wand is its birth as a new entity, and the process is one of awakening rather like birth in our own lives. In astrology, the Ascendant is the sign that is rising at the moment of birth. It casts its power over the whole personality. The sun represents the higher self and the source of life, so its placement in a fire sign is the most powerful placement. Aries, Leo, and Sagittarius each have their distinctive character, and a wand with a nativity in one of these times of the year will take on the spiritual character of whichever sign the sun is in.

The moon may also be in a fire sign, which I generally feel is beneficial, as it links the fire of will with the water of feelings; thus the energies are balanced, and the transmission of the will of the mage is enhanced.

Check on the location of Mercury also, because that planet rules magic. Air signs are also well suited for wand enchantments. Gemini, Libra, or Aquarius all will lend their intellectual qualities to the wand and give it greater subtlety. Water or earth signs may be chosen too, and they will imbue the wand with the power of those elements. I do not believe that lack of fire signs will weaken the wand's usefulness as a conduit of will. A wand with many planets in fire signs will strongly pull the mage's will into alignment. You may wonder if a wand has a will of its own; yes, it does. You will feel it if you ever get it miffed at you or try to do something it thinks is wrong. Trust the wand's intuition.

Finally, the most basic matter of timing is the phase of the moon. As in most enchantment or spellcasting, one should perform the enchantment when the moon is waxing or full. Increasing light boosts any spell directed toward manifestation. However, a wand that is intended to do work with the dark or waning moon energies (banishing or eliminating negative habits or influences, losing weight, or diminishment of any kind) could be enchanted under a dark or waning moon. The process of carving can also be done under a waning moon, as carving removes wood from the wand stock or branch, and the process of removal sympathizes with the lessening of the visible light of the moon.

There is one more bit of preparation necessary, even after the wand has been finished and sits before you on your altar ready for enchantment. This is the preparation of two liquids that will draw into the wand the powers of the sun and the moon.

In the ceremony of enchantment, I use two anointing liquids. One stands in for the element of water and the light of the moon. The other stands in for the power of the supernal light, which we experience in the material plane as the light of the sun. This light is the source of all life—and so all magic. The moon, which reflects and focuses this light through the astral plane, is the most immediate power we feel in the night. When the moon is precisely opposite the sun, it is a full moon, perfectly round and bright silver. There is nothing more magical than moonlight. Sunlight is considered yang, or masculine, and moonlight yin, or feminine. The positions of the sun and the moon within the constellations of the zodiac have a strong influence on the power and character of the wand, just as they do in human beings. Preparing these anointing fluids emphasizes that truth.

Oil of the Sun

Mix into 8 ounces of almond oil 6 drops each of the following essential oils: frankincense, orange, and cinnamon.

Bless and consecrate this oil with this invocation:

> *The sun's light is the source of all growth and life on earth. May*
> *this oil be consecrated to the sun and the supernal light; may it be*
> *filled with power to make all things grow and prosper.*

Leave it in the bright sunlight for six days beginning at noon on a Sunday, when the sun is in a fire sign (Aries, Leo, or Sagittarius). It is best made at or just before Midsummer Day, June 24.

Water of the Moon

Water has natural affinities with the moon because of the influence of her tides on the oceans. Water and the moon both carry the power of the Divine Feminine because of the moon's influence on a woman's menses. You will want to use pure spring water for this purpose, or at least filtered water. If you can get water from a sacred spring, so much the better. Add to the water three pinches of sea salt. You can find sea salt from the Isle of Anglesey in Wales, which is an ancient and sacred druidic island full of the spirits of our ancestors and the heroes of British legend. I found this salt in a gourmet shop.

Set the bottle of salt water in the light of the full moon for three nights (include the night before and after the night that the moon is technically full). It is best if the nights are clear and the bottle is set outdoors in the moonlight. It is best of all when the full moon rides high towards the zenith in the sky.

After it has absorbed the light for three nights, cast a circle as indicated above (or according to your own tradition) and, once done, hold your palms open toward the bottle of water. Enchant it with the following triple blessing or something similar:

Waters of the moon,

Be blessed with the light of Arianrhod, the silver wheel!

Be blessed with the power of Llyr, the deep lord of the seas!

Be blessed with the joy of Dylan, son of the wave!

I consecrate you for the great work.

Awen, awen, awen.

Such a triple blessing is characteristic of druid magic and many other forms, three being a sacred number in many magical systems. I use the names of Welsh divinities in this example, but you may substitute any other suitably water-related deities, angels, saints, etc. The important thing is that these aspects relate to water in nature; to the emotions, which are the astral part of the element; and to the moon. The repetition of *awen* is a sort of druid mantra to invoke and strengthen the imagination. It does not have the same meaning as "amen" or "so mote it be," which both mean "so be it." Those words would serve for the wizard who is not of a druidical persuasion, and so would a Latin phrase such as *Lux Aeternam*.

The water of the moon and oil of the sun may be used to anoint people, objects, and candles, as well as wands. Just don't get the sun oil in your eye by accident, and do not take either of them internally, obviously. Other planetary oils can be purchased or created for anointing wands if you so desire. Incenses dedicated to particular planets or elemental forces can also be employed. I tend to stick to Nag Champa incense, but it is entirely a matter of taste and how far you wish to go in getting correspondences just so. You can enhance the experience of wand enchantment by draping your altar with an indigo cloth. When enchanting moon water, you may drape it in a white or silver cloth.

With these fluids and your other altar equipment, you are ready to perform the final part of wandmaking: the enchantment and dedication.

Enchantment and Dedication

𝒩OW THAT WE understand existence as changing energies that may be approximately measured by chronology, let us turn to the moment of birth and the rite of wand enchantment itself. The verb "to enchant" comes from the Latin word *cantare*, meaning to sing. It is the same root as *chant* (*chanson* in French). The Latin prefix *en-* means "into," and so *enchant* literally means "to sing into" an object. This is an important point to keep in mind. You don't have to be a great singer, but the power of the voice lies at the roots of enchantment.

When I enchant a wand before sending it off to a client, I am casting magic into it from my own wand, which was previously enchanted. So, in the act of enchanting a wand, a string of magic is spun out from one wand to the next and one enchantment to the next. If you enchant your own wand, that is a little different process. You will employ your hands and draw the elemental energy through them and into the wand. You are still drawing magic from a source within yourself and beyond your finite temporal being.

What does this magical current do? As I have pointed out, the branch from which you make a wand already has the tree and all its ancestors in it as a spiritual current. The wandmaker unites his or her own spiritual lineage with that of the dryad. The spirit may lie dormant and asleep, but the maker's interaction with the wood in the process of carving it and finishing it as a wand of magic will arouse many a dryad from slumber.

The dryad's sleep is quite natural. When a branch has become severed from its parent tree and then begins the process of dying—just as when our human bodies begin to decay—the spirit slowly dissolves again into the astral dimension. But when a branch is turned into a wand so that it will not decay, its spirit can be reawakened, and the act of enchantment allows it to become a separate being. It needs a separate being from the parent tree, a separate identity, in order to have any spiritual cohesion. The enchantment of magical objects is something like the formation of an ego in the psyche of a child—the ego is a psychic complex that permits the child to separate itself from its parents and take on a life of its own.

The wand needs to take on its own identity, not that of the wandmaker. I have poured a lot of energy and intention into the wand in the act of creation, but in the enchantment that connection needs to be ceremonially severed. That is why I make a distinction between the act of enchanting a wand and the act of dedicating it. Dedication is the process of declaring the purpose of the wand and establishing a new bond with the wand's intended user. If you are enchanting your own wand—that is, one you have made for your own use—then dedication can become part of the enchantment; you don't need to do two different rituals. But if you are making a wand for someone else to use, it is important to awaken the dryad spirit of the wand and then sever the ties you have established in the act of making.

As an example, I will lay out the enchantment I employ. Bear in mind that the act of enchantment is a magical act and therefore partakes of words and ritual movement. I cannot convey the movement very well in a book, and to some extent it doesn't matter so much what you do so long as you do it in the spirit of ritual. The "spirit of ritual" means that you are going through the words and gestures in a state of mind that is focused on your intention and that is energetically conscious of the dryad spirit and the etheric forces you are directing through your hands and your own wand (if you are using a wand).

Finally, let me note that my own enchantment ceremony is based in traditional British druidry, but its structure should be easily adaptable to other traditions.

A Ritual for Wand Enchantment

PART I: *Preparation*

Seat yourself before an altar arranged with manifestations of the four elements:

- ☾ A red votive candle (representing fire)

- ☾ A censer of incense or a feather (representing air)

- ☾ A stone or bowl of sand (representing earth)

- ☾ A bowl of water of the moon (representing water; see page 208)

These objects are placed according to their directional associations as shown in the following illustration:

On the altar, also have the following:

- ☾ A bell (I use a Tibetan singing bowl)

- ☾ A bottle of oil of the sun (see page 207)

- ☾ A dagger (set on the east side by the incense, as this tool is used as an instrument of elemental air)

- ☾ A large beeswax pillar candle in the center

Set the wand you are going to enchant on the altar in front of you as you face north.

PART II: *Marking Sacred Spacetime*

A: CASTING THE MAGIC CIRCLE.

With a wand, staff, or your index finger, cast a circle around the space that will include you and the altar, visualizing a circle of lambent blue light. Circle three times, intoning three times:

> *I cast this circle round me now*
>
> *And with protective force endow*
>
> *With ethereal flame sublime*
>
> *Marking sacred space and time.*

B: CONSECRATING WITH FIRE AND WATER.

Consecrate your ritual circle with water and fire by asperging water and carrying fire (a candle or incense) around the circle, saying:

> *May this circle be consecrated with the element of fire.*
>
> *May this circle be purified with the element of water.*

C: GIVING PEACE TO THE QUARTERS.

Take up your bell. Ring the bell once as you turn to each of the four directions and back to the center. Let the sound resonate fully. The sound clears the astral sphere around your circle, repelling all disturbance. Facing center, say:

> *Let all disturbing thoughts and entities be banished from this circle,*
> *and let there be peace, for without peace can no work be.*

Face north and ring bell: *Let there be peace in the north.*

Face south and ring bell: *Let there be peace in the south.*

Face west and ring bell: *Let there be peace in the west.*

Face east and ring bell: *Let there be peace in the east.*

Face center and ring bell: *Let there be peace throughout all our lands.*[39]

D: INVOKING THE POWERS OF THE FOUR QUARTERS.

Setting down the bell, pick up your wand (or, again, if you are enchanting your first wand, you will need to use your hands for this). Face east and, raising up both arms, salute the east, saying:

> *In the name of the Hawk of Dawn, I summon you, O powers of the east and the element of air. Send your ministering sylphs unto me in this circle to aid in this work of art. Bless me with your wisdom, your protection, and your strength.*

Face south and, with the same gesture, say:

> *In the name of the Stag of Summer in the heat of the chase, I summon you, O powers of the south and the element of fire. Send your ministering salamanders unto me in this circle to aid in this work of art. Bless me with your wisdom, your protection, and your strength.*

Face west and, with the same gesture, say:

> *In the name of the Salmon of Wisdom in the deep of the pool, I summon you, O powers of the west and the element of water. Send your ministering undines unto me in this circle to aid in this work of art. Bless me with your wisdom, your protection, and your strength.*

Face north and, with the same gesture, say:

> *In the name of the Starry Bear of the winter sky, I summon you, O powers of the north and the element of earth. Send your ministering gnomes to me in this circle to aid in this magical work. Give me your wisdom, your protection, and your strength.*

Turn to the center (facing west), and say:

> *Welcome, all ye blessed spirits, to this circle, this place of enchantment.*

PART III: *Consecrating and Anointing the Wand*

Sit before the altar, facing north. Take up the wand you are going to enchant in your right hand, and hold it over the candle flame. Move it back and forth gently, without putting it into the flame directly. Say:

---

39 This peace formula is taken from OBOD druid rituals.

Wand of oak (or whatever wood it is), *I consecrate you with the secret fire ...*

Wave the wand in the smoke of your incense. Say:

With the clear intelligence of air ...

Hold it against your altar stone or bowl of sand. Say:

And with the manifesting power of earth.

PART IV: *Anointing with Water of the Moon and Oil of the Sun*

Dip your finger into the water of the moon you have on the altar and stroke the water over the length of the wand, saying:

I anoint you with the lustral waters of the moon ...

Uncork your bottle of oil of the sun and, using your finger, again run a small drop of oil along the shaft of the wand, saying:

... and the oil of the sun.

PART V: *Giving the Breath of Life*

Put the reservoir end of the wand to your lips and breathe on it gently and whisper:

I breathe into you the breath of life. Awaken!

With your breath, envision the core of the wand glowing with light much as a hot ember would glow if you blew upon it.

PART VI: *Introducing the Core*

Still holding the wand in both hands, with the reservoir end to your lips, breathe on it a second time and visualize the core material you wish to enchant into the wand. Say:

I enchant into you a core of phoenix feather (or whatever the core is).

At this point, your concentration must bridge the worlds, taking from the astral plane the phoenix feather, unicorn hair, etc., and moving it etherically in the plane of its astral existence into the astral dimension of the wand in your hand. This is another bit that is hard to explain and cannot even be shown in the normal sense. You will have to experiment and practice until you can feel and visualize this happening.[40]

PART VII: *Charging the Wand with Sound*

If you have a wand you are using to perform the enchantment, touch its tip to the pommel or reservoir stone of the wand being enchanted and tap it three times, visualizing the prana flowing through your hand and wand into the new wand. As you tap it, say:

Magnum Mysterium. Omnium Magica Erat.[41]

Next, place the wand between your hands, with the wand's tip in the center of your left palm and the wand's reservoir or pommel in the center of your right palm. Chant *awen* or *om* to focus your attention into your own light-body, and then create a current of prana between your palms, passing through the wand, charging it with life and light. The palm points are called *lao gong* points by Taoist wizards and masters of chi gong.[42]

40 There is a palpable difference between imagining that such a thing is happening (as a writer does when writing a fantasy novel, for instance) and actually moving the essences in the astral dimension of things. It may be helpful to study yoga, tai chi, or chi gong and learn to feel the flow of energies as a first step to feeling in the ethereal and astral dimensions. Practice meditating and astral traveling to otherworlds.

41 The point of the incantation is to signify that you are passing the magical current of all magic into the new wand. The language of the incantation is not as important as its meaning to you. Using Latin or another language you do not use in mundane affairs is a way to keep your mind in the altered consciousness of magic. Latin has long been traditional for wizards, but some modern druids prefer Irish or Welsh, while other Neopagans and magicians use Greek or Old Norse. Those who actually know Latin grammar will perhaps object to the construction of the above phrase. The repetition of the -um ending is intended to add alliterative power, and the verb is intentionally ambiguous—this is *grimoirie* rather than grammar, where sound is more important than ordinary sense, and bad grammar aids us as a departure from mundane rules.

42 It is a matter of speculation whether the ancient druids may have understood these energetic systems. It does not seem to me too dramatic a stretch of the imagination to believe they did and that this is how they performed their magical art. In any case, it is how modern druids work.

PART VIII: *Sealing the Enchantment and Receiving the Name*

After you have chanted long enough to feel that the wand is charged and aware, take it again in your right hand and lift it over the candle flame, declaring:

The maker of trees (or God) *has made you a branch of oak* (or whatever).
I, (your magical name), *have made you a wand of magic.*

Now, touch the side of the wand to your brow chakra, or third eye, and ask politely:

Spirit of this wand, if it be thy will, reveal unto me thy secret name.

Listen. If the spirit wishes it, you will hear a whispered name in your mind's ear. In my experience, this name can take almost any form, coming from various magical traditions and languages, or it may be simply a strange and mysterious name. This takes some careful listening. Once you hear the name, say:

(Name), *thou shalt be called.* (Name), *go well, do good work, harm no one.*

Kiss the wand farewell (or if it is to be your wand, in greeting and affection), and set it aside to your left or back upon the altar with your left hand. The kiss and the use of the familiar "thou" form in English are signs of affection and intimacy, as well as an acknowledgment that the wand is now a living being with a life of its own. The kiss is also a ritual gesture of parting.

PART IX: *Closing*

Reverse the invocation of the quarters. Step to each of the cardinal directions from north to east, moving counterclockwise, thanking the spirits of the directions and elements, and closing the open gates to the otherworlds with a gesture like closing a curtain.

In the north, raise your arms in blessing and say:

In the name of the Starry Bear of the winter sky,
I thank you, powers of the north and the element of earth.

In the west, raise your arms in blessing and say:

In the name of the Salmon of Wisdom swimming in the clear pool,
I thank you, powers of the west and the element of water.

In the south, raise your arms in blessing and say:

> *In the name of the Stag of Summer in the heat of the chase,*
> *I thank you, powers of the south and the element of fire.*

In the east, raise your arms in blessing and say:

> *In the name of the Hawk of May, soaring in the sky,*
> *I thank you, powers of the east and the element of air.*

At the end, ground yourself by touching the earth or floor of your sanctum and deliberately feeling any excess accumulation of magical power going into the earth. Eating a snack is also grounding; chocolate is recommended.

Witches or magicians of ceremonial orders can adapt the above details to suit their own systems. There is nothing magical about the exact form of the ritual. The magic lies in its gestures and words suiting you and empowering your own belief.

Wand Dedication

A ceremony of dedication may be done after the wand has been enchanted and charged, especially if the wand you are dedicating comes to you as a gift or is made by someone else's hands. The purpose of a dedication is to bond your wand to you and to solemnly state your intention with regard to how you will use the wand. In form, it is otherwise similar to the ceremony of enchantment. Essentially, however, one enchantment is a birthing spell of creation, while the ritual of dedication is a binding spell.

PART I: *Preparation*

On a Sunday in the hour of the sun, on a night when the moon is full or waxing and either moon and sun are in a fire sign, prepare an altar indoors or outdoors, with symbols of the four alchemical elements placed in each of the four directions according to the correspondences.

PART II: *Creating Sacred Space*

Using your finger, cast a circle around the altar sunwise, or clockwise. After this has been done, stand at each point of the compass and address the powers there, lifting your palms upward in attitude of prayer and welcoming.

Face east and say:

> *In the name of the Hawk of Dawn (or Sky Father),*
> *I summon you, O powers of the east and the element of air.*

Face south and say:

> *In the name of the Stag of Summer (or Lord of the Greenwood),*
> *I summon you, O powers of the south and the element of fire.*

Face west and say:

> *In the name of the Salmon of Wisdom (or Goddess of Wisdom),*
> *I summon you, O powers of the west and the element of water.*

Face north and say:

> *In the name of the Starry Bear of the winter sky (or Mother Earth),*
> *I summon you, O powers of the north and the element of earth.*

Face center and say:

> *Here is all space. Here is all time. This circle is the seat of eternity. Welcome, Shining*
> *Ones, and grant me your wisdom, protection, and strength in this act of dedication.*

Pause for a period of silent meditation or the intonation of a chant or mantra.

PART III: *Consecration*

Sit on the south side of your altar with the candle in front of you, as you face north. Hold the wand in both hands at the level of your heart.

Ground and center your energies by meditating and focusing on the candle, then on the wand. Raise the wand over the candle flame with your right hand and say:

> *Wand of magic, I consecrate you with the sacred fire and the purity of divine light.*

Hold the wand so that its point is in the center of your left palm and its pommel or reservoir stone is in the center of your right palm. Intone the mantra *awen* (ahhhh-OOOOOO-ennnnnn) or your personal mantra repeatedly while dropping into trance. Feel your prana flowing through your palms and through the wand from right to left. In your inner eye, see the wand glowing with inward light, the magical core scintillating with its particular colors, spiraling from the handle of the wand to its point and out into your left hand. Feel this current of power, this current of magical force, running through the wand and your body. Visualize the flow increasing in speed and volume.

PART IV: *Dedicating the Wand*

Raise the wand to the level of your forehead and say:

> *I dedicate you to the art of magic, to goodness, and to the direction of my will.*

Say the wand's secret name when you address it this way. Then say:

> *Join with me and serve no other, in love, trust, and companionship.*

Then kiss the wand and rest with it in your lap for some time, listening to the dryad spirit of the wand. If it speaks to you, engage it in conversation.

PART V: *Closing and Grounding*

When you are finished, close your ritual circle, reversing the above invocations, and withdrawing the boundary of the circle antisunwise, or counterclockwise, thanking instead of summoning the powers. Ground yourself by eating and drinking something to celebrate.

Following the dedication ceremony, spend as much time in physical contact with your wand as you can for several days. Sleep with it under your pillow (or, if you are a restless sleeper, somewhere safe nearby). Keep it within the immediate proximity of your aura for seven days or, if you wish, for one full month or for nine months. All are good mystical time periods.

As before, you may adapt the preceding invocations with divine names according to your own tradition or religion. The formula is correct when you decide it is correct. The important thing is not the outward form of words but the contact you make with the wand's spirit. So, you must make sure that you are 100 percent certain and comfortable that doing magic is consistent with the tradition within which you wish to work.

Bardon, in *The Practice of Magical Evocation*, gives an excellent discussion of various ways to approach the charging of a wand. The section is too long to quote in its entirety, but suffice it to say that he discusses charging with willpower, with special qualities or faculties, with magnetism, with elements, with akasha, and with the "universal light," which is the light from which all things are created constantly. This supernal light is accumulated into the wand by means of imagination. In the mind's eye—the astral vision—the wand will shine like the sun. Bardon considers a wand charged in this way to be well suited to "theurgical purposes." *Theurgy* in this sense means "the evocation of higher beings of the light and intelligences" (54). The supernal light gets the attention of beings existing in the higher planes, not the material body of the wand.

Using a Wand

PROFESSOR FLITWICK, IN *Harry Potter and the Sorcerer's Stone*, instructs his students to "swish and flick" as the proper wand technique; Professor Snape sneers at wand "waving." These descriptions do describe a valid way to use a wand. The swish gathers up one's intentions and the flick directs them. It's rather like good form in golf: don't forget the follow-through! The point of using a wand at all, rather than just your finger or your eyes, is mainly to direct your magical intention more forcibly. You could golf without clubs, too, but not drive the ball so far.

Once you have prepared all the other elements of your spell—colored candles, herbs, incense, some object to represent the recipient of the spell, proper astrological timing, and all that—there is usually an incantation that sums it all up in a nice rhyme. There are many other books that can give you the basic method of constructing spells (see Illes, Cunningham, and Sutton and Mann). My only advice is to study poetry before writing your incantations. They work better magically if the meter and rhyme scan well.

How you move your wand will depend upon the purpose of the spell. The entirety of the spell is a symbolic structure that you are building up to contain magical forces—the power of your imagination and spirit. In many acts of the magical arts, you will be directing cosmic forces. In other words, the energy doesn't come out of your being, but your being acts as a channel through which the force—or etheric fluid—is directed. Your highly polished intention is the lens through which that astral light is beamed, and if it is foggy or smudged, the beam might go astray or fail in its purpose. The thing about magic is that, like a laser beam, it will probably have *some* effect, even if it isn't the one you intended. Remember, never point your wand at a mirror, either literal or metaphorical. You could put an eye out.

A wand is most often used in a gesture of pointing in order to project magic in a specific direction. If you want peace in the Middle East, cast your spell in that direction. But if you want to affect a particular person, you might point your wand in the direction of that person, or you might point it at an object or photograph on your altar that represents that person. When the wand is pointed in this way, the actual magical process going on inside your mind, body, and spirit is invisible to the ordinary eye and indescribable in ordinary language. Moreover, different mages will experience the thing differently. When I point my wand, there is a very particular focusing of my attention—my eyes, my ears, and my other senses—toward the object of my spell. If I'm doing it right, I will feel my prana being directed through the wand and my intention focusing it.

It is tempting to say that one imagines one's prana (*nwyfre*, élan vital, chi, or whatever you want to call it) flowing through the wand, but it isn't quite so much *imagining* as it is just letting it happen and not *thinking* about it too much.

There is an element of visualization, but there is a difference between conjuring the image or vision of prana and just letting it flow through you. Again, I will make the analogy to correct form in golf. You don't arrive there by *thinking about it* but through training your mind and body to move in the desired way. Moving prana means training your etheric and astral bodies in a similar manner. If you feel your spell sailing away in a beautiful line toward the goal, that is what counts. And then all the magic pros can sit around the nineteenth hole with a Scotch and soda and argue about what is really "correct" form.

In the case of sports, the muscles have their own sort of memory in the part of the brain called the cerebellum. In magical work, one uses other parts of the brain, parts that are deep, primordial, and mysterious. In anatomical maps, these regions of the brain are marked "Here Be Dragons." In the old days, it was called working from the heart or the liver. The latest medical opinion seems to be that the brain's temporal lobes might do the trick.

Another way of using your wand is as a meditation tool. In this case, you direct your intention through the wand and use it as a companion and guardian while walking between the worlds. The physical wand has its astral component just as the human being does, and when you step off into the otherworlds, you can take your wand with you. At the same time, your wand also guards your body while your consciousness journeys. There is much comfort to be derived from holding your wand while meditating or astral traveling.

Tapping is a tried and true method of transferring power through a wand. In the old Irish and Welsh legends of druids and denizens of Faerie, a tap on the head was all that was needed to turn a prince into a pig. If you have the object of your spell right in front of you, a tap may be more appropriate than pointing or swishing and flicking.

Finally, in some actions, prolonged contact between the wand and the object of enchantment is useful. For example, in wand enchantment itself, contact may be maintained between the point of the wand doing the magic and the reservoir of the wand receiving it. The same technique may be applied to charging talismans, balancing chakras, or to healing in general. Here again it is the contact between the etheric bodies of the wand and the object of healing that counts.

Wands are used to invoke or evoke spirits and deities. In such cases, simply hold the wand upright in front of you. Do not point at gods—it's not polite. Pointing a wand at daemons is appropriate because the mage is commanding them. A wand is pointed outward and downward to cast a magic circle or to draw pentagrams in banishing rituals; this inscribing in the air may be used for writing runes or other signs also. A wand is often used to astrally stir potions and to charge them with intention. It may move over the surface of the potion or point straight down into it to imbue it. Likewise, it may swirl the astral energies of a bowl of water for scrying or bless a goblet of mead.

In the end, the wand's usefulness lies in motion and direction. Its shape and structure assist in the movement of ethereal forces. The movement of the wand is a ritual movement and after practice becomes a key to unlocking the inner depths of the mind. Those depths are the doorways to the higher realms, and within those higher dimensions of existence, the gesture of pointing or creating a swirling vortex of power becomes an irrevocable force—a force indeed that changes what happens in the world. As above, so below.

Final Thoughts

THE CRAFT OF wandmaking is a branch of the art of enchantment, and the creation of one's ideal wand is only one step in the pursuit of a magical life—that is, a life that accepts wonders and acknowledges that there is more to human existence than the material plane. I hope that through the reading of this book you have found food for thought and have come to recognize that there really is no separation between the world of magic and the mundane world. They are the same world looked at from different angles and with different vision.

In truth, there is no such thing as a "nonmagical" world, for the cosmos is always and everywhere structured around patterns of thought and feeling, geometry and poetry, and woven with countless imaginations. From our private studies and laboratories to the parks, streets, and lakes of our cities, to the wilderness and the depths of the oceans and the great sea of stars, the cosmos is chock-full of intelligence. Spiritual beings are everywhere around us and often very interested in us. Why? Simply because we too are beings of spirit and magic. Even if we do not realize it, our minds and souls extend across space and time, intersecting with those of other beings. Each of us is vastly extended beyond our small ego-consciousness and intricately interconnected to many worlds. It is knowing this that makes one a member of the magical community.

My student, go forth. Do good work, and harm no one.

Magical Alphabets

$\mathcal{T}$HE FOLLOWING ARE examples of some of the most common magical alphabets. The Irish ogham is most common in the druid traditions, though it is gaining more attention in other traditions as well. Theban letters are primarily used by witches. Norse runes, or the Futhark, as they are called, are used by Pagan mages working in the Norse traditions—Asatru, Odinism, etc. Norse runes likewise have become well known among wizards today, including druids.

Bear in mind that in any magical alphabet, each letter is used to convey more than just a single phonetic value. Each letter is part of a web of meanings that encompasses the entire cosmos, both materially and spiritually. Consultation of the books in the bibliography will lead you to more details about the esoteric meanings of these letter signaries.

Irish Ogham Letters

≣	N	Nuin (Ash)
≣	S	Saille (Willow)
⊨	F	Fearn (Fern)
⊢	L	Luis (Rowan)
⊢	B	Beith (Birch)
≣	Q	Quert (Apple)
≣	C	Coll (Hazel)
≡	T	Tinne (Holly)
⊒	D	Duir (Oak)
⊐	H	Huath (Hawthorn)
⫽	R	Ruis (Elder)
⫽	St	Straif (Blackthorn)
⫽	Ng	Ngetal (Reed)
⫽	G	Gort (Ivy)
⫽	M	Muin (Vine)
≣	I	Ioho (Yew)
≣	E	Eadha (Aspen)
≢	U	Ur (Heather)
≠	O	Onn (Gorse)
+	A	Ailim (Fir or Elm)

Theban Letters

𝔑	A	𝔪	O
𝔮	B	𝔪	P
𝔪	C	𝔮	Q
𝔪	D	𝔪	R
𝔪	E	𝔥	S
𝔴	F	𝔪	T
𝔳	G	𝔭	U, V
𝔶	H	𝔭𝔭	W
𝔲	I, J	𝔳	X
ℭ𝔩	K	𝔪	Y
𝔶	L	𝔪𝔥	Z
𝔪	M	𝔶𝔷	full stop/ period
𝔑𝔪	N		

Norse Futhark Runes

Rune	Name	Rune	Name
ᚠ	Fehu	ᛇ	Eihwaz
ᚢ	Uruz	ᛈ	Pertho
ᚦ	Thurisaz	ᛉ	Algiz
ᚨ	Ansuz	ᛋ	Sowulo
ᚱ	Raido	ᛏ	Teiwaz
ᚲ	Kenaz	ᛒ	Berkana
ᚷ	Gebo	ᛖ	Ehwaz
ᚹ	Wunjo	ᛗ	Mannaz
ᚺ	Hagalaz	ᛚ	Laguz
ᚾ	Nauthiz	◇	Inguz
ᛁ	Isa	ᛟ	Othila
ᛃ	Jera	ᛞ	Dagaz

Magical Powers of Stones and Metals

MINERAL (COLOR)	PLANET, DEITY, ZODIAC SIGN	MAGICAL PROPERTIES
Agate (banded red and brown)	Mercury Gemini	Protection, victory, attracts love, promotes fertility, turns away lightning or evil spirits, finds buried treasure, cures insomnia, gives pleasant dreams, unblocks chakras, gives strength to mind and body, increases balance, gives bursts of energy
Tree Agate (white)	Mercury	Purification, light, branching paths of causation and choice
Moss Agate (green)	Taurus Venus Gemini	Eloquence, persuasion, fertility, magnetism, eternal life, knowledge, astral travel, scrying, contacting spirit guides, wealth, happiness, finding friends
Amber (golden)	Sun	Excellent fluid condenser, combines yin and yang, protection, attraction, sensuality
Amethyst (purple)	Aquarius	Averts intoxication, protects against losing oneself/losing control/false infatuations, clairvoyance, prescience, dispels illusions, attracts women, protects from evil sorcery, brings good luck and success, increases spiritual senses

MINERAL (COLOR)	PLANET, DEITY, ZODIAC SIGN	MAGICAL PROPERTIES
Aventurine (green)	Earth	Protection, good luck in gambling, releases anxieties, inspires independence and positive attitudes, enhances visualization/writing/art/music, attracts prosperity/love/unexpected opportunities
Bloodstone (green and red)	Mars	Links root and heart chakras, stimulates kundalini, guards against deception, preserves health, creates prosperity/abundance/self-confidence, lengthens life, gives fame, aids invisibility, removes obstacles, controls spirits, causes storms, gives help in court cases
Calcite (multicolored)	Venus	Clears negative energies, intensifies mental and emotional clarity, attracts love
Carnelian (red)	Mars Aries	Protects against the evil eye, fulfills all desires, speeds manifestations, revitalizes the body and spirit, strengthens concentration, increases sense of self-worth, brings career success, balances creative and organizational abilities
Citrine (pale yellow or clear)	Mercury Pluto Scorpio	Protects against intoxication/evil thoughts/ overindulgence/snakes/plagues/epidemics, gives clarity of thought, aligns ego with higher self, strengthens one's ability to deal with difficult karma, opens channels of intuition
Fluorite (multicolored)	Pisces Capricorn	Grounds excessive energy, enhances the astral senses, provides healing through the chakras, enhances abstract understanding/meditation/studying/dreaming
Hematite (shiny gray)	Mars Aries Aquarius	Aids in favorable hearings or judgments in winning petitions before those in authority, protects warriors, energizes the etheric body, gives optimism/confidence/ courage, repels negativity, gives strength to the body
Jade (green)	Aries Gemini Libra	Strengthens the heart/kidneys/immune system, increases fertility, cleanses etherically, balances the emotions, dispels negativity, gives courage and wisdom, also gives vivid and accurate precognitive dreams

MINERAL (COLOR)	PLANET, DEITY, ZODIAC SIGN	MAGICAL PROPERTIES
Jasper (red or brown)	Jupiter	Weatherworking, brings rain, cures snakebite, heals stomach ailments, balances chakras, stabilizes energy, protects from negativity, may drive away hallucinations/evil spirits/nightmares, grounds, can build up steady energy for long periods of time
Lapis Lazuli (blue)	Jupiter Isis	Opens the throat chakra, removes painful memories, brings good fortune, releases tension and anxiety, increases mental clarity/creativity/clairvoyance, helps overcome depression, aids communication with spirit guides, enhances astral awareness
Malachite (green stripes)	Venus Minerva	Gives ability to understand animal languages, protects, revitalizes body and mind, repels evil spirits, inspires tolerance and flexibility, opens communication, stabilizes energy, enhances creativity through magic, acts as a psychic mirror by reflecting the energy one projects into it
Onyx (banded black, white, or brown)	Saturn Gaia	Balances male and female polarities, gives spiritual inspiration, helps face past-life problems and transformational challenges, expands the imagination, deflects negative energy
Quartz Crystal (clear and colorless)	The Zenith and the Center	Amplifies etheric energies, draws together the Divine Sphere and the Material Sphere, enhances meditation/communication with spirits/telepathy/clairvoyance/visualization, creates life itself
Rose Quartz (translucent pink)	Venus Libra	Creates love, heals emotions, gives compassion, reduces anxiety, enhances creativity and self-confidence, heart chakra
Smoky Quartz (grayish brown, translucent)	Pluto	Root chakra, grounds and centers, breaks up pranic blockages (and negativity caused by them), helps transform dreams into material manifestation, counters spiritual adversaries

MINERAL (COLOR)	PLANET, DEITY, ZODIAC SIGN	MAGICAL PROPERTIES
Milky Quartz (translucent white)	Moon Cancer	Nurtures feminine energies, promotes good spirit guides for astral travel and freedom for women and their independence, all workings to do with mothers and their children, family, emotions, moods, and feelings
Rutilated Quartz (gray, translucent, woven with threads or needles)	Venus Thetis Gemini Taurus	Enhances life energy, increases clairvoyance, transmutes negative energy, aids in communication with one's higher self, increases the efficacy of magic, protection
Tourmalinated Quartz (clear with inclusions of tourmaline)	Moon Cancer	Absorbs negativity, grounds, balances, protects, dispels grief and sorrow, heals traumas, transforms emotions
Rhodonite (opaque rose pink with veins or patches of gray or black)	Isis Minerva	Reduces stress, calms the mind, enhances energy and vitality, deters interruptions, aids in reaching one's maximum potential, promotes emotional healing and love, warns of danger, protects, root and heart chakra
Serpentine (opaque mottled green)	Mercury	Protection against serpents, increases prudence and self-restraint, good for indirect travel/ quests/increasing knowledge and wisdom
Tiger's-Eye (chatoyant striped yellow and golden brown)	Leo	Protection through the inspiration of courage, enhances emotions/self-confidence/luck/ assertiveness, gives clear insight to eliminate fears and anxieties, grounds, centers, strengthens the will
Turquoise (sky blue or light green)	Venus Jupiter	Conducts energy from one person or place to another, attraction, abundance, elemental air, Egyptian Hathor, Celtic Boann, brings love and prosperity, green or blue magic

Appendix III

Table of Beast Symbolism

$\mathcal{M}$ANY ARE THE mythical beasts that wander the moors and mountains of the astral plane. They are the beasts of dreams who speak to us, who guide us from one world to another, and who counsel us or thwart us, according to our merits and intentions. Here is a summary of the creatures whose hair, skin, or feathers are most often used in wands.

CREATURE (PART USED)	CHARACTER AND QUALITIES
Dragon (splinter or shard of a scale)	Light will vary depending on the color of the dragon; black has strong ultraviolet light. Use red for passion, protection, and vengeance; green for prosperity, earthworking, treasure-finding, and finding spells generally; black to intensify intelligence, cunning, and vision into other worlds; and gold for weatherworking, prosperity, wisdom, guidance, friendship, and fertility.
Gryphon (feather or hair)	Sacred to Nemesis, the Hellenic goddess of vengeance. Symbolizes high nobility and power. Combines the hearing of dogs, the eyesight of eagles, and feline temperament. Carnivorous, sudden and aggressive, royal, deadly, king of beasts and monarch of the skies combined, loyal guard of treasures and spiritual riches, has the powers of vigilance/ferocity/perception/strength/dependability/clairvoyance/wisdom/clairaudience, and, on the negative side, avarice.

CREATURE (PART USED)	CHARACTER AND QUALITIES
Hippocampus (hair)	Watery magic, works to combine elemental water and earth. Emotional and physical healing, strength, service, and calm. Develops clairvoyance, prophecy, imaginal vision, and dreams.
Hippogriff (feather or hair)	The wild energy of running or flying free—taking a determined path or soaring into the realms of imagination. Union of opposites. Aggressive, assertive, eager to help. Actions of elemental air or earth—the mental and material. Mind-body healing.
Phoenix (feather)	Spirit of fire, renewal, death and rebirth, endurance, healing. Also, hope for immortality and the power of beauty to enchant. Transformative passion, remaking oneself. Herbivore, gentle and intelligent. Very strong healing powers. Enhances the power of the will and treats fevers, physical or emotional.
Spirit Owl (feather)	Minerva/Athena, wisdom, assertion, aggression, protection, disguise, secret aid, digestion, cleansing, secrecy, and stealth.
Spirit Raven (feather)	Odin and the war goddess Babh; wisdom, cunning, intelligence, spying, making good of something seemingly dead, vision flight, conflict resolution, swiftness in thought/action/self-protection, prospering at someone else's expense, business dealings and opportunities.
Spirit Snake (skin)	Wisdom and healing (especially white snakes); represented in a spiral or helix, snakes can symbolize the whole cosmos.
Unicorn (hair)	Aggressive, protective, pure, integrity of spirit and unspoiled essence. Able to cleanse all poisons with its horn. Nobility of spirit, the untamable spirit of the horse; service to women and true virtue. Healing disease and detecting poisons. Finding treasures, purifying. Creates all virtues: love, faith, hope, justice, wisdom, truth, and fortitude. Attuned to the Divine Feminine.

Alphabetical Table of Trees and Their Magical Qualities

TREE	ELEMENT & KEY CONCEPT	SACRED TO	MAGICAL PROPERTIES
Alder	Water Preserving	Pisces, Deirdre, Bran	Oracular magic, seership, dreamwork, preservation, concealment, crossing or bridging worlds, emotional bridges, music, enchantment, preservation from flooding/water damage/drowning
Apple	Air Singing	Lughnasadh, Rhiannon, Epona, Pwyll, King Arthur, Vivian (the Lady of the Lake), Avalon, Venus, throat chakra	Faerie, protection, blessing, calling, sending, opening doorways to other worlds, travel, revealing deception, illumination, love, harvesting, abundance, inspiration, enchantment
Ash	Earth/Water Journeying	Virgo, Artemis, Diana, Mercury, Llyr	Calling, direction of art and craft, moving toward a goal, healing, crossing bridges to other worlds

TREE	ELEMENT & KEY CONCEPT	SACRED TO	MAGICAL PROPERTIES
Beech	Fire Learning	Mercury, Minerva, Lugh, Ogma, Belenos, sun, solar plexus chakra	Solar and positive magic, the enhancement of creativity, learning, the search for information, books, languages
Birch	Water Beginning	Vernal equinox, spring, flora, bards	Purification, discipline, create spells of youth and fresh starts, bardic enchantment, creativity, procreation, birth, renewal and rebirth, purification, spells for discipline and service
Blackthorn and Plum	Earth Blocking	Babh, the Crone, Pluto, Hades	Curses, protection, communication and collaboration with Faerie and dark powers, overcoming creative barriers or blocks, persistence, patience, divining of precious metals
Cedar	Air Cleansing	Imbolc, Brighid	Enchantment, clearing negativity, dedication of sacred space, poetry, smithcraft, healing
Cherry	Fire Desiring	Mars/Ares, Aries, Teutates	Protection, conflict, sex, attraction, assertiveness, aggression, love, confidence, daring, union of opposites, root chakra, healing of injuries from conflict or loss
Chestnut	Water Producing	Zeus, Gaia, Ouranos, Aphrodite, Cancer, Dana, naiads, undines	Fertility, feminine powers, motherhood, the sea, protection of families, protection of waters, reflection, introspection, meditation, abundance, nurturance, cleansing, relationships (especially mother and child)
Ebony	Earth Dominating	Hecate, dark moon, Pluto/Hades, Circe, Cerridwen, Arawn	Leadership, domination, penetrating to the core of any problem, control, sexual assertion, aggression, concealing, revealing, healing dark diseases, dragon energy, seduction

TREE	ELEMENT & KEY CONCEPT	SACRED TO	MAGICAL PROPERTIES
Elder	Earth Regenerating	Taurus, Venus, Boann	Enchantment, healing, protection, regeneration, wealth
Elm	Earth Containing	Saturn, Dana	Healing, fertility, growth, rebirth, destiny, wisdom, passage from one life (or phase of life) to another, metamorphosis, endurance
Hawthorn	Air Guarding	Aquarius, the White Hart, the Green Man, Bealtaine	Fertility, rebirth, renewal, union, wildness, human being as animal, detects magic, counter-jinxes, counter-curses, accuracy of magic, protection, strength, control, warding, sending, detection, concealment
Hazel	Air Understanding	The White Goddess, Arianrhod, full moon, Sophia, the Salmon of Wisdom, Virgo	Female autonomy, feminine power, magic of wisdom/beauty/charm/love/stars/navigation/summoning/attraction/creativity
Holly	Fire Penetrating	Holly King, Hades, Arawn, Persephone, Demeter	Protection, works against evil spirits/poisons/angry elementals/lightning, averts fear, allows courage to emerge, dream magic and eternal life, the overthrow of old authorities, success in business or endeavors in hunting or quests, holly energy moves us to progress to a new stage of development
Juniper	Earth Transforming	The Morrigan, the Cailleach, Samhuinn	Transformation, transition, crossing to other worlds, cloaking, revealing, letting go, yin power, shadow, meditation, seduction, binding, geas, fate
Lilac	Air Imagining	Mercury, Gemini, Gwydion, vernal equinox	Magic of union, attraction, intellectual enhancement of sexual pleasure, cultivation of creative bliss, intellectual pursuits, imagination, information, mental power, creation of harmony, travel, illusion, detection, verbal wit, writing, charm, work with the Fair Folk

TREE	ELEMENT & KEY CONCEPT	SACRED TO	MAGICAL PROPERTIES
Linden	Air Attracting	Dierdre, Oengus Og, Eros, Aphrodite, heart chakra	Creation, transmutation, illumination, love, attraction, binding, obligation, healing wounds, enhancement of beauty, peace, enchantment
Maple	Earth and Fire Changing	Autumnal equinox, Libra and Virgo, John Barleycorn, Green Man, Mabon (son of Modron), Cerridwen, the moon, Minerva	Control, finding, binding, transformation, creation, ambition, passion, revolution, rebirth, poetry, beauty, harvest, healing, abundance
Oak	Fire Opening	Leo, sun, Center, Oghma, Hu, Arthur, Belenos, Apollo	Leadership, wise rule, personal sovereignty, authority, power, protection, sealing or opening doors, endurance, invocation of wisdom, fertility, abundance
Poplar	Water Feeling	Arianrhod, Dylan, Poseidon, Proteus, Psyche	Emotions, feelings, the unconscious, sensitivity, reading body language, sense of humor, intuition, empathy, dance magic, instincts, all senses, attraction, repulsion, fear, self-doubt, panic, emotional healing
Redwood and Sequoia	Fire Aspiring	Cernunnos, Stag of Summer, Gaia, Sagittarius, Centaur, Chiron	Striving upward, travel to higher spheres, drawing down power from heaven to earth, religious seeking, discipline, mystical union, hunting, martial arts, wild animals, wisdom, experience

TREE	ELEMENT & KEY CONCEPT	SACRED TO	MAGICAL PROPERTIES
Rowan	Earth Quickening	Capricorn, winter solstice, Govannon the Smith, Brighid, Pan, belly chakra	Unites fire and earth elements, bridges worlds, transforms raw materials into art, astral vision, protection, warding off evil spirits, averts storms and lightning, brings peace, invokes form and order, ritual, growth, fertility, rebirth, women's autonomy, poetry, metalwork, stone carving, weaving, spinning, geomancy, work with ley lines
Spruce, Pine, and Fir	Water Turning	Winter solstice, Arawn, Pwyll, Hades, Cerridwen, Hecate	Battling evil, astral flight, cleansing, purification, creation, making potions, witches' brooms, transformation, shapeshifting, wisdom
Walnut	Air and Fire Illuminating	Jupiter, Mercury, Taranis, crown chakra, Odin	Wind and weather magic, expansion, vortices, enhancement of the powers of breath, spells to conjure or avert lightning/ hurricanes/cyclones, teleportation, astral travel, inspiration
Willow	Water Weaving	Moon, Luna, Phoebe, Diana, Artemis, Selene, Hecate, Cerridwen, Arachne	Dowsing, divination, seership, rain-making, funerary rites, love, easing childbirth, fertility, female sexual organs, healing, glamour, bewitchment, concealment, secrecy, germination, herb-weaving, making potions, melody, combination
Yew	Air and Earth Remembering	Arawn, Maeve, Hermes, Hecate, Indra, the Dagda	Death, grieving, travel between worlds, ancestors, trance, seership, divination, healing, transformation, knowledge, eloquence, persuasion, mediumism, necromancy

Further Reading and Works Cited

Animals

Beer, Rüdiger Robert. *Unicorn: Myth and Reality.* Trans. Charles M. Stern. Van Nostrand Reinhold, 1972.

Davies, Marion. *Sacred Celtic Animals*. Capall Bann, 1998.

Green, Miranda. *Animals in Celtic Life and Myth*. Routlege, 1992.

Nigg, Joe. *The Book of Gryphons*. Applewood Books, 1982.

Ransome, Hilda M. *The Sacred Bee: In Ancient Times and Folklore*. Dover, 2004. (Originally published in 1937.)

White, T. H. *The Book of Merlin*. University of Texas, 1988.

———, trans. *The Book of Beasts*. Dover, 1984. (Reprint of 1954 edition. Originally written in the twelfth century.)

Astrology

Alexander, Skye. *Magical Astrology*. New Page, 2000.

Bayley, Michael. *Caer Sidhe, Vol 1: The Celtic Night Sky*. Capall Bann, 1997.

———. *Caer Sidhe, Vol. 2: Hanes Gwyddionaeth Crefydd; History, Science, and Religion*. Holmes, 2002.

Clouter, Gregory. *The Lost Zodiac of the Druids*. Vega, 2003.

Ellis, Peter Berresford. "Early Irish Astrology: An Historical Argument," http://cura.free.fr/xv/11ellis1.html.

O'Dubhain, Searles. "Celtic Astrology," http://www.mythicalireland.com/astronomy
/celticastrology.php.

Paterson, Helena. *Celtic Moon Signs: How the Mystical Power of the Druid Zodiac Can Transform Your Life*. Element, 2004.

Warnock, Christopher. "The Planetary Hours," http://www.renaissanceastrology.com
/planetaryhoursarticle.html.

Deities and Myths of the Hollow Hills

Briggs, Katharine. *A Dictionary of Fairies*. Penguin Books, 1977.

D'Aulaire, Ingri, and Edgar Parin D'Aulaire. *D'Aulaire's Book of Greek Myths*. Delacorte Books, 1992.

———. *D'Aulaire's Book of Norse Myths*. New York Review of Books, 1967.

Ford, Patrick K., trans. *The Mabinogi and Other Medieval Welsh Tales*. University of California Press, 1977.

George, Demetra. *The Mysteries of the Dark Moon: The Healing Power of the Dark Goddess*. Harper Collins, 1992.

Kirk, Robert. *The Secret Commonwealth: An Essay on the Nature and Actions of the Subterranean (and for the Most Part) Invisible People, Heretofore Going Under the Name of Elves, Fauns & Fairies*. New York Review of Books, 2007. (Originally written in the seventeenth century.)

Neeson, Eoin. *Celtic Myths and Legends*. Mercier Press, 1998. (See "The Children of Lir" in particular.)

Ross, Anne. *Druids, Gods & Heroes from Celtic Mythology*. Peter Bedrick Books, 1986.

Stewart, R. J. *Celtic Gods, Celtic Goddesses*. Blandford, 1990.

Walton, Evangeline. *The Mabinogion Tetralogy*. Overlook Press, 2002. (A one-volume collection of four novelizations of the Mabinogion, including The First Branch: Prince of Annwn; The Second Branch: The Children of Llyr; The Third Branch: The Song of Rhiannon; and The Fourth Branch: The Island of the Mighty.)

Druidry

Bonwick, James. *Irish Druids and Old Irish Religions.* London: Griffin and Farran, 1894.

Carr-Gomm, Philip. *Druidcraft.* Thorsons, 2002.

———. *The Druid Mysteries: Ancient Wisdom for the 21st Century.* Rider, 2002.

———, ed. *The Druid Renaissance: The Voice of Druidry Today.* Thorsons, 1996.

———. *The Druid Way.* Element Books, 1993.

Carr-Gomm, Philip, and Bill Worthington. *The Druidcraft Tarot.* St. Martin's Press, 2005.

Ellis, Peter Berresford. *The Celtic Empire: The First Millennium of Celtic History, 1,000 BC to AD 51.* Running Press, 2001.

———. *The Druids.* Trans-Atlantic Publications, 1994. (Reprinted by Running Press in 2002 as *A Brief History of the Druids.*)

Evans-Wentz, W. Y. *The Fairy-Faith in Celtic Countries.* New Vision, 2009. (Originally published in 1908.)

Greer, John Michael. *The Druid Magic Handbook.* Weiser Books, 2008.

———. *The Druidry Handbook.* Weiser Books, 2006.

Rees, Alwyn, and Brinley Rees. *Celtic Heritage: Ancient Tradition in Ireland and Wales.* Thames and Hudson, 1961.

Spence, Lewis. *The Magic Arts in Celtic Britain.* London: Rider, 1945; Constable, 1995.

Sutton, Maya Magee, and Nicholas R. Mann. *Druid Magic.* Llewellyn, 2000.

The Elements

Lipp, Deborah. *The Way of Four: Create Elemental Balance in Your Life.* Llewellyn, 2004.

McArthur, Margie. *Wisdom of the Elements: The Sacred Wheel of Earth, Air, Fire, and Water.* Crossing Press, 1998.

Yoga Therapy of Michigan website. "Dosha Theory," http://www.yogatherapy-om.com /ayurveda/dosha-theory/prana.htm.

Kabbalah

Bardon, Franz. *The Key to the True Quabbalah: The Quabbalist as a Sovereign in the Microcosm and the Macrocosm*. Peter A. Dimai, trans. Wuppertal, Germany: Dieter Rüggeberg, 1975.

DuQuette, Lon Milo. *The Chicken Qabalah of Rabbi Lamed Ben Clifford*. Weiser, 2001.

Fortune, Dion. *The Mystical Kabbalah*. London: Ernest Benn, 1935.

"Gematria." Wikipedia article, http://en.wikipedia.org/wiki/Gematria.

Regardie, Israel. *The Golden Dawn*. Llewellyn, 1982.

Stewart, R. J. *The Miracle Tree: Demystifying the Qabalah*. New Page, 2003.

Magic

Abra-Melin. *The Book of the Sacred Magic of Abra-Melin the Mage*. S. L. MacGregor Mathers, trans. Aquarian Press, 1976. (Originally in Hebrew, thought to date from 1458.)

Abram, David. *Spell of the Sensuous: Perception and Language in a More-than-Human World*. Vintage Books, 1997.

Agrippa, Henry Cornelius. *Three Books of Occult Philosophy*. (Kessenger reprint of the English translation by "J. F.," originally published in London by Gregory Moule, 1651. Also see the edition in the Esoteric Archives: http://www.esotericarchives.com/agrippa/agrippa1.htm.)

Ankarloo, Bengt, and Stuart Clark. *Witchcraft and Magic in Europe: Ancient Greece and Rome*. Athlone Press, 1999.

Bachelard, Gaston. *Water and Dreams: An Essay on the Imagination of Matter*. Edith Farrell, trans. Dallas, TX: The Dallas Institute of Humanities and Culture, 1994.

Bardon, Franz. *Initiation into Hermetics: A Course of Instruction of Magic Theory and Practice*. A. Radspieler, trans. Wuppertal, Germany: Dieter Rüggeberg, 1981.

———. *The Practice of Magical Evocation: Instructions for Invoking Spirit Beings from the Spheres Surrounding Us*. Peter Dimai, trans. Wuppertal, Germany: Dieter Rüggeberg, 1991.

Betz, Hans Dieter. *The Greek Magical Papyri in Translation*. University of Chicago Press, 1997.

Bonewits, Isaac. *Real Magic: An Introductory Treatise on the Basic Principles of Yellow Magic*, revised edition. Creative Arts Book Co., 1971.

Buckland, Raymond. *Buckland's Complete Book of Witchcraft*. Llewellyn, 1992.

Carroll, Peter J. *Liber Kaos*. Weiser, 1992.

Cicero, Chic, and Sandra Tabatha Cicero. *Secrets of a Golden Dawn Temple: The Alchemy and Crafting of Magickal Implements*. Llewellyn, 1995.

———. *Self-Initiation into the Golden Dawn Tradition*. Llewellyn, 1995.

Crowley, Aleister. *777 and Other Qabalistic Writings of Aleister Crowley*. Israel Regardie, ed. Weiser, 1973.

Cunningham, Scott. *Earth Power*. Llewellyn, 2000.

Denning, Melita, and Osborne Phillips. *The Llewellyn Practical Guide to Astral Projection: The Out-of-Body Experience*. Llewellyn, 2001.

DuQuette, Lon Milo. *The Key to Solomon's Key: Secrets of Magic and Masonry*. CCC Publishing, 2006.

Friedlander, Walter J. *The Golden Wand of Medicine: A History of the Caduceus Symbol in Medicine*. Greenwood Press, 1992.

Ginzburg, Carlo. *The Night Battles: Witchcraft and Agrarian Cults in the Sixteenth and Seventeenth Centuries*. Trans. John and Anne Tedeschi. London: Routledge & Kegan Paul, 1983. (Original Italian edition: *I Benandanti: Stregoneria e culti agrari tra Cinquecento e Seicento*, 1966.)

Grimassi, Raven. *Hereditary Witchcraft: Secrets of the Old Religion*. Llewellyn, 1999.

Hall, Manly P. *Symbolic Essays*. Philosophical Research Society, 1986.

Henson, Mitch, ed. *Lemegeton: The Complete Lesser Key of Solomon*. Metatron Books, 1999.

Illes, Judika. *The Element Encyclopedia of 5000 Spells*. Element Books, 2004.

Lantiere, Joe. *The Magician's Wand: A History of Mystical Rods of Power*, revised edition. Olde World Magic, 2004.

Leadbeater, C. W. *Man Visible and Invisible*. Theosophical Publishing House, 1969.

Mathers, Samuel Liddell MacGregor, trans. and ed. *The Key of Solomon the King*. Weiser, 1989. (Translated and edited from manuscripts on the British Museum; Latin title is *Clavicula Solomonis*.)

Peterson, Joseph H. "The Magic Wand," http://www.esotericarchives.com/wands/index.html.

Runyon, Carroll R., Jr. *The Book of Solomon's Magic*. CHS, Inc., 1996.

Skinner, Stephen. *The Complete Magician's Tables*. Golden Hoard, 2006. (See Table R on colors.)

Sutton, Daud. *Platonic and Archimedean Solids: The Geometry of Space*. Wooden Books, 2002.

Zell-Ravenheart, Oberon. *Grimoire for the Apprentice Wizard*. New Page Books, 2004.

Minerals and Metals

"Alloys" article from the 1911 edition of the *Encyclopædia Britannica*, available online at http://en.wikisource.org/wiki/1911_Encyclopædia_Britannica/Alloys.

Backyard Metal Casting website, a website that describes ways to create your own foundry and cast metals, at http://backyardmetalcasting.com/.

Conway, D. J. *Crystal Enchantments: A Complete Guide to Stones and Their Magical Properties*. Crossing Press, 1999.

Cunningham, Scott. *Cunningham's Encyclopedia of Crystal, Gem & Metal Magic*. Llewellyn, 1988.

Eliade, Mircea. *The Forge and the Crucible: The Origins and Structure of Alchemy*. University of Chicago Press, 1979.

Fernie, William T. *The Occult and Curative Powers of Precious Stones*. Rudolf Steiner Publications, 1973.

Gienger, Michael. *Crystal Power, Crystal Healing: The Complete Handbook*. Cassel, 1999.

Melody. *Love Is in the Earth: A Kaleidoscope of Crystals*. Earth-Love, 1995.

Metallium, Inc., website, http://www.elementsales.com.

Pack, Robert. "Stone Thoughts" in *Rounding It Out: A Cycle of Sonnetelles*. University of Chicago Press, 1999.

RotoMetals website, a company that sells metal casting supplies and most of the planetary metals, at http://www.rotometals.com.

Tolkien, J. R. R. *The Two Towers. Book II of The Lord of the Rings*. George Allen and Unwin, 1965.

Twintreess. *Stones Alive! A Reference Guide to Stones for the New Millennium*. Tree House Press, 1999.

Signs, Symbols, and Correspondences

Blamires, Steve. *Celtic Tree Mysteries: Secrets of the Ogham*. Llewellyn, 1998.

Crowley, Aleister. *777 and Other Qabalistic Writings of Aleister Crowley*. Israel Regardie, ed. Weiser, 1973.

Ellison, Robert Lee (Skip). *The Druids' Alphabet: What Do We Know about the Oghams?* Earth Religions Press, 2003.

Govinda, Lama Anagarika. *Psycho-Cosmic Symbolism of the Buddhist Stupa*. Dharma Publishing, 1976.

Graves, Robert. *The White Goddess: A Historical Grammar of Poetic Myth,* amended and enlarged edition. Farrar, Straus and Giroux, 1966.

Jackson, Nigel, and Nigel Pennick. *The New Celtic Oracle*. Capall Bann, 1997.

McManus, Damian. *A Guide to Ogam: Maynooth Monographs No. 4*. Maynooth, Ireland: An Sagart, 1997.

Mountfort, Paul Rhys. *Ogam: The Celtic Oracle of the Trees; Understanding, Casting, and Interpreting the Ancient Druidic Alphabet*. Destiny Books, 2002.

Murray, Colin, and Liz Murray. *The Celtic Tree Oracle*. St. Martin's, 1988.

Pennick, Nigel. *Magical Alphabets: The Secrets and Significance of Ancient Scripts—Including Runes, Greek, Ogham, Hebrew and Alchemical Alphabets*. Red Wheel/Weiser, 1992.

———. *Ogham and Coelbren: Keys to the Celtic Mysteries*. Capall Bann, 2000.

Salt, Alun. "The Coligny Calendar," http://alunsalt.com/2005/05/23/the-coligny-calendar/.

Skinner, Stephen. *The Complete Magician's Tables*. Golden Hoard, 2006.

Sutton, Daud. *Platonic and Archimedean Solids: The Geometry of Space*. Wooden Books, 1998.

Thorsson, Edred. *The Book of Ogham: The Celtic Tree Oracle*. Llewellyn, 1992.

Trees and Herbs

Black, Susa Morgan. "Blackthorn," http://www.druidry.org/obod/trees/blackthorn.html.

Blamires, Steve. *Celtic Tree Mysteries: Secrets of the Ogham*. Llewellyn, 1998.

Chetan, Anand, and Diana Brueton. *The Sacred Yew: Rediscovering the Ancient Tree of Life Through the Work of Allen Meredith*. Arkana, 1994.

Cunningham, Scott. *Magical Herbalism*. Llewellyn, 1985.

Hageneder, Fred. *The Spirit of the Trees: Science, Symbiosis, and Inspiration*. Continuum, 2001.

Kendall, Paul. "Mythology and Folklore of the Alder," http://www.treesforlife.org.uk/forest /mythfolk/alder.html.

———. "Mythology and Folklore of the Willow," http://www.treesforlife.org.uk/forest /mythfolk/willow.html.

Loudon, John Claudius. *Arboretum Et Fruticetum Britannicum: or, the Trees and Shrubs of Britain*. Nabu Press, 2010. (Originally published in 1838.)

Paterson, Jacqueline Memory. *Tree Wisdom: The Definitive Guidebook to the Myth, Folklore, and Healing Power of Trees*. Thorsons, 1996.

Petrides, George A. *Eastern Trees* (Peterson Field Guides). Houghton Mifflin, 1998.

Tompkins, Peter, and Christopher Bird. *The Secret Life of Plants*. Harper and Row, 1973.

Trees of Mystery website, http://www.treesofmystery.net/sequoia.htm.

Uyldert, Mellie. *The Psychic Garden: Plants and Their Esoteric Relationship with Man*. Thorsons, 1980. (Originally published in Amsterdam as *Plantenzielen De Driehock*.)

Wilson, Ernest H. *Aristocrats of the Trees*. Dover, 1974.

Zalewski, C. L. *Herbs in Magic and Alchemy: Techniques from Ancient Herbal Lore*. Prism Press, 1990.

Woodworking and Carving

Bütz, Rick, and Ellen Bütz. *Woodcarving with Rick Bütz.* Stackpole Books, 1998.

Cicero, Chic, and Sandra Tabatha Cicero. *Secrets of a Golden Dawn Temple: The Alchemy and Crafting of Magickal Implements.* Llewellyn, 1995.

Cipa, Shawn. *Carving Fantasy & Legend Figures in Wood: Patterns and Instructions for Dragons, Wizards, and Other Creatures of Myth.* Fox Chapel, 2005.

Congdon-Martin, Douglas. *Tom Wolfe Carves Wood Spirits and Walking Sticks.* Schiffer Books, 1992.

Ellenwood, Everett. *Beginning Woodcarving* DVD.

Gregory, Norma. *Step-by-Step Pyrography Projects for the Solid Point Machine.* Guild of Master Craftsman Publications, 2000.

Harris, Eleanor. *The Crafting & Use of Ritual Tools: Step-by-Step Instructions for Woodcrafting Religious & Magical Implements.* Llewellyn, 2002.

Hasluck, Paul N. *Manual of Traditional Wood Carving.* Dover, 1977.

Jackson, Albert, and David Day. *Good Wood Handbook,* second edition. Popular Woodworking Books, 1999.

Jones, Andrew, and Clive George. *Stick Making: A Complete Course.* Guild of Master Craftsman Publications, 1998.

Milburn, Bob, and Orville Milburn. "French Polishing: A Hands-on Tutorial," http://www.milburnguitars.com/fpbannerframes.html.

Pye, Chris. *Lettercarving in Wood: A Practical Course.* Fox Chapel, 2003.

Robertson, Betty. *How to Carve a Wood Spirit* DVD. CreateSpace, 2008.

Sayers, Charles Marshall. *The Book of Wood Carving.* Dover, 1978.

Index

*If you seek the kernel, then you must break the
shell. An likewise, if you would know the reality
of Nature, you must destroy the appearance,
and the farther you go beyond the appearance,
the nearer you will be to the essence.*

⮌ Meister Eckhart

To Write to the Author

If you wish to contact the author or would like more information about this book, please write to the author in care of Llewellyn Worldwide, and we will forward your request. Both the author and the publisher appreciate hearing from you and learning of your enjoyment of this book and how it has helped you. Llewellyn Worldwide cannot guarantee that every letter written to the author can be answered, but all will be forwarded. Please write to:

Alferian Gwydion MacLir
℅ Llewellyn Worldwide
2143 Wooddale Drive
Woodbury, MN 55125-2989
Please enclose a self-addressed stamped envelope for reply (or $1.00 to cover costs).
If outside the United States, enclose international postal reply coupon.

Many of Llewellyn's authors have websites with additional information and resources. For more information, please visit our website:

HTTP://WWW.LLEWELLYN.COM